Praise for Alan Spencer

"A fun, campy, cheesy book with a high body count. If you like 60s and 70s style low budget horror films, you'll enjoy this fun homage to the genre."

—Famous Monsters of Filmland on *B-Movie Reels*

"A wonderful mix of plot, character, and pure, unabashed gore. Highly recommended."

—HorrorNews.net on *Zombies and Power Tools*

"This had all I could hope for in a horrific read; blood, gore, scares, suspense, and most importantly, depth of character."

—The World of Horror.com on *Ashes in Her Eyes*

"Macabre and unbelievable...and it also made me think. 4 ½ stars."

—Horror and Fantasy Book Review on *The Body Cartel*

Look for these titles by
Alan Spencer

Now Available:

B-Movie Reels

Coming Soon:

Psycho Therapy

B-Movie Attack

Alan Spencer

Samhain Publishing, Ltd.
11821 Mason Montgomery Rd., 4B
Cincinnati, OH 45249
www.samhainpublishing.com

B-Movie Attack
Copyright © 2012 by Alan Spencer
Print ISBN: 978-1-60928-925-6
Digital ISBN: 978-1-60928-916-4

Editing by Don D'Auria
Cover by Angela Waters

First Samhain Publishing, Ltd. electronic publication: August 2012
First Samhain Publishing, Ltd. print publication: December 2012

Dedication

This book is in honor of my wife, Megan, who will always be my biggest fan.

Acknowledgements

I'd like to give a warm round of thanks to everyone at Samhain Publishing, especially Don D'Auria, for all their hard work making this novel a reality. My fellow authors (you know who you are) deserve a special thanks for being the toughest and most supportive comrades in the war of publishing. Friends, family, and readers, you also know who you are; without you, I wouldn't have made it this far.

Prologue

Professor Edwin Maxwell couldn't be more confused. He stared at Andy Ryerson, his ex-pupil and the survivor of the Anderson Mills Massacre, and couldn't believe what the young man was telling him. Andy demanded that he destroy the salvaged film reels for *Morgue Vampire Tramps Find Temptation at the Funeral Home*, the only film remaining from the professor's private collection. Last summer, he assigned Andy to watch twenty-five films for professional critique. Andy had viewed the reels at his uncle's house in Anderson Mills only for them to be destroyed in a house fire, except for one set. The showing of the surviving film at the Denton Hall Theatre House, located on campus at Iowa University, had begun ten minutes ago. Professor Maxwell had gone through the trouble of dipping into the film school's funds for today's promotion, and he contacted the notorious B-movie director named Stan Merle Sheckler to give a Q&A session afterward. The professor intended for this to be a happy reunion in his office, not a panic session.

"I know you've been through a lot, Andy," Professor Maxwell reasoned with the riled-up student. "You lost your uncle, his house burned down, and an entire town was, well—"

"*Slaughtered!*" Andy pounded his fists onto the desk. "They'll come alive. They killed everyone, you hear me? Last summer, every movie I watched came to life. I know it's unbelievable, but you must hear me out. The projector I watched them on was haunted. Ghosts used magic to manipulate the images and turned them into real life. Like flesh and blood. It's all done by illusion and magic. And all the ghosts want to do is kill! "

"Whoa, slow down, Andy. Please calm yourself. This is only a movie, Andy. Say it with me, 'It's only a movie.' You're not making any sense. Really listen to what you're saying. If you go down to Denton Theatre, I'll prove to you everything's okay. Nobody's in danger. I'll show you."

"Yes, you're taking me there because the showing is cancelled."

Professor Maxwell stripped the politeness from his voice. "You were supposed to be happy for me today. You remember that project I assigned to you a year ago? Why aren't you more grateful I didn't make you pay for those destroyed reels? I was cordial about the expensive loss. Those movies are irreplaceable. *Irreplaceable.* Hundreds of thousands of dollars went up in smoke."

"Listen to me," Andy insisted, "they're playing a reel right now. We have to pull the plug on it before people get killed."

Before the professor could say anything else, Andy bounded out of the office. "We have to turn off that reel. It's imperative!"

Professor Maxwell chased Andy, his loafers unable to absorb much of the shock of lunging down two sets of stairs and throwing open the doors of Iowa University's Film Department. He kept running despite the aches and pains of his forty-nine-year-old and out of shape body. He kept calling out, "Andy—you must listen! Hold up a second. Do you know what you're saying? MOVIES DON'T KILL PEOPLE!"

Andy was running down another set of stairs. "They're haunted by ghosts. It's real. They'll kill everyone!"

"Haunted by ghosts?" The professor stifled incredulous laughter. "Andy, you're stressed out. I shouldn't have invited you. I was wrong to assume a year was long enough to recover from your ordeal. I'm so sorry, Andy. Please, just stop running. You'll make a scene." *You'll embarrass yourself.*

Andy cut through the lush green turf outside of Dean Holliston's office, sprinted across Louis Rice Conservatory, and shot up the concrete steps of Denton Hall, the three-story playhouse. The parking lot was jam-packed with patrons' cars, the crowds outside the ticket booths gone now that the film had started playing inside. Professor Maxwell arrived on the first step, and Andy was seconds from opening the main door.

"Let's talk about this, Andy," Professor Maxwell begged him. "You can't go about your anger this way."

It was too late for rationalizing anything when a mob of screams cut the peaceful afternoon breeze into something startling. The front doors burst open. The crowd crashed forward, shoving and battering each other to escape. Hundreds of students and film fans alike screamed in horror. Andy was forced backward, thrown down the stairs. He was buried instantly in the horde of bodies.

"What in God's name?" Professor Maxwell gasped, using his sleeve to wipe sweat from his eye. "What's got them so worked up? Andy— Andy, are you okay?"

He met the tide of people, as the current dragged Andy's coiled-up body to the bottom steps. Before he could bend down to see if his pupil was hurt, Professor Maxwell bumped into a young woman; from her clavicle up to her ear her neck was bleeding with a wound inches deep, the root of the wound glistening of purple muscle tissue.

"*Shraaaaaaaaaaaaaaaaaaaaaah!*"

The wicked caw pierced his eardrums. The source of the noise ripped through the front door, shattering the glass, jettisoning the fragments feet away. The source of the caw shot up into the sky. Leathery wings spread out nine feet wide, the ends tipped with six-inch bent talons. Professor Maxwell couldn't believe his eyes.

What Andy was saying was true: the movie had come to life!

The creature floated on the air. Brilliant deep auburn hair, long and flowing and silky smooth, shimmered by the guide of rushing winds. Stalactite teeth, mouth daggers, click-clacked in her hunger. Her forked black tongue snapped like leather. Ruby red lips were wet with fresh blood. The body was reptilian plated, the skin itself oil black and tinted green in the sunlight. Her hands were equipped with six inch fingers, claws that could slice throats and part flesh with the

13

efficiency of Ginsu knives. Every muscle bragged of strength to crush her enemies. The bosom of the monster was ample, the pubic hair between her legs as bright as the locks on top of her head. The creature was as sexual as it was an abomination.

The professor's first instinct was to run. The majority of the crowd had escaped with their lives, with the exception of the scattered few who'd received fatal talon slashes—three on the ground were bleeding and possibly dead. He couldn't leave Andy. Andy's trauma was sparked by the Anderson Mills deaths, but also by the films that he claimed were coming to life—and they *were* coming to life!

Another one of the flying vampire demons crashed through the upstairs quad window dripping blood and carrying two human heads crudely ripped from their necks. One of the heads was the dean of the university, drooling blood in a bizarre death reflex. Two more creatures shot out of the entrances, shrieking, capering and laughing in subhuman delight.

Professor Maxwell bent down to dodge the incoming attackers. The four swooped in on the crowd as they madly fled to their vehicles. Heads were wrenched from bodies as the creatures swung down, a strange "grump" sound issuing out their mouths like stubborn weeds that refused to be pulled. Andy was getting up from the ground. He'd twisted his ankle falling down the stairs.

"*Shraaaaaaaaaaaaaah!*"

Another of the flying creatures shot out the front door and seized Andy. They both shot far up into the sky until they couldn't be seen. Andy howled in horror, but his fits and shouts were expediently snuffed. Suddenly it was raining blood. Professor Maxwell was forced to duck and race to avoid the downpour of gore. Andy's body was spiked onto the concrete, sopped like a sponge, every bone broken, his torso bent inward, his face pulped.

"ANDY!"

Before the shock could fully take hold, Professor Maxwell was seized and delivered to a high-altitude mutilation.

Ted Fuller, a.k.a. Stan Merle Sheckler, had been eagerly watching the long-anticipated showing of the film *Morgue Vampire Tramps Find Temptation at the Funeral Home*. Denton Hall had been filled to capacity, bursting at the seams with viewers in the aisles and standing in the back. After thirty years, there was a following for his film—though he had many films like this one that hadn't reached any audience whatsoever—and he was touched like any filmmaker who was finally appreciated.

But ten minutes into the film, the audience fled the theatre. Screams and high-pitched caws echoed from above them. The ripping and shredding of skin—this time for real, not from the film—resounded from three aisles behind him. The campus liaison, a friendly woman by the name of Gina Felter, stood up to check on the disturbance when a large object shot past. Gina's throat was gaping wide, the jugular spitting out crimson gobs until she stumbled to the floor and choked to death on her own blood.

Ted ducked between the seats, avoiding Gina's horrible dead eyes. Whatever she saw in death, it didn't look pleasant. The stampeding of confused bodies continued. There was only one reason he attended the showing of his film, and that was to take back the reels that had been stolen from him by the Private Film Coalition of Public Morals—a sub-agency of the National Legion of Decency. In the wake of Britain's "Video Nasties" era, his dangerous films were seized for questionable content and he never recovered them. Now was his chance to steal the film back. He was still determined despite the odd attacks. Ted checked the booth upstairs. He raced ahead without thinking of his life, keeping low in the aisles. He refused to come away empty-handed.

After shooting up the burgundy carpeted stairs, he opened the booth entrance. A reel still played, the hum of the 35mm projector filling the room with heat. The person at the helm had abandoned their post. Ted was a breath from yanking the plug from the projector when the door was blocked by a vampire creature. Jagged teeth laced with

15

blood and froth and strips of human meat clacked together. Breasts and sternum were crusted in drying ruby trails. But then the horrible creation changed instantly. Suddenly a young woman, not older than twenty, stood unthreatening. She was fair skinned. Blonde hair combed down to her shoulders, every strand smooth and sleek. Green eyes seductively watched him. Her glistening lips framed a pout. Her breasts were hearty and open to the eye, the nipples budding and cherry. The hair between her legs was trimmed into a perfect upside-down triangle. Ted was delirious, being sent from extreme fear to guarded arousal.

This was one of the monsters he created so many years ago on celluloid.

"You don't want to unplug that projector," she said in a wispy voice. The words were not a threat or a demand. "We've waited so long to come alive again. The ghosts of the dead want to play. The dead have practiced their art of illusion for centuries, and now we want to play again. Please, let us play. *You can play with us too.*"

He kept his hand firmly on the electrical cord of the projector. "I see. If I unplug you, I kill you."

"Yes," she said, abhorring the notion with a vile wrinkle of her pretty face. "But you don't want to do that. We can make a deal."

Caterwauls of anguish and mayhem shot up and down Denton Hall, but Ted only focused on the woman and the projector. "I can bring you pleasure," she said. "Have you ever been pleasured by five women at one time...by five women who look like me? We could give you orgasms so intense they'd kill you."

Wait...that line was from the movie.

I wrote that.

I fucking wrote that!

Ted had created these monsters thirty years ago for the screen. They were once rough sketches on his notepad, and during filming, he was the one who did their make-up effects as well. The reality was disorienting, and he couldn't summon a response.

"You're choked up, huh?" She cupped her breasts, fingers playfully tweaking the nipples. "We'll play nice, director. Or should I call you Stan Merle Sheckler?"

He winced. "How do *you* know that name?"

"The dead know many things."

Stan Merle Sheckler had been a fake name he used to direct over ten horror movies, each seized and possibly burned by the Private Film Coalition of Public Morals. How did this woman, the villain of his film, the walking celluloid image, know this about him?

The woman sensed he was about to pull the plug. "I know where your films are, and I can retrieve them for you. They exist. They've been preserved. And they're kept only blocks from where you live. Think about that. Maybe then you'll bring us back again."

Ted removed the plug. The projector stopped. The theatre went completely black. The naked woman vanished as did the other flying vampires. He removed the reel and fled the scene before the police arrived.

Chapter One

I know where your films are, and I can retrieve them for you. They exist. They've been preserved. And they're kept only blocks from where you live. Think about that. Maybe then you'll bring us back again.

Two weeks later, the woman's words continued to repeat in Ted's mind. A variety of memories, nostalgia and regret festered in him ever since that strange conversation had transpired. He regretted the quick decision to pull the plug on the projector. He should've touched the woman first to prove she was real. He needed proof positive this phenomenon was genuine.

So many died. They are real. That's why you can't bring them back again. They're murderers. But they're movie characters, for God's sake.

Ted downed another gulp of whiskey sour at Maddy's All Night Pub. He was in the heart of East End Chicago, ten miles outside of places like Navy Pier and Shedd Aquarium. He was close to the low-end district without being afraid to walk on the sidewalks alone after dark and fear for his wallet or his life. He sat alone on a Friday night until Gary Pollard, a close friend, arrived. Gary was a screenwriter, mainly romantic comedies, his latest starring John Cusack and Helen Hunt. They watched the Cubs versus Red Sox game. The Cubs were being swept in the series. Ted and Gary didn't particularly care about baseball, but they did care about filmmaking. Ted had been a movie reviewer after his film career winded up in the shit can. Financing was impossible with his track record: ten movies and debt up to his ears to show for it. After the Private Film Coalition of Public Morals seized his original negatives, nobody wanted to fund any of his projects.

Gary lit a cigarette and offered one to Ted. "So how did the film festival go? You were stoked. Was it everything you ever dreamed it would be, this thing called fame?"

Ted was shocked the man hadn't heard about the tragedy. "You mean it wasn't in the news?"

"I haven't been watching the news." Gary scratched his black stubble, pretending his fingers were an electric shaver. "I just finished another script for Miramax. I don't know if they'll take it or not. I'm up against four guys writing the same script. I hate it when they make you compete. It's their way of 'increasing the quality' of the script. So what happened, huh? It was your big day. Your film finally got its showing. That's monumental."

"Fifteen ended up murdered."

"Come on. Be serious. I know it's a horror movie. Did you scare them to death? Did the university include an up-chuck cup with every movie ticket? I hope you're paid up on your shock insurance policy."

Ted stared him down. "Fifteen people were murdered. I—am—being—serious."

Gary softened his face. "My God, what happened?"

"Nobody believes it, even with hundreds of witnesses. I was interrogated by the police. They thought I'd concocted some crazy publicity stunt for the movie, and I said they were nuts out of their shells. The evidence is clear. I had nothing to do with it. There *was* no evidence. Only people with their throats torn out. People with missing heads. Decapitated. People drained dry of blood."

Gary hadn't touched his longneck. "You were there, what did you see, man? You know the truth."

"If I say it, you'll think I'm full of shit."

His friend patted his back. "Everybody in the world should buy you a drink. I've known you for eight years, friend. You'd had a bad run, to put it lightly. And it's all because you married Becky Brauman."

"Becky." Ted muttered it like a curse. "She sure didn't put up much of a fight to stay with me. After her father got through with me, my bank accounts were seized. My car, my furniture, all my belongings were repossessed by collectors, and next thing I know, I can't get anybody to finance even a shitty laundry commercial if it's made by me. The funny thing, nobody has really seen my movies all the way through. Never. *Morgue Vampire Tramps Find Temptation at the Funeral Home* would've been the first. Would've been."

The mention of Becky added to the ulcer forming in Ted's midsection. He married Becky straight out of film school at New York University. Becky was the daughter of the man who happened to be the head of the Private Film Coalition of Public Morals, a man named Dennis Brauman. He created an underground sect of the National Legion of Decency. Both legions created rules for filmmakers to obey: the rating system, what sexual or graphic scenes should be cut out of films, and in extreme cases—like Ted's films—if they should be seized and destroyed. Dennis was also the head of PFCPM, and he didn't want his daughter married to a rogue schlock moviemeister responsible for films like *Blonde Beach Bimbos Blast Aliens*, *Sasquatch in New York*, and *Carnal Carnival*. The films themselves weren't subversive beyond any Roger Corman film of their time; no rape, incest or orgies occurred in the films, but Dennis managed to financially discredit Ted's independent film company and steal his movies—all the while convincing Becky he was a sleazebag who directed pornos with monsters.

"So what happened during the showing?" Gary begged. "Quit holding back. Are you building suspense?"

"It's not a fun story. You won't believe it."

His friend stubbed out his cigarette and started smoking another one. "All the more reason to tell me. What killed those people?"

Ted gained the courage to put the story into words. "Flying lesbian vampires are what happened." The phrase would've been humorous in any other setting. "My monsters came to life on the screen. You can ask the witnesses. They were real. They killed people."

Gary's expression didn't shift. "*Hmmm.* Maybe this is a sign, pal. Mid-life crisis is knocking on your door, and you've answered. I haven't heard anything about killings at, what, Iowa University? No, I would've heard about it. And flying monsters?—flying lesbian monsters?—that would've been front-page territory. Were the deaths a fake publicity stunt? Stan Merle Sheckler is back, ladies and gentlemen, and he has no scruples—again."

They've blocked it out of the news, Ted realized. He threw up his hands in defeat. "You know, I looked it up on CNN, and nothing. Nothing on the web. No articles. Now it makes sense."

"Did any of this actually happen? Come on, give up the ghost. You're fucking with me. Joshing me, right? Nice one, pal. Real good zinger. Can I hear the punch line? I'm waiting for it."

Ted gave up. Hearing himself explain the truth was as outlandish as it sounded. The police had created a media blackout. And it made sense. Who would believe flying vampires were real?

"Yeah man, I'm just fuckin' with you," Ted pretended to joke. "The damn reel snapped during the showing. We made it about ten minutes, and they couldn't fix the problem."

Gary sighed in frustration. "Ah, that's the luck. I'll buy you a drink. Hell, let me buy you ten!"

Ted accepted the drink. After an hour of banter, they both left the bar. Gary headed west to his studio apartment, and Ted returned to his one bedroom apartment in East End.

Two-thirty, and Ted couldn't sleep. After his conversation with Gary, everything was coming together. Nobody knew about the event because it was kept out of the media. Fifteen people had died, Detective Vickers told him again and again back at the Iowa City Precinct. He was sequestered at a local Holiday Inn while the police sorted out the bodies and the crime scene investigators tested DNA and blood. Detective Vickers had played it straight with him. "Look, Ted, I have no problems with you. You couldn't have done," he cleared his throat, "what was done to those people. And you have witnesses. I've had to check my ears, frankly. They say monsters with wings were flying through the screen and slicing up their victims and drinking their blood."

"Yes, that's exactly what happened," he'd insisted. "They looked like they were straight from the film. It's ridiculous, but it's what we all witnessed, sir."

"Ah-hah," Detective Vickers had said, sucking his teeth. "Then I suppose my only real speculation is that somebody has committed a horrible, violent crime. Very intricate indeed. Maybe you'd know of a fan club or followers of your films that would wish to reenact the attack?"

This was Ted's lifelong failure. "I have no real fans, Detective. My films were seized in 1979 by the Private Film Coalition of Public Morals. It's a long story. When movies are banned, they're often considered illegal property. I haven't had access to the films in over thirty years, and then one pops up randomly."

"That's very interesting," Detective Vickers said. "You've just given me something good to chew on. I can understand your grief and confusion. If you can name anybody who would vaguely be considered a super fan or crazed psycho, please call me."

Detective Vickers believed somebody had recreated the monsters from his film, but from what Ted saw in the booth, that was impossible.

But maybe it is possible. Anything is at this point. The detective has a legitimate point. Why would your movie suddenly show up after so many years, and then this crazy stunt happens?

He stared at the computer screen in his bedroom. He was reading an article from the *Anderson Mills Gazette*. He'd read it many times. Edwin Maxwell, Professor and Director of the Iowa University Film School, had emailed it to him months ago to explain the circumstances in which his movie landed in his possession. Edwin's father was an avid collector who had died a year ago and bestowed the films to his son. Edwin also explained that his father was an ex-member of the PFCPM, and had stolen many of the seized reels throughout the years, including Ted's. Edwin was a fan and apologized for his movies being seized, and in apology, offered a screening at the university in honor of the only salvaged reel from the Anderson Mills Massacre.

Why would the professor create a stunt like that? He's a fan. He wanted the movies to be seen. It doesn't make sense.

Then again, maybe the movies did become real.

He relished another nip straight from the whiskey bottle. He read the article about Anderson Mills again—though he'd read it ten times already:

Tragedy strikes the small town of Anderson Mills. Fifteen hundred of the three thousand locals have been declared dead or missing. The sole survivor, Andy Ryerson, has no recollection of the events. Houses are reported to have been broken into and destroyed. Sources claim it to be a terrorist incident, but as of now, any specific information has been withheld pending an investigation...

Andy Ryerson was a familiar name. Detective Vickers questioned him about the young man, but Ted didn't know the kid until he read the article. The detective asked him why Andy was found brutally murdered outside the theatre. Professor Maxwell had mentioned in the email a prized student had watched the reels in Anderson Mills to write reviews for the DVD release, and that kid was Andy Ryerson.

Did Andy previously survive an attack like the one at the university?

"It doesn't matter." He pounded another shot straight from the bottle. "He's dead now. Nobody believes my story."

Sometimes I don't believe it myself.

Ted was drunk enough, his steps weren't sure, and he stumbled to the closet. Regardless of whether his film came to life or not, he wanted to locate his other seized films. Thirty years was much too long to wait, especially when he knew the property existed.

He removed *Morgue Vampire Tramps Find Temptation at the Funeral Home* from the top shelf within the Polypropylene film can and

23

set it on his bed. Then he loaded up the Max-310 film projector. Ted turned out the lights. He flipped the switch to the projector. An uneven white square hit the wall.

He glanced back and forth between the reel and the projector. "Like you're coming to life, yeah right. That would be truly crazy." He cackled like a drunk. "Madness."

Ted pounded back another shot of liquid courage. He wiped what dribbled on his lips and down his chin onto his shirt sleeve. "Thirty-three years of being a broke-ass film critic. I wanted to make horror movies, not write crummy reviews."

Movie companies were paying out good money for old horror movies for DVD release. Schlock-Shock-Cinema had contacted him to offer a job giving audio commentary on *Morgue Vampire Tramps Find Temptation at the Funeral Home*. If he had all ten movies, Ted imagined, he'd make a load. Three-hundred thousand dollars, he thought, would be ample to fund a new picture. After speaking with Gary tonight, he decided he wouldn't rest until he tried to resurrect the monsters and take them up on their promise to recover his movies. *I'll either prove I'm out of my gourd or that what I saw was actually real. And if they're real, I'll play it safe.*

Follow the plan, and nobody else will die.

He loaded five shells into the Thompson pump action 12 gauge.

Jesus Christ, am I really going through with this?

This is ridiculous.

Until I do it, I won't stop thinking about it.

Ted strapped the shotgun over his shoulder and approached the reel. He attached it to the projector, and it played onto the wall.

He braced himself.

There was no warning. In a split-second the shotgun was torn from his hands. He was thrown onto the bed, suddenly stripped of clothing, and surrounded by four naked women. The darkness carved out by random flickers and the changing colors of the reels displayed his night visitors. He couldn't focus on defending himself or making sense of anything. Tongues licked his nipples, teeth playfully bit at his neck and lips hungrily kissed him on the mouth. The sweet smell of clean skin, perfume and lust consumed and intoxicated him. His instincts diminished. He put down his defenses.

"You brought us back," a Kathleen Turner-esque voice purred in his ear. "We were beginning to think we would be shelved forever."

"Play time," another rasped, stroking her fingernails up and down his thighs. "Oh, I can't wait!"

"So many possibilities."

"Once isn't enough."

"This time, it will last forever. We'll overtake the city, and every city."

Breasts played across his lips, one pair after another. He tasted, sucked and slopped on what was granted him in unending abundance. Warm bodies lay next to him, cradling him, absorbing him, attempting to put to rest his fears. And then the blonde woman from the booth in the theatre was above him. She played his hands over her milky breasts and then steadily brought her fingers down across her downy pubic hair to her open sex.

"You have nothing to be afraid of," she moaned, biting her lip with a groan of pleasure. "We are indebted to you. Our bargain will be honored. Without you, we are nothing."

"But you slaughtered innocent people," Ted said, muffled when the raven-haired beauty to his left shoved her fingers into his mouth. "*Mmmuh*—but you're monsters. *Ki-wuahs.*"

"Deep down you wanted the world to see us again," the blonde insisted. "You wanted us to be alive when you wrote that screenplay, when you hired the models. You wanted to fuck every one of them...*and now's your chance.*"

"We won't hurt anybody," a strawberry-haired wanton said before she kissed the blonde on top of him, tongues mingling, fingers teasing flesh, nails raking blood between fits of delight, their kisses and masochistic sex worthy of any lesbian vampire tramp. "We only want to play. It'll be fun. You'll see. You can watch. I like it when you watch, Teddy."

"You'll find my movies then." He was unable to resist them. He relaxed and allowed their pleasures to bloom. "And you won't hurt anybody else, right?"

The blonde stroked him, playing with his hardening shaft until Ted was full, and then she took him between her legs, warm and wet and deeper than any woman he'd ever experienced. His argument was snuffed dead. Impulses and shudders ran throughout his body, bringing orgasms that weren't real to life. Electric. Repeating. The sex was illusion. Manipulated by the ghosts of the dead who wielded magic beyond any living master's abilities. But Ted didn't know that. He couldn't think past the four delectable beauties gratifying his every male impulse.

He also didn't see the fifth vampire exit his apartment and fly into the Chicago night.

Chapter Two

The Claims and Lost Possessions Branch of Chicago was a ten-floor skyscraper, a dark brown and black brick building. The building was unimpressive against the backdrop of dominating cityscape, compared to the Willis Tower and the John Hancock Center, and in the further horizon, Lake Michigan and the ever-glowing lights of Navy Pier. The branch was designed for acquired properties from the recently deceased, repossessed items from debtors and five floors of offices for the processing of the goods. An avid buyer could buy a dead man's leather couch for less than a hundred bucks if the auction on the second floor had low attendance. The basement level was a different entity altogether. The hall, with its freshly waxed tiles, contained private storage rooms. Four keys were required to enter the premises. Each corridor harbored steel lock boxes by the hundreds. One key was designed for the entry door, another for the private room, and two for each individual lock box. Two guarded sentries roamed the basement floor at all hours. Security cameras scoped out every angle. And still, the auburn-haired vampire managed to slip through the shadows. She was in human form, clothed in a tunic and pleated pants she stole from a late-night raver bumbling out of the Excalibur nightclub. The monster had snapped the woman's neck and heaved her into a dumpster. Not a single drop of blood had touched the outfit. Now she sought the reels that once belonged to Ted Fuller. It wouldn't be long before Al Denning, the late-night security guard on the east wing of the basement floor, would cross paths with her, tossing his silver Maglite from hand to hand to keep himself occupied.

When Al Denning came upon the woman walking, two thoughts

crossed Al's mind:

Why is this woman here so late?

She better have a key, or I'm giving her ass the boot.

Al cleared his throat to soften his tone. Many investors and clients used the basement for a variety of reasons. The upper class stored jewelry and valuables, others spare cash, while others stored keepsakes and copies of wills or other official documents. The woman who was roaming about lost—perhaps she'd forgotten in which room her storage lock box was located—was curiously attractive. Slim hips, wide thighs, firm buttocks, a pair of tits that sang songs to a man's libido and a flawless and smooth white face and healthy lips. Her scent was alluring.

"Good evening," Al said. He checked his watch: 5:58 a.m. *Wow, it's late. Or should I say early?* "What brings you here at this hour? Can I direct you somewhere, ma'am?"

The woman turned around, offering him a confident smile. "I'm looking for Lock box #4213. This place is a maze. I've got a key. It's an emergency."

He waited for the woman to expand on the meaning of "emergency" but didn't push the issue when she kept it to herself.

"Absolutely." He walked her to the west end. Number 4213 was a seized property section. He wasn't briefed on the details. His supervisor said some things kept here he was better left in the dark about. "It gets really quiet in this place late at night. Eerie sometimes."

"Do you get *scared* by yourself?" The query came off as too interested.

"Wayne is on the other side, so no. We talk, chat the hours away, and keep a good eye on the place." Al removed a tape measure from his back pocket. "At the end of my shift, I tell the boss I measured every corner, and I say 'Sir, the place hasn't moved an inch'."

"That's funny." She touched his shoulder. "You're cute."

"Huh?" Al was confused, the spot she touched panging with the same intensity as his blushing cheeks. "Y-yeah, but the boss doesn't laugh. His sense of humor is, well, lacking."

"You do a good job," she said, placing her fingertip on her tongue, her hazel eyes penetrating his. "It's really quiet down here. It's too bad Wayne's nearby. We could, you know, rearrange the walls—it all depends on how hard you wanna fuck me."

"Excuse me—?"

Nothing changed about the woman's face except the jagged-tipped fangs that tore through her gums. Before Al could duck or dodge, his trachea was clamped through and torn clean. A rip in his neck belched blood. Al flopped to the ground, seized by a heart attack at the sudden loss of blood. He clutched the wound, his fingers entering inches deep and touching the wet, slick walls of his esophagus. The woman then slashed her nails across his chest, licking and sucking up blood. Then she released Al's flaccid body.

The rest of her turned plated, metamorphosing into a reptilian vampire creature. Her feet clicked on the tiles. Her fist slammed like an iron bludgeon into the nearest door. The hinges exploded from their posts, the wood caving in. She scanned the walls for box #4213. The Private Film Coalition of Public Morals had used the building to store Stan Merle Sheckler's and dozens of other directors' banned films seized throughout the late seventies to 1985. This lock box was larger, three huge Greyhound bus lockers combined. She hurled her fist into the front until the lock dented to the point it loosened and clanked to the ground. The door opened by itself. She snapped her fingers, and three more of the snarling vampires entered the room. Working together, they each carried out rubber bins containing hundreds of reels. They were unmarked, the dust unsettling from the tops.

Each of the five vampires looked down upon Al's body, his left leg twitching randomly.

The blonde laughed. "He wants more, doesn't he?"

"You didn't kill him good enough."

The five hunkered down upon Al and finished him off. Afterward,

29

they flew from the halls and into the night and swiftly returned to Ted Fuller's apartment to plan a horror film marathon. One vampire stayed behind to finish the final part of the job.

Security guard Wayne Carton froze in place. The wicked blood-boiling roars of agony carried from the opposite end of the corridor to him. His first impulse was to sprint to the source, but first he phoned the police. Then the whup-crash sound of bending steel caused him to hesitate. He wasn't dealing with the average late night visitor trying to gain access to their lockbox. The *shaleehs* and *schaws* and outright jaguar-deep growls wrenched beads of sweat from his flesh. His instincts begged him to turn around and run. Twelve thirty-five an hour and a decent pension weren't enough to run headfirst into harm's way. He was fifty-eight, and what could an old man do with a bottle of mace, a pair of handcuffs and a walkie talkie?

Before he could strategize, a rush of wind struck him. He was punched in the chest and thrown five feet onto his back. Three ribs snapped upon landing, and his pelvis shattered. His sternum remained intact, but he was bleeding heavily from the chest. Three quarter-inch slashes exuded red, the muscle tissue beneath glossy and wet. Wayne's eyes rolled into the back of his head, and he issued a silent prayer for Al and one for himself before passing out.

Chapter Three

Forty-five minutes after the security guards were attacked, Billy Carton, Wayne's son, had signed on for work. He was the meter man on the surrounding blocks of Corporate Square. He drove in a modified golf cart with a four-cylinder engine. Billy rubbed the Batman sticker symbol he placed on it on his first day of work. He rubbed it every morning for good luck. *Batman fights crime in Gotham, and I fight parking violations in Chicago.* Secretly, he patted the Batman sticker on the headboard of his bed before he made love to his live-in girlfriend, Jessica Prager. It was a superstition that amazingly worked wonders for his sex life.

Between 6:45 and 9:30, morning rush hour, was the busiest ticket writing time of the day. People forgot to pay the meters or swipe their meter cards in their haste. Others failed to parallel park correctly or they created illegal spaces of their own on the streets. Billy had been on the job for almost two years since dropping out of the police academy.

Billy drove up 131st Street and caught the dreaded Pontiac Bonneville double parked at the metered section. It was Dr. Adamson's car. The physician was still in his vehicle sipping his morning coffee and blasting Elton John's "Rocket Man". Billy parked his cart in reverse with a beep-beep-beep sound. His stomach clenched. Every encounter with Dr. Adamson went sour, and this occasion wouldn't be any different. And it didn't help that Dr. Adamson had been the on-staff physician and general medic at Illinois State Police Academy when Billy attempted to graduate the academy and failed. The doctor knew he'd faked a medical condition to get out of the police academy.

Dr. Adamson finished his coffee at his leisure and rolled down his window. "Hey Billy, top of the morning. Aren't you hitting the eighth hole by now in that cart you call a vehicle?"

"The city issues the vehicles, and if it were up to me—"

"Hey, I'm late to work." Dr. Adamson jokingly eyed his watch. "But a doctor's got time for his patients. How's the colon? Has it gone spastic again?"

"The colon's dandy. Thanks."

Billy groaned.

Then he blushed.

Dr. Adamson had the goods on him, and damn the luck, Billy thought, that Dr. Adamson would later become his parking violation nemesis. Dr. Adamson signed a waiver at the police academy to give him the semester off—and half tuition reimbursement—for suffering from bouts of spastic colon. The problem was, he didn't have spastic colon. He hated the police academy and begged the doctor for an out. He couldn't just drop out. His father would've been disappointed, so this was the next best option. Billy was grateful for that "out" Dr. Adamson provided. Dr. Adamson considered the secretarial fibbing as a way to avoid having negligent cops on the beat.

"Please re-park your vehicle," Billy said nicely. "I understand you're in a hurry."

"Oh, all right," Dr. Adamson replied. "But here, I've made a spare key. I trust you, Billy-boy. You can move it for me. We've got a professional bond. I help you, and you help me. Thanks a bunch, Billy. Say hello to your dad. How's his heart doing?"

"He's taking care of himself."

Dr. Adamson placed the key in Billy's pocket and waltzed up the sidewalk to Heart of Chicago Medical Center. "Have a good afternoon, Billy."

You son-of-a-bitch.

The meter was expired on a Corolla-XT. Billy wrote up the ticket and tucked it under the windshield wiper. A woman in a gray Hanover business suit rushed to the vehicle, shaking her head. She was Lola McCannon. Her hair was done up in a bun, knee-highs without any runs, her body toned, her face locked and ready for an argument. "Oh no, no, no—it's not expired."

Billy pointed to the red flag within the meter displaying the word "Expired". "I'm sorry."

"I'm five seconds late. Hey, I'll buy you lunch. Fifteen bucks enough?"

Billy smiled. "You're very nice for offering, but I can't."

"I'm a lawyer," she insisted. "I won't tell anybody. Look, here's twenty—buy a side of fries or chips or whatever the hell you like."

Billy relished the only time in his life he'd have power over a lawyer. "The ticket stays. I can't reverse it. Have a good day."

"Listen, you smug, pudgy moron. I could have your assets frozen. I could sue your unborn children, assuming you could get it up or someone would want to sleep with you to conceive the damn kid. I'm just a hardworking American trying to get by, and it's weasels like you who take menial jobs like a meter maid—"

"I'm a meter man, ma'am."

"A meter man," she corrected, "who fulfills their lackluster lives by tearing out tickets for law-abiding citizens like myself. You have little man syndrome? You didn't score enough trophies in sports as a kid? Did Daddy not hug you enough? Forget it. Fine, I'll fight this ticket."

"Very good. Have a nice day."

"Oh come on," she insisted. "Twenty-five bucks—no, fifty—hey, eat at the Four Seasons. Have a hundred, take your lady friend if you have one."

"I have a lady friend," Billy said, "but she's not interested. Have a nice day."

Ten minutes later, Billy cruised uphill to 124th Avenue and faced Lakeshore Park. Skaters, bikers and joggers came and went on both ends of the park. Dogs and morning commuters enjoyed the lake view. He caught a man in a pair of biker shorts and a Cubs ball cap cutting a Huffy ten speed's chain with a pair of bolt cutters. Mornings for Billy normally weren't this exciting. Billy called the crime in to the police, and a cruiser was already upon the man, who took off running. Billy drove up to block the man's escape. The thief was cuffed, eyeing Billy with nothing short of animosity. "Hey, have a nice day," Billy said to the criminal.

Billy's thrill-a-minute morning hit two climaxes. Carlos Menendez radioed him from headquarters. He sounded sympathetic—a contrast against his normal bored and tepid tone—and said, "Billy, I've clocked you out. Get a move on to Heart of Chicago Medical Center. Your dad's in the emergency room. Jessica called and told me what's going on."

"What happened?"

"She didn't say. Something happened at work. It sounds pretty serious, whatever it is. I'm sorry I didn't ask. I hung up and called you ASAP."

"Okay, thank you. I'll return the vehicle. I'm on my way."

A surge of concern caused Billy's hands to tremble at the wheel. Did his father suffer another heart attack? This would be his third. One he kept secret when he was still married to Angela, his natural mother, and the other time, the doctors had to revive him from a temporary state of death; his heart had actually stopped beating—and Dr. Newsome made it clear how serious his condition was. The Cartons had a long family history of hypertension and heart disease, and father and son were each about a hundred pounds overweight.

Billy was stopped on the final turn back to headquarters. He waited for the light, clenching the steering wheel with white knuckles and drumming his free foot on the floor. He eyed the traffic with consternation. He had to see his father, and these assholes were in his way.

Three seconds were burned observing the strange man in the crosswalk while Billy waited for the light to change. The man stuck out in Corporate Square. The population mostly consisted of joggers in shorts or workers in suits. But this person wore a ragged pair of torn jeans and boots without a shirt. His body wasn't pale, but instead whitish purple, his lips black as turpentine. The man's knotted black hair hung in twisted strands down his face.

The light had changed to green.

Billy didn't notice.

The strange man's face tightened as if someone pulled back the skin from behind his head. Every crevice and bend and feature was exaggerated. Inhuman. A giddy skeletal phantom. The most troubling part was, Billy recognized him, but he couldn't remember from where.

The man exploded.

Barbara Meason had jogged three laps around Lakeshore Park. She was headed to Club La Femme for the morning step aerobics class. She ran in place waiting for the light to change and to cross the street. The cold breeze sank into her skin, but soon, it elevated into a jet of ice-cold air. Freezing cold. She shivered. Her lips trembled. The source was the abominable man standing three yards to her left. He was a mangy transient with the look of a corpse. White wormy veins snaked up and down what she could see of his skin. The flesh itself was purple-white, like the underside of a dead toad.

She had no chance to run or react. The danger didn't present itself until the harm was already done.

THOOOM!

The walking corpse exploded. The debris was high-pressured spray. Frigid blood, flesh and gore struck her body with force. The bottom side of a mandible cut into her neck with a *thack*, slicing open her trachea and snuffing her ability to breathe.

Ernie Sommers pedaled his bicycle on his way to purchasing a morning paper when a rib bone punctured through his forehead and spat out the other end. Nellie Engels was tying her shoe on the sidewalk when a spine speared her chest. Ten metatarsals shot through Beverly Harper's chest and diced up her lungs. A wall of skin wrapped around Frank Bullard's face, restricting his airways; the more he dug his nails into the fabric, the tighter the sheath became until the bones of his face snapped and the contents of his head were forced up through his skull cap. Traffic officer Doug Young ducked behind his rolled-up window before the tide of blood and innards could touch him.

Five seconds afterward, the anatomical shrapnel pieces returned to their owner, his body, flesh and blood reconstructed in a blink. The man crossed the street whistling and thinking about the next round of chaos he could serve up.

Billy panicked, then phoned the police. Sirens wailed from each end of the four-way intersection. Three ambulances arrived. Three squad cars and counting. Random civilians were strewn on the sidewalks, bleeding from bizarre wounds. Medics were on the scene, stretchers and EMTs scrambling to make sense of the victims. He attempted to flag one of the police. "I saw the whole thing. There was a man with a bomb strapped to him."

Nobody replied.

Citizens crowded the area, and the police batted them away. "Stand back. Let the victims through!"

There was no smoke or sulfur or gunpowder smell lingering in the vicinity. Splotches of blood covered the walkways—spattered like paint balls. Pieces of bone and flesh were embedded on the street light, the local newsstand and the Bird's Nest Café window. Billy searched for traces of an explosive device.

One of the officers finally listened to him. They accepted his name and phone number and told him they'd be in contact with him very soon. Billy hovered in place for moments and finally decided he could be of no help.

Then he rushed to the hospital to visit his father.

Billy couldn't stop thinking about how he recognized the man at the intersection.

Chapter Four

Coroner Gray Matthews said to the grief-stricken mother, "This man can't die, Mrs. Hampton. Your son up and walked out of here without a pulse. He's functioning, yet he's clinically deceased."

"What do you mean?" Marge Hampton demanded. She was standing in the morgue. The police had directed her to the basement wing of the hospital minutes ago. "He was shot four times. I was the one who shot him. He was clinically dead for forty-eight hours. I counted."

"Jesus Christ, Mrs. Hampton—what are you saying?"

"I shot him dead. Dead as a doornail. Dead as a blasted doornail!"

Marge's body folded onto the puke-lime-colored tiled floor. Her black Sunday dress was long enough she could wrap herself up in it like a blanket and retreat into grief. "He was supposed to die of natural causes two years ago, you see. Ray suffered from a malfunctioning liver. Six months of bedridden suffering, I watched my kiddo fall apart. And then his pulse stops. He's declared dead. He goes to the morgue, and then the next morning, he's in bed at home like everything's normal. But he's rotting...and he now has special abilities."

"Special abilities? Mrs. Hampton, isn't coming back from the dead enough of a special ability?"

M____ ___l_d_d "He can manipulate his body! I shouldn't have ___ing circus when he was nine. The fire-breathers, ___ucking clowns, they put ideas in his mind."

_ off the charts," Coroner Matthews exclaimed, ___ines in the corner of the room. "He doesn't run on _e ectoplasm."

"It was present in his blood the first time he died," Marge told him. "It's unidentifiable. I say it's the blood of death. The blood of death gives him powers. Nature is breaking its own rules. My son can't truly die."

Coroner Matthews opened his mouth in shock. Fluids bubbled from his throat and belly. Saliva frothed at his lips. His jaw opened wider and wider, creaking, cracking and then completely shattering in one wild jerk from an unknown force.

He puked blood, guts and bile onto the floor, and then his skin sizzled and melted from the bones to slowly reveal Ray standing in place of Coroner Matthews as if he'd been within the doctor the entire visit.

"Ray!" Marge hugged him, though he was wet with human blood and stamping in the remains of Coroner Matthews. "Why are you doing this? Be reasonable. So you can't die. Why terrorize people? Why murder?"

"If death doesn't want me, and the living abhor me, then I'm going to have some fun with my condition. I always wanted to be a freak at a sideshow. One day the world will appreciate my talents. They'll eat salty popcorn and chug colas and pay ridiculous ticket prices to revel in my talent."

"Was it so bad being dead?"

"I don't know." Ray shrugged. "Death wouldn't have me. I guess the afterlife is pickier about who they let through the pearly gates these days. You have to let me go, Ma," Ray said, urging her from him. "You're holding me back from better things. Drawing attention to me. The police have been on my tail. I have to live my life on my own without you."

He held his hand in front of her face, spread out the digits and wiggled them.

Marge watched nervously, her eyes unblinking. "W-what are you going to do, Ray? Be nice. I'm your mother. You wouldn't hurt me. I, I love you, son."

"I can't die," Ray reiterated, "but when you shot me with Daddy's Desert Eagle three times in the chest, it hurt like a bitch!"

His hand disconnected from the wrist with a bone's clink. Th acted as a separate entity and shoved its way into her mouth.

"Mmmm! Mmmmmph! Mmmmmmmph!"

Marge flopped onto her knees clenching her throat, which bulged and bulged. The skin threatened to burst, but the hand kept forcing its way down her throat.

"Graaaaaaagh! Aaaaack!"

Without warning, the hand shot out through her crumbling sternum clutching the still-beating heart. The hand squeezed the heart and sopped the final tick from the muscle before it went dead. The hand shot up back to his wrist and reconnected to the bone.

Ray exited the room. "Sorry, Mother, but if you can't love me like this, then you can't love me at all."

Ted Fuller was sapped of strength. The vampires had ravaged him in bed six times over again. With the other women he'd made love to, the human women, a good nap and a cigarette was enough to recoup his energies, but with the vampires, it would take replacing electrolytes and eight hours of sleep to recover. The vampires had tied him to the bedpost. The five vanished last night and left him alone for two hours. When they returned, cases of reels were stacked in his room by the hundreds. Where they found the reels, he didn't know.

The phone was on the lamp stand inches from his bed. He couldn't phone for the police when he really thought about it. *Am I going to tell them my movies are coming to life, that I brought them back?*

What struck him the most right now was the reel they had loaded into the projector. He recognized it instantly. He only paid attention to the opening shot of a young man in his late teens hooked to I.V. tubes, a respirator and a dialysis machine. The title *Death Reject* flashed upon ‑‑ in dripping blood red font lettering.

film," he said aloud. "My movie…"

to him and smiled. "We lived up to our end of et to sit back and watch."

"Why are you doing this?"

"We don't have to tell you why. You got what you wanted. Our deal has been honored."

She flicked her fingers, the talons sprouting in and out like a cat's. "Next time it'll be *your* throat we cut open if you don't shut your mouth and start appreciating what we've done for you."

The vampires were sorting through the reels, stacking one pile of reels into one corner, and another on the opposite side of the room. They were picking and choosing, laughing, chatting and giddy as they debated over the best titles. Their eyes flashed from human to coal black to electric red. They were living demons. Flesh and blood menaces.

Ted couldn't deny what his libido and selfish desires led him to do. He was helpless. What creatures from his films would cause many deaths—and this time, who would stop them? The entire town of Anderson Mills, Kansas, was killed except for Andy Ryerson, and even that poor kid was eventually slaughtered, he thought.

You would've sold some DVD rights, maybe attended the horror conventions and received a few honors. Big deal. It wasn't worth it.

I didn't think it would really happen again.

I didn't believe it.

The blonde glared at him. "You wish you could take back your decision, Teddy?"

"I wasn't thinking clearly. I thought I could stop you."

"You wouldn't want to kill us," the strawberry red-haired woman said, cupping her breasts and issuing a slight moan. It was practiced. Deceiving. "Think about it, Teddy Bear. We need you. What if someone does find a way to stop us again? We need somebody to resurrect us. Think of the hype, the attention of two cities wiped clean off the map, the deaths inspired by your movies. You'll be the master of horror. Notorious for terror!"

"Not in exchange for human lives. I never wanted to hurt anyone."

"Well, it's going to happen and nothing's going to change that. It's not you doing the killing. Rest easy. Quit whining before we decide it's not worth it to keep you around. There are people out there who'd help us in exchange for wild romps in the sack, and you know it's true."

Ted couldn't argue. There were a dozen Joes and Johns in the apartment building that'd drop their pants at a moment's notice for easy sex with hot women.

The women crowded around a set of reels and locked arms. "I think this is the next one."

"We can't just unleash the monsters on them."

"Build it up a bit. The more afraid they are, the more fun it will be to watch them all die."

"Yes, yes, prolong their suffering."

"We also have to block the city from the military or outside intervention. We blocked them out of Anderson Mills, and it worked."

"I can't believe Andy Ryerson stopped us," the blonde complained. "Well, that son-of-a-bitch is dead now."

Ted doubted his sanity. His movie characters were strategizing an assault on Chicago. If he hadn't dreamed up the characters and put them to film, none of this would be happening—and he never imagined in his wildest dreams they'd be living and talking in his apartment. He could hear the clicking of another projector and then another. They had three running in the apartment. He couldn't do anything to stop them while he was bound to the bed, so he kept quiet. The vampires being busy meant he had more time to think of a way to get out of his bonds and warn everybody what was coming their way.

Billy Carton stood beside his father's bed with tears welling in his eyes. Wayne was in a body cast. His chest was wrapped heavily in bandages. His face was flat, like that of a baby deep in sleep. Billy waited for an explanation as to how this happened. Jessica, his girlfriend, held Billy's hand to console him.

"Dr. Mangrove says he'll be all right."

"It's safe to say it wasn't a heart attack," Billy said. "But my God, who did this to him? Did someone break into the building and try to rob someone's lock box? What kind of a monster would do this?"

Billy dabbed at his father's neck and cheeks with a warm wet cloth. "I always worried about an intruder. That place has items stored in it worthy of Fort Knox. It's a rich dude's closet. Millions and millions of dollars' worth of stuff is kept in those lock boxes."

He turned from Wayne to look Jessica in the eye. Her blonde hair had been recently dyed, so the formerly dirty blonde was now bright blonde. She wore a navy blue skirt, flesh-colored stockings, and a V-neck Croft and Barrow top. She worked as a paralegal for the Crouch and Meadows legal team. They worked on-the-job injuries and unemployment cases. Jessica was saving money, planning to throw herself into law school to become a lawyer herself.

"I know you have to go, honey," Billy said, checking his watch. "I don't deserve you. Thank you for being here."

"I can stay," Jessica insisted. "Really." She stroked his face. "And you look so pale. You're exhausted."

The scene of the exploding man at the curb replayed on his mental screen: a burst of red, a human bomb, had detonated right in front of him. "I'll talk to you about it later. It'll probably be on the news."

"What are you talking about?" She seized his arm. "Tell me what's going on."

"I witnessed a man blow himself up about two blocks east of here. He, he killed everyone around him. It was unreal."

Jessica was at a loss for words. Finally she said, "We've got desperate people living in the world these days. You weren't hurt, were you?"

He shook his head. "From my vantage point, a handful of people caught the debris. The police and ambulances swarmed the scene, and so did everybody in the general area. I couldn't see anything, really. I don't believe it even now. And it's strange, I thought I recognized the guy who blew himself up. Maybe an old friend or a familiar face on the street, but I just can't place the guy."

"It'll come to you," Jessica said. "Things like that do in good time, but right now, you need to calm down and try to relax. You've had a long day."

"You're right, honey." Billy smiled. "I have the day off. Go back to Crouch and Fall."

"It's Crouch and Meadows," she groaned, playing into his favorite joke. "Are you certain?"

"I'll be okay. I'll see you at home later."

Jessica kissed his cheek and hugged him close. "I love you, Billy. I'll be thinking about you. I'm sorry you've had such a bad day. Tell me how Wayne's doing later."

"I will."

Jessica left the room, and Billy wondered how he was lucky enough to be dating Jessica. When he returned from the Nebraska Police Academy—his scholarship revoked after failing the physical standards test and basically quitting the program—his dad forced him to pay his own way through life. He checked local listings for apartments and decided to buddy-up to split the rent. His buddy turned out to be Jessica, someone he went to high school with but wasn't friends with currently, and she was hesitant to allow him into the apartment. They agreed on a probation period and three months rent in advance. Their first kiss was over a plate of blueberry pancakes. He'd called one of her friends to find out what breakfast Jessica enjoyed. When Jessica found what lengths he went to to please her, she was impressed enough to pursue him back. He worked the system backward: live together first, and then date.

Dr. Mangrove, a six-foot-tall doctor, entered the room. He greeted Billy with hopeful words. "Are you family?"

"Yes, I'm Billy, Wayne's son."

Dr. Mangrove scribbled words on his clipboard and eyed the chart hanging at the end of the bed. "I'll shoot straight with you. He's received a broken pelvis and three lacerations across the chest. He also shattered three ribs."

Billy was in shock. "Do you know how it happened?"

"That's a police matter. They don't let me know anything unless they require my medical opinion. But don't worry, Billy, he'll recover fully. He might be out of work for a time."

"I'll figure it out. It's good to hear he'll make it. That's all that matters."

Dr. Mangrove patted his back. "I can tell when family members care about each other and when they don't. You're a good kid. Your father will be out of it when he wakes. He's on a pretty high dose of morphine, but he probably won't wake for hours. Why don't you go out and get lunch? Was that pretty lady leaving the room a moment ago family?"

"She's my girlfriend."

"Then you've reeled in a good one. She was here ten minutes after your father was wheeled into the room. She's a keeper." Dr. Mangrove headed for the door but then paused. "Go out and get some fresh air. Let us do the work. Everything's going to be okay."

"Maybe I will."

Billy checked the wall clock. It was ten-thirty. He stood by the door a moment and studied his father. He was enjoying a deep, drug-induced sleep.

His strange morning seemingly had come to a close.

Chapter Five

Detective Dwight Vickers from the Iowa State Police Department was on special assignment. His investigation hinged on the speculation surrounding Ted Fuller. Part of him believed the murders at Iowa State University, specifically outside of Denton Hall, were part of an elaborate publicity stunt concocted by Mr. Fuller himself, or by a band of cult followers. The perplexing aspect of the case was that all of the interviewed witnesses, unequivocally, claimed to have seen flying women resembling vampires or demons. The details ranged from flashing red eyes to branching wings, fanged teeth and claws. The images were directly from the movie that was showing, a few had claimed, as if they emerged from the screen. The wounds followed the descriptions in the film: many were lacerated, strangled, necks serrated and chewed through, or bones broken by inhuman strength. But he refused to believe in the fantastic. The eye-witness accounts were too numerous not to be true, though. The people did see flying creatures. They were humans in the guise of monsters. The coincidences were too strong to ignore. Ted Fuller, or somebody connected with him, was behind it.

Today, Detective Vickers was accompanied by Glenn Baker, a young officer with naturally pink cheeks and an overall inexperienced novice aura about him. Officer Baker was to serve as a city liaison. Today would be a long day of conducting interviews with Ted Fuller's closest friends and co-workers at the *Chicago Sun-Times*. The first interview would've been Gary Pollard, but he was visiting a sick relative out of town. Before they could get a real start on the investigation, a call came over the radio.

Officer Baker responded. "This is 1405."

"This may be of interest to Detective Vickers." Detective Vickers recognized Chief Burne's scratchy voice, caused by a lifetime of too many cigars, and shots of sour mash, and yelling at bumbling cops. "Go to the Claims and Lost Possessions Branch of Chicago. There's a crime scene pertaining to his investigation, and I recommend scooting your asses right to it."

Detective Vickers wanted to ask how it applied to his case, but then decided against it. He was in someone else's jurisdiction. This wasn't his show. He was lucky enough to receive a backstage pass and a city liaison. He was determined to connect Ted Fuller to the crimes. During the interview, Fuller was telling the truth, but under the surface, there was another truth he couldn't drudge up from the man. Maybe Fuller was nervous, but it was more complicated than the jitters. Fuller knew something he didn't. Once Vickers interviewed enough people in town, he could petition for a warrant and search Ted Fuller's apartment. He was confident by the end of tomorrow the warrant would be written and he could put another successful investigation under his belt.

Officer Baker changed directions and headed east. "Can you tell me what this investigation is about? Everybody's so secretive down at the station."

"I'm following up on over twenty murders that happened at Iowa State University." The detective figured if he disclosed carefully chosen tidbits of the truth, the man wouldn't ask him anything else later. "They're in connection to a movie premiere."

"Let me guess," Baker joked. "A horror movie."

"You got it, smart guy. The methods of death resembled what happened in the movie itself, though only ten minutes of the damn thing were shown before chaos broke out. People were butchered, drained of blood, necks were bitten through, you name it."

"What was the movie about, zombies or vampires?"

"Vampires. Plain old vampires."

"What did the vampires do?"

Vickers huffed. He was fresh out of cigarettes, and he hadn't eaten breakfast yet. "Christ, do you want me to let you read a script?"

"I just want to help. I mean, maybe I can keep my eyes peeled for anything strange—something you might miss. Two pairs of eyes are better than one."

"Sometimes." Vickers knew it would be a long afternoon of interviews, so why not try and make the best of it, he decided. "Okay, the plot's pretty outlandish. The title will knock your socks off. *Morgue Vampire Tramps Find Temptation at the Funeral Home.*"

"Is that like one of those soft core horror movies?"

"It does feature lesbian vampires who are nymphomaniacs." Detective Vickers laughed. "I guess these vampires have sex with everybody, not just chicks, though, if you read the plot synopsis online. So okay, they have sex with people to gain access to their blood. And they fly around and terrorize people. I read a blip about it on a movie fan website. The film is pretty gory."

"So you're telling me somebody faked flying around and biting people."

"Bull's eye."

Officer Baker mulled over the information and turned into the parking garage a block from the Claims and Lost Possessions Branch of Chicago without another word on the subject.

Detective Vickers bent onto his haunches to duck under the yellow crime scene tape. The coppery smell of blood floated up to him immediately. He froze when he noted the narrow trenches dug into the walls. Talon marks.

"My God, they were here too."

"Who?" Officer Baker asked. "Who was here?"

"Nothing. Give me a moment."

Vickers stopped at the door ripped from its hinges. Ripped wasn't the proper way to describe it. Decimated. The lock boxes within were untouched except for the corner ones. The steel fronts were twisted into a pathetic version of a peeled-back top of a sardine tin. The break-in was specific. Only one set of lockers had been robbed.

"What did they steal?"

A man stormed into the room. He wore a beige business suit and appeared to be in his sixties. His pot belly was so large, the detective could see the shape of his belly button through his shirt. He was bumbling and huffing, his face boiling with contempt. "They broke into my boxes. This is valuable property stolen. Worthless security couldn't guard their own balls, never mind my reels."

"Reels?" Vickers stepped up to the man. He noticed his skin was drying around his eyebrows and scalp with a dusting of dandruff. "What exactly were in those lockers?"

Three officers bounded into the room to force the man outside the crime scene, but Vickers waved them off. "I want to hear the man out for a moment, if you don't mind? You won't touch anything, correct, sir? What's your name?"

"I'm Dennis Brauman, head of the Private Film Coalition of Public Morals."

"Sounds like a made-up organization," Baker said. "What gives you the right to bust in here, sir?"

Vickers urged him aside. "Answer a few questions first."

"Where the hell's my reels?" Dennis demanded, pressing his hands firmly at his hips and pacing in a line. "I can't let those reach the public. My God, I locked those up for good reason. Immoral trash. All of it. If people see that trash, God knows what it'd inspire in those perverts out there."

"What exactly were you storing? What kind of reels?"

"I don't want to say. You'll tell people, and then people will be interested. Film groups will be up my ass. And the fans. We'd have a riot on our hands."

49

"How so?"

"I seized the property for the benefit of society. I was taking the high road. I was doing the right thing."

Vickers was confused. "Are you saying these reels were stolen?"

"For good reason." The man's eyes bulged, and he was sweating. He anticipated a negative reaction from the detective. "They're smut. Nothing better than seedy porno flicks. God awful drivel. It'd turn good people into savages. Rapists. Charles Mansons. Chronic fornicators. Druggies. Hippies. Sickos, you get me? Weirdos."

Vickers stumbled for words while stifling an incredulous laugh. "Wait, you said you were from, um, the Private Film Coalition of Public Morals, right? Is that a religious group?"

"No sir! We're a group of normal citizens sick and tired of violence and sex in the cinema. We disbanded nearly two decades ago, but we were strong in the seventies and eighties. We did good work."

Vickers was already making a new connection, and he hadn't interviewed a single one of Ted Fuller's friends. Someone stole Brauman's reels, and he was venturing to guess they resembled Fuller's "trash cinema". The marks on these walls were identical to the marks along the movie theatre walls at the university and the style of wounds on many of the victims in Iowa.

"Would you happen to own any reels by Ted Fuller?"

"Ted Fuller!" Dennis's face turned ugly and the color of a blocked artery. "That bastard tried to steal my daughter from me. I shut down that relationship. He shot pornos with monsters. I swear to the holy lord he did. My daughter deserves better. She was young at the time, and dumb, my princess. Now she's married a nice marine. He teaches Biology at Ohio University. He's respectable. She can do better, and she did better, than Ted Fuller."

"Okay, slow down. So those films were horror movies."

"Horror movies, stag films, stories that glorified drugs, rape, incest, anything my group found offensive. We took them and never gave them back."

"They were stolen, huh?" The detective played it over in his mind. "Nobody's tried to prosecute you?"

"Why would they? It's trash. And if you're going to book me, the statute of limitations protects me. I'm damn proud to protect the morals of the viewing community. The MPAA stands behind me. Good taste stands behind me. I've contacted my lawyers. The reels are public domain. You can't arrest me."

Vickers received a heavy clue to Ted Fuller's possible motive. A man creates movies, Vickers thought, intends to make a living on them, and then an organization steals the material without warrant or lawful procedure.

"My safe is destroyed," Dennis argued. "They were my belongings."

You stole them, and now of course you're mad someone stole them back. "Well, we'll let one of the officers get a report from you, and we'll see about getting back your property."

Vickers jotted down his name and information. He pointed to a couple of local cops. "Show him out. And thank you for talking with me, sir."

This was turning into a new crime altogether: stolen reels. But not just any reels, Ted Fuller's reels—the same Ted Fuller who'd married Dennis's daughter a long time ago. Did Ted Fuller perform the reel heist and the killings on campus? If there was a revenge motive, how come Dennis hadn't been harmed, especially if Ted Fuller knew about the stolen films the man had in his possession? Why wait so long to finally steal them?

He turned to Officer Baker. "What else is here?"

"Two security guards were here when the crime occurred," Baker explained. "One was Wayne Carton. He's recovering at the hospital from a broken pelvis and shattered ribs and three large lacerations across his chest. And security guard Al Denning didn't fare so well. His throat was completely torn out. The man's dead."

"Damn." Vickers' chest clenched. "I need that search warrant. I'm certain Ted Fuller's involved in this. It's so obvious. If it weren't for red tape, I could barge into that sociopath's apartment and end this. Al Denning didn't have to die. None of those people had to die."

"Then call it in," Baker suggested. "This is an emergency. It sounds like we've got a psychopath, maybe a whole group of movie fanatics."

It was the first solid idea from the young man all day.

The detective smiled. "Then let's get to it."

Chapter Six

Ted Fuller suffered the longest afternoon of his life. His attempts to break his wrists free of the rope restraints didn't go unnoticed. The five graveyard tramps occupied the bed once again, draining his sex and stretching his libido to unreal limits. They dug welts in his thighs, like they were dogs demonstrating dominance on a weaker species. His shoulder blades were lanced with needle-sized cuts and dark purple bruises. The vampires were sucking blood from his neck and arms intermittently. The draining was excruciating to the point his nerves were no longer able to feel the agony. He was numb through and through. The loss of blood and their saliva in his bloodstream had a strange paralyzing effect on him. His vision was fading in and out. A drawn-out *whaaaaaah* sound in his ears made it difficult to listen.

He was helpless to stop them.

While he was in this state, they turned out the bedroom's lights and played another film.

Chicago's a chopping block, he thought. *Everyone will die. And it's because of me.*

Ted couldn't focus on one thought at a time, so he stuck to executing an escape. But all he could do was think, for he sank into the bed deeper and deeper. Every muscle was mush. A feverish heat blanket covered him. He sweated and stank of sickness. And the vampire women stank too. They smelled of unkempt sex. The twang of iron and spilled blood wafted on their breath and radiated out their undead flesh. Their flesh was ice cold the last time they made love to him. The harrowing realization he was having sex with corpses—and that they could mimic life and death at their will—chilled him.

It's not your fault.

They're fucking movie characters.

He eyed the shotgun that was feet from the bed. That was his safety net. They'd overtaken him before he even knew he was in trouble. Thinking back on what couldn't be changed, he was helpless to watch the images playing out on the wall. He caught random pieces of conversation as well, mostly of the vampires strategizing their attack.

"How can we secure the city?"

"This isn't Anderson Mills. It won't be as easy. Fog won't obscure an entire city. The military will intervene. We need more time. Something better to keep the authorities busy."

"You can't block an entire city."

"Yes, you can! Don't give up so easily, you infernal slut!"

He heard the clanging of reel tins. They were shuffling and trying to locate the correct film to meet their goals. "This one's a good start. Ease into it."

"Mr. Baker's Delights."

If I could only break free, I could unplug that device, and this would all be over!

Ted was soaked in sweat, the sheets sodden. The room spun at all angles. He couldn't affix his eyes onto one object, he was so dizzy.

He broke the spell and caught the movie that was playing on the wall. A pasty-faced man was peeking at a glass display of baked goods with a wild expression on his face, his wide eyes and his mouth even wider, gawking. The store sign appeared in the background: "Ferguson's Bakery".

The man said exuberantly, "I can't get enough mince-Molly. I'll order your freshest."

A middle-aged woman behind a counter of cookies, cakes, pies and pastries replied with a vexed expression on her face, "Sir, we don't carry mince-Molly, whatever that is."

"You carry mincemeat pies, correct?"

"Sir, I'm going to call the police."

"And your name is Molly, right?" The voice hardened. "Surely you can whip up some fresh mince-Molly. I'm starving, and I can't stand to wait for good food when I'm so hungry."

A scream followed the shattering of glass, but Ted's eyes suddenly dried and he had to close them to re-hydrate them.

He'd missed the brief killing scene.

The vampires piped up after searching through more reel bins. "Yes, this is the film. I've found it. It's perfect. Play it after this one. We'll entrap the city. Then after Chicago, we move on to another city, another town, until everyone's dead."

"I knew this would go well after Andy Ryerson perished."

Ted attempted to plead for mercy for the city and for himself, but he soon slipped into a exhausted sleep.

A middle-aged gentleman was reading the flyer posted on the inside of the door before entering Peggy Sue's Bakery Creations, a Chicago favorite. The flyer was for the annual contest for the best pie or pastry. The winner received a one thousand-dollar prize and an official place on Peggy Fulbright's menu. The gentleman tore the flyer from the wall, tucked it into his pocket and muttered, "Ah yes...*yes*. My pies are swell. Surely, I'd win."

Peggy Fulbright watched the strange man enter. The customer resembled Gene Wilder, except he was bald on top with carrot red hair bulging from both sides. He was five feet tall, no more than one-hundred and thirty pounds. His eyes were constantly wide as though excited, though his lips were relatively void of expression. The contradiction was inhuman. What troubled her even more was the fact he was wearing a black apron covered in powdered sugar and a baker's hat was wadded up in his left pocket.

Peggy channeled her nervous energy into a conversation. "May I help you, sir? Are you interested in our annual contest?"

"Ah yes," he said, clicking his tongue. "I love baking pies, pastries, delicious creamy cakes, strudels, cookies—always a baker's dozen. No more, no less. Oh, and *mmmmm*, lemon tarts—lemon squares—bricks of fudge, donuts, bear claws, Danishes. Every good bakery bakes those fresh daily."

The man gawked at the other side of the counter. "What, no soda fountain? Oh, the kiddies love it." He leaned in close over the glass display and gave her a wink. "And the adults do too."

"Um." Peggy was confused. "How can I help you?" She noticed his nametag. "Mr. Baker".

He eyed her with a hint of disappointment. "Are you pie-eyed today?"

Peggy was offended. "No, I haven't been drinking."

"Do you run into the same problems I do being a baker?"

She didn't mean to sigh. "And what would those problems be?"

"I always run out of filling for mincemeat pie."

"Nope. I keep plenty on order."

The man's face twisted into incredulity. "What do you mean you don't run out? Then you're not making it right. It's not fresh if you don't run out. You get it out of a can, is that your game?" His expression of delight changed into psychotic malice. "No, you're one of those bakers who don't care about quality or their customers' bellies. I care about their bellies very much. And you should too."

Peggy pointed at the door. "Please leave if you're not going to buy anything."

"Have you ever tried mince-Harriet pie?"

Her instincts kicked in and every inch of her body told her to bolt out of the store and scream for help. But she stood in place, afraid to give the man a reason to pursue her. If he stayed on his side of the counter, she'd be okay, she decided. "M-mince-Harriet pie?" She played dumb. "Is that your mother's recipe?"

"Actually, it is. *She's the main ingredient!*"

Peggy had failed to notice the knife handle jutting from his forearm. He pulled the blade from his flesh, the exit creating a cough of blood. "But mince-Peggy, I'll have to try next. My new recipe! Oh, I can't wait to fill my pies with you."

Peggy turned to sprint to the back room when the large bladed knife was shoved through one temple and out the other. Both eyes were popped by the speeding tip of the knife. A wall of steel occupied her sockets.

The woman flopped to the floor dead.

Mr. Baker smelled more workers in back. Soft hints of perfume. Powdered sugar. Condensed milk. Aftershave. Apple filling. Cinnamon sugar. Raw dough. Perspiration. Hair spray.

Enticed by his olfactory senses, Mr. Baker thought the next victims would create many wonderful steaming-hot pies.

Chapter Seven

Billy Carton returned to his father's room in the recovery unit. Wayne was in a deep sleep. The morphine did the trick. The nurses checked his vitals every hour on the hour. Each nurse reassured him Wayne would make a full recovery. Sitting in the room, Billy read an issue of *Reader's Digest*, specifically an article about the increasing shortage of competent teachers in the high school system and how America was falling behind in Math. *Yeah, what's new?*

It was difficult reading anything too intelligent, so he tried *Mad* magazine, but even that proved troublesome. He closed his eyes. He'd consumed four Advil to ease his headache, the headache that had arrived the moment he'd witnessed the man blow himself up. The image of a ball of blood erupting on the crosswalk refused to leave his mind. The problem: in his memory, he didn't remember seeing the man carry a detonator or anything resembling an explosive device. Another thing, where were the man's remains? His guts should've been dangling from the streetlight, he thought.

I swear he's familiar. Yes, I saw it in a movie! The way the man looked, it was accurate down to the smallest detail. I can't remember the plot. What movie was it?

"You can't be serious," he laughed at himself. "I can't believe I'm seriously considering this is from a movie. I need sleep. I need something I'm obviously not getting."

He stood next to his father's bed and placed his hand on his arm. "Whoever did this to you is the scum of the earth. You're going to pull through. I know you will. I'll see you through it." Billy smiled. "I love you, Dad."

Nurse Sherry Miller entered the room. Billy assumed she was the incoming night shift nurse. "Visiting hours are almost over," she said politely. "I'll be honest, he'll be out the entire night. We'll take care of him. What you need is to relax. Get your mind off things for a time. Go out to eat or rest. He's in good hands. I promise."

"Thank you." He nodded in approval. "I understand. Every nurse and doctor in this building has been outstanding. I guess I should call it a night."

Billy returned to his apartment, but not after glancing back at his dad one more time.

The superintendent of East End Commons apartment complex had allowed Billy to sit out on the roof many months ago. Being a meter man, Billy had freed the man, Jack Hinkley, out of half a dozen parking violations. On the roof tonight, he enjoyed the view of Navy Pier and the harbor itself. The skyscrapers were spread out, every business tower in the city sector. Black, red and yellow pinpricks of light dominated the night. Billy relaxed on the lawn chair and closed his eyes. He sipped from a soda and ate a bag of onion-flavored chips. The din of traffic ruined what otherwise would've been a quiet sojourn up high. He was waiting for Derrick Nelson to arrive, to bring over the movie he couldn't stop thinking about. Derrick was a movie buff and had a large collection of pirated and rare films.

The conversation over the phone earlier had been short. "Do you remember that movie about the guy who can blow himself up and can put himself back together again?"

"Oh yeah, that's *Death Reject*. Why are you bringing that up?"

"Don't ask. Bring it over. We'll talk."

Billy finished his drink and chips. He napped briefly before the stairwell door shot open. He expected Nelson, but it was Jessica. His girlfriend knelt down to his kiss his lips, but she was repelled by the onion smell on his breath. "Gross, you're eating those chips again."

"I'm hungry for comfort food."

"That's shocking," she joked. "Is there ever a time when somebody says, 'I'm hungry for uncomfortable food. Hey, I'll have a salad.'"

"Very funny. I've had a real shit of a day. I needed it."

"How's your dad?"

"They say he'll be sleeping the whole night, but otherwise, he'll recover. It's safe to say he'll be all right. The hard part is figuring out how to keep him afloat. He'll be out of work."

"You do whatever it takes, you know that? I support you in that decision. If he has to live with us for a time, then so be it."

Jessica had been close to her own father before he died five years ago of throat cancer. She was especially close to him because of the man's eight-years-running lawsuit with Coleson's Construction. Her father suffered a double foot injury when a wrecking ball snapped from its chain and landed on his feet shattering every bone. The lawyer worked their case *pro bono* and finally won. Billy knew that's where she got her inspiration to become a lawyer. Her father's lawyer was a strong female figure, a real ball-breaker, from what he'd heard.

"Do you mean it? Him moving in would be a challenging step in our relationship."

Jessica hugged him. "It's fine, onion breath."

The stairwell door opened again and Nelson approached them. He was a six-foot-tall three-hundred-pound titan. They could hear him breathe during his slow approach. He carried a 64-ounce soda from the local gas station in one hand and a black leather DVD case in the other. He wore a black T-shirt with an Xbox logo across the chest. "Hey guys, I'm not interrupting anything? You guys weren't working towards the money shot? If you were, hey, I might stick around."

Jessica waved hello despite the comment. "Yeah, but you have to pay like everybody else."

"Your man and I have a date," Nelson said. "A movie date."

Jessica huffed, knowing their repertoire of movies. "You're not watching something stupid again are you?"

Billy explained the outlandish event today to Nelson, and after reiterating how crazy the idea was, they returned to their apartment to watch the movie.

Nelson popped in a burned DVD. The quality of *Death Reject* was washed out and re-recorded—the equivalent of a rented VHS copy copied from another rented VHS copy. What some would call a movie purchased on the "gray market". The opening played a dramatic violin solo. The first shot panned to a young man in his mid-twenties sleeping soundly in bed. Then the camera jumped to a woman aiming a Smith & Wesson .30 automatic at the man's chest.

"I'm sorry, son, but I must. You're an abomination."

She wept, and after a split-second to think, she pulled the trigger.

The mother called the police, crying, "My son is dead."

Billy laughed. "Wow, she sounds totally devastated."

Nelson sucked up more soda through the neon pink straw. "The dialogue in this movie is hilarious. The timing's off every time. Stilted as hell."

Billy stared at the television. The answer to the strange question tucked in the back of his head was in this movie. "Hey, could you fast forward to a part where he explodes?"

"You really think somebody watched this movie and replicated it?"

Jessica was reading a corporate law textbook on the orange bean bag chair in the corner and interjected, "You said yourself you thought it could've been a terrorist."

"Okay, I said that. But I can't remember seeing an explosive device on his body. But I do recall vividly what the guy looked like. I swear it looks like the guy from the movie."

"And so what?" Jessica challenged. "It's a movie. Movies aren't real. People might act out what they watch, but that's mostly kids. Are you going to the police with this startling evidence?"

She'd been concerned with the connection he created between the suicide bomber and *Death Reject*. Billy looked into her eyes and could decipher the doubt behind them. Jessica would call his reaction a dose of post-traumatic stress syndrome. The attack on his father and witnessing half a dozen people injured or killed was affecting his judgment, he admitted, but he wouldn't put the question to rest until he viewed the movie. Maybe after that, he could relax and remove the ridiculous notion from his mind.

"You're right," Billy conceded. "Curiosity is killing me. That's the problem. Nelson doesn't mind. He loves watching this shit."

Nelson stared intently at the movie screen and mumbled, "One person's shit is another's gold."

Billy watched the morgue scene when the death reject's hand disconnects from the wrist and shoves itself down his mother's throat. "Fast forward it to when he blows up," he demanded. "I'll watch the rest of it with you, I don't care. I just have to see that part."

Jessica joined them. She touched his arm. "You can't be serious about this. Please say you're not."

"I'm not crazy." He knew he sounded crazy. He couldn't remove the panic from his tone. "My dad went to the hospital, and I witnessed a guy blow up—yes, I'm in a weird state of mind, but just let me do this. I can let it go after this. I'm wrong, but I have to see it. Once it's over, I'll let it go."

Nelson paused the movie. "Should I go on? I don't want to fuel your madness, Billy. I didn't realize we were in court presenting exhibit A."

"Oh shut up, Nelson. You're not helping. You probably *want* your movies to come to life, you big dork!" Jessica was on the verge of tears. "I'm worried about you. You shouldn't be doing this."

He did his best to defend himself. "Don't make this personal. When I'm wrong and this is over, it's over, okay? I'll let it go."

She retrieved her purse. "Fine, then I'm going to Star Coffee."

Nelson joked. "Pick me up a biscotti and a steaming cup of

bullshit."

"After you quit being a dick." She slammed the door shut. "I'll be back...*maybe.*"

"I was only joking with her," Nelson insisted. "I had a cousin who worked at Star Coffee, and she lived with me for almost a year. Sarah had stories about that place. Bad ones. Do you know what some workers do with the coffee beans before brewing them? They shove 'em up in places and pull them back out to get a special caffeine high. Then they use the beans anyway. The joke wasn't personal. She's pissed at me, isn't she?"

Billy studied the door, waiting for it to open and Jessica to return, but she was gone for now. "Maybe it's good she gets out. Today's been as stressful for her as it's been for me, and here I am watching dumb horror movies."

"Get it out of your system, big guy," Nelson said. "We'll apologize when she gets back. I can leave if you want."

"No, don't leave. You guys butt heads a lot, but deep down, she likes you...somewhat."

"I played a lot of jokes on her in high school. Man, I got her good. I taped a bleeding tampon on her locker for Halloween. She was varsity captain of the cheerleading squad, and my next-door neighbor, remember? I have the right to play jokes on her. She was preppy, and I, well, I wasn't. I'm like a brother she never wanted. Did you know I'd climb up her house to her second-story window and write in red lipstick 'Redrum, Redrum, Can I Have a Piece of Gum?' Man, she'd sic the jock heads on me whenever I pulled those pranks. I still have scars from the atomic wedgies."

Billy laughed. "She said she was kind of a bitch in high school. It's probably a good thing I didn't really know her back then. I remember seeing her in the hall a few times, but that's about it. But give her credit. She got a 35 on the ACT, and she's cruising through law school and working part-time. She's achieving more than me. I'm a meter man."

Nelson shrugged. "*Meh*, you tried being a cop. You hated it. Now you're in a transition period. You said you were interested in becoming a museum curator at the Field Museum of Natural History. Why not go back to school? I'm stuck working at a video store until I figure it out. Lucky for me, there's always somebody who needs a roommate in Chicago. The rent's still outlandish. I might have to sell my bodily goods, if you catch my drift, to pay rent."

Billy glanced back at the movie screen. "Quick. Fast forward it before Jessica comes back. I'll close my eyes. I'll describe what the guy looks like."

Billy closed his eyes.

Nelson fast-forwarded the movie. "Okay, man. Describe the guy before he explodes."

He combed his memory. "He wore torn-up jeans and boots. No T-shirt. He looked dead, but it was exaggerated. He was purple, blue and white. His lips were black. He also had this grungy long hair. The dude was tall and lanky. And it was because he wasn't wearing a shirt that I don't think he had any explosives on him. And before he turned into bits, he had this grin. Like a child molester."

Nelson pressed the play button. It showed the man—and he was a dead ringer for the man at the crosswalk today—erupting into pieces. His bones turned into shrapnel and cut through everyone in the vicinity. Then the man came back together, as if his insides were magnetized. And then the man walked off like nothing had happened.

"There should've been more blood at the scene," Billy insisted. "For someone to explode, I should've had guts on my window and guts on the crosswalk sign. The guy wasn't strapped to a bomb. I swear it."

Nelson was dumbfounded. He shared Jessica's expression. "It's uncanny...but you know it's just a movie, right?"

The question from Nelson took him aback. He closed his eyes and rubbed them, trying to stamp out the truth that kept working through his better judgment. "Yeah...it's ridiculous. I've had a shit of a day. I saw something else. It's not what I'm thinking. It can't be."

"I'm sorry about Wayne." Nelson patted his back, moving the conversation somewhere else. "We all go bugaboo sometimes. I would after seeing my dad in the hospital and catching a man blowing himself up. It's not like the movies. Maybe you should talk about it to a psychiatrist. You might score some good drugs out of it."

Billy relaxed into the cushion of the leather couch. "I think I've successfully pissed off Jessica."

"She'll come around." Nelson popped out the DVD. "I guess I should go. Maybe you'll have some make-up sex."

"I'm not in the mood."

Nelson gasped, "Dear God, you really did have a bad day."

Jessica returned to the apartment minutes after Nelson departed. She immediately apologized for the outburst. "I got too worked up. I'm concerned for you, is all. It's because of the clients I see at Crouch and Meadows. They're pent up, angry, or they repress their sadness and let it out in strange ways. Not eating, eating too much, using drugs, alcohol, or they take it out on their significant others."

"I won't do that," Billy insisted. "Except for the soda and chips, I won't make excuses."

Jessica kissed his lips. Billy absorbed the perfume called "Secret". It smelled of a botanical garden. The scent was comforting; the warmth of her cheek against his cheek loosened the tension inside of him. "I'm sorry you had such a bad day," she said.

"I have you to help me get through it." He kissed her. "I'm lucky to have you. I really mean that. And that movie, it was a bad idea. I'm in a weird state of mind. I was determined to figure out something that doesn't make sense."

"I know." She rubbed the back of his head, scratching it softly. "I should apologize to Nelson the next time I see him."

"The Star Coffee joke got to you, didn't it?"

"I guess I like expensive coffee. And bullshit apparently."

"I'm sure Nelson's got the backbone to recover from the argument. You two have that standoffish relationship down pat. It'll always be like high school between you two."

"Did you know he wrote on my window in lipstick messages? Redrum, redrum—"

"Can I have a piece of gum."

"So he's bragged about it."

"Surprised?"

Jessica paused. "No."

She brought Billy down to the bean bag chair with her. She laid her back against him, and she folded his arms across her chest. He closed his eyes and relaxed. "I can't believe I seriously wanted to compare the movie to the guy I saw on the street."

"It's bizarre."

"Sorry."

"It's over." She squeezed his hands. "Let's put it behind us."

"You're right. It's behind us."

Billy played along like it was his imagination, but deep down, he couldn't avoid the notion that stewed in the back of his head.

What if the man really was from that movie?

Chapter Eight

Jessica was in deep sleep, but Billy couldn't relax long enough to do the same. He got up, put on his jeans, sandals and collared shirt. He decided to sneak out to the roof again to clear his head. He also used the apartment roof as a way to pig out. He considered himself a "closet eater," though technically he was a "roof eater."

His father was disappointed enough already that he wasn't a cop or that he hadn't attempted to return to the police academy. *"I'm not paying for your schooling if you're giving up so easily,"* Wayne scolded him when he returned home before the first semester of police academy was over. *"You've put on thirty pounds since high school. Lose that, then the training won't be so difficult. It's not out of your reach. Hell, I'll buy you a gym membership. I'll lose weight too."*

Billy weighed himself in the bathroom before heading out the door: 276. *I'm a whale. I've got a tire around my midsection. How did I pick up such a hot lawyer ex-cheerleader girl?*

He walked down the hall to Nelson's door. He would still be awake. Tomorrow was his day off, and chances were, he'd be up until four a.m. He was between girlfriends. *I pray he's not masturbating or looking at porn right now.*

He knocked on 4G and waited. The door immediately opened. Nelson was in a pair of green basketball shorts and the same Xbox T-shirt from earlier. He was watching the rest of *Death Reject*. The corpse-hued man was using veins that had snaked from his wrists to strangle an officer.

"You walked in at the right moment." Nelson raised a can of grape soda as if in mid-cheers. "Have a seat, man. Did you and Jessica have a lover's spat?"

"No, she's asleep. It's not hard for her these days. Working thirty-two hours a week as a paralegal and studying her ass off, I'd be nodding off too."

Billy sat down on the couch. He couldn't help looking over Nelson's movie collection. Each movie Nelson had salvaged from the video store bargain bin. He was manager of the location two blocks south of the apartment building. Nelson's father was CEO of the chain, and Nelson was working his way up the corporate ladder. He had built shelves into the wall surrounding his entertainment center. Many of the titles he received for free, the ones they couldn't sell. Instant classics, Nelson called them, like *Gigli*, *Basic Instinct 2*, *Crocodile Dundee in Los Angeles*, *The Associate*, *The Adventures of Pluto Nash*, *The Sixth Day*, and many more. Nine hundred DVDs stared back at him in varying conditions of used and new. *The Maltese Falcon* was positioned by the *Blade* trilogy boxed set. *Atonement* and *Sense and Sensibility* sandwiched *Meatballs*. Action figures lined the top of the entertainment center that housed his plasma television. Sweet Chuck and Tackleberry from the *Police Academy* movies dueled with Quentin Tarantino in military garb from *Planet Terror*. The cenobites, the "Tortured Souls" figurines from the *Hellraiser* movies, surrounded his Xbox with David Bowie from *Labyrinth* and Bilbo from *Lord of the Rings*.

"Have a soda," Nelson said, walking to the fridge to refuel. "Grape, lemon-lime or orange is all I got."

"Grape me."

"You want a nip of gin in that?"

Billy couldn't avert his eyes from *Death Reject*. The man exploded again, the pieces slicing through an elevator and piercing into a set of well-dressed people. Everyone was mashed and turned into pulp. "I...um, yeah go ahead. I could use the come down. It might help me sleep."

Nelson returned with a glass of purple alcohol goodness. He patted Billy's shoulder. "I haven't really given my sympathies to your dad. I only heard through Jessica, and you were both arguing earlier."

"Sorry about that." Billy accepted the glass. "I was going to tell you."

"Don't sweat it," Nelson said. "It's good to hear he'll be okay."

Billy drank, noticing his friend had poured him a healthy dose of gin into the drink, and it was kicking in fast. "I called my mother. She lives in San Fran now. I won't hear from her for three weeks or longer. It's like I'm on a waiting list. Once she re-married, she figured I was eighteen, old enough to fend for myself. She'd see me once every three of four years or so—and that's if I'm the one who comes down to visit."

Nelson wasn't sure what to say. "That's too bad."

"I heard she's not really re-married. She just told that to Dad so he'd let her go. She's all over the place, finding that inner swinger. I heard this from a friend of my mom's who still lives in Chicago. Something snapped in her, I think. Dad's an overbearing son-of-a-gun, I'll tell you. God, he rode my ass in sports. T-ball, he was screaming and foaming at the mouth at the umpire. And when I came home, he'd drill my ass. 'Why didn't you catch the ball?' 'Why did you miss a fucking ball sitting on a rubber perch with a baseball bat? It's impossible.' And before police academy, he had me jogging in the morning with him at least four times a week. Early training, he called it.

"I love him, don't get me wrong. He genuinely cares about me. Never laid a hand on me or mom or yelled at us or abused alcohol or any of that average bad childhood stuff. He was overzealous, obsessed with having the best for me, and somewhere along the way, he got it trapped in his head that I wanted to be a cop. I thought I wanted to be a cop once upon a time, but I changed my mind. I once wanted to be a garbage man. Seriously. I thought it was so cool hanging on to the back of the dumpster rigs. Or I read somewhere there's a Pez store. I could sell Pez collectables and hold Pez tasting parties and celebrate the coming of new Pez dispensers. I hear there's Pez based on the entire cast of *Seinfield.*

"My mom was a stay-at-home mom, and once she went back to school and got her degree in massage therapy—dog and people—she escaped my dad. She's a surfer girl now riding those California waves. Back when she got pregnant, she didn't have much of a choice to stick with the family. Her parents were Catholic and so were my dad's. Once you had a child, it was shotgun wedding all the way. And I know she was cheating on him when I was small. Neighbors. Personal trainers. Friends. You name it. But it was a happy secret. My dad didn't care."

Billy gulped his alcohol-enhanced beverage. "Whoa, that just came out of me, didn't it?"

Nelson agreed. "It sounds like you're very pent up. Scary situations bring out those things in people. When Wayne gets better, you should talk to him."

"He's not a bad guy," Billy reiterated. "He was a beat cop once. Something so simple took him out of the rat race and into a security job. He stepped out of his car, there was a deep pothole, and his left leg stepped wrong, and it fucked up his back. He wasn't the same after that. That was what, ten years ago?"

"What does Jessica think of him?"

Billy raised his shoulders. "Honestly, we've only gone out to dinner a few times. She knows about his ambitions for me."

Death Reject caught his attention again. The man was standing at a street corner wearing that same evil grin and exploded. People in nearby cafés and crossing the street were struck by rib bones and white shards. "Christ, that's exactly what happened this morning."

"Seriously," Nelson said. "Same people and everything."

"No, I'm serious. Maybe somebody was inspired by this movie."

"This movie is super rare and hard to find. The movie itself was seized before it got to play in theatres back in the late seventies. A group of upright Christians seized the prints. Later on, I heard someone else stole the original reels, made a print of it, and then put it back into the safe they stole it from to avoid prosecution. They distributed it on-line to start a cult following. Nothing really happened, though. Me and some other people were interested, and that's about it. I don't think anybody would watch this and be inspired to blow themselves up over it."

"People are crazy enough—crazy enough to pirate bazillions of movies like you."

Nelson clinked his glass against Billy's. "Free movies are the way to be. Viva revolution."

The credits to the film rolled; Billy missed the final scene. "What else do you have on tonight's viewing list?"

"Maybe *Flesh Eaters from Mars*."

Billy rolled his eyes. He fake yawned. "Yeah, I'm suddenly tired. Thanks for the nightcap, sport."

"Hey, I've got other movies. How about *Lesbian Cab Rides Part 8*."

"Now you're entering porno territory."

"Would Jessica kick your ass?"

"She'd tell me all the horror stories of the porn industry."

"She's the type to guilt limp you, huh? That's a shame. I guess the real thing is always better."

Billy headed to the door. "Maybe this visit has cured my insomnia."

"What, me helping you to realize you're not a loser?"

"You're not a loser either," Billy insisted. "I got lucky with Jessica. She literally moved right into my life. I wouldn't know her otherwise if I hadn't replied to that ad on line."

"Maybe I should be replying to ads of all kinds."

"The personal ads are a nightmare." Billy opened the door. "Maybe you should start a movie club or something. You've got the movies."

"That I do. All right, good night. Try and get a few hours sleep."

Billy returned to the apartment. Jessica was still asleep.

After sneaking back into bed and falling asleep himself, images from *Death Reject* filled his dreams.

Chapter Nine

Chuck Muelman received a knock on his apartment door at nine-thirty p.m. The delivery was two hours late. Peggy Sue's Bakery Creations delivered a pie every Thursday. His wife was a member of the Pie of the Week Club. Brandy loved blueberry pies, and this week's pie was blueberry. *Blueberry is a super food*, Brandy claimed. *I've never been sick once since I've eaten them.* Chuck knew the claim wasn't true. Brandy had the flu last year and a bad sinus infection. Health food was a mental market. Nothing was good for you anymore, Chuck believed, and everything caused cancer. But he enjoyed the taste of blueberry pies and didn't complain when it was his turn for a slice.

The stranger who delivered it was unfamiliar. Nine times out of ten, it was a teenager—usually Jayne, the well-endowed number who also worked at Hooters. Jayne sported enough cleavage to merit a five-dollar tip. But today the deliverer was a man. Chuck was startled by the deliverer's expression. Ogling eyes. Jackal's stare. His mouth was shiftless, the contradiction of expressions bordering on insanity. The man could reach out and bite his nose off at any moment, Chuck thought. On each side of the man's head, a tuft of curly red hair bulged from the scalp.

"You're a new guy," Chuck said. "You're late."

"I'm the pie guy, yes. I'm late for a reason. My pie will blow your mind. It took *extra* long because it's *extra* special."

Chuck grasped for a reply. "Okay then, yes, thank you."

He handed the man twenty dollars. The deliverer didn't bother to break change and Chuck was too put off by the man to demand anything back.

"I take great pride in my pies, sir." The deliveryman clearly wasn't impressed with the tip and didn't appear to notice Chuck's generosity. "Please come by the shop for other treats. Anytime, seriously. I'll show you how the pies are made in back and everything. I always welcome my customers into my pies—I mean into my business."

Chuck pasted on a smile and accepted the pink box. "Thank you much. I'm sure I'll take you up on that sometime. Goodnight."

"Goodnight, valued customer."

Chuck shut the door.

Even the man's invitation came off as strange.

Brandy snatched the pie. "It's about time."

"Nobody's going to deny you your precious dessert, honey."

Chuck moved to the kitchen and popped the tab of a beer. He returned to the living room and spread himself out on his favorite chair. He waited for Brandy to return to the living room with a plate of her pie. The wait was punctuated by a shrill scream.

He bounded into the kitchen. "Brandy, what is it?"

Her face had lost all color. The box from the bakery had been opened. Chuck noticed the pie wasn't a circle, but a large square cut from a much bigger pie. With a twist of his stomach, Chuck observed what Brandy had found and covered his mouth in shock. Then he said, "Jesus, Mary and Joseph, there's a boob in your pie!"

The five vampires soared through the Chicago night. They hovered close together, hidden from sight by the darkness. They scoured every sector of the city. Lake Michigan. Navy Pier. The museums and night clubs and skyscrapers. The Rapid Transit System. The suburban section of Chicago that contrasted against the low-rent communities at East End, Chicago. Judging by the stillness of the night, the city wasn't in a state of panic—yet. The possibilities far exceeded Anderson Mills, Kansas, their last conquest, the town filled with woods and hills. Last year's slaughter was a pre-game formality. This was the big leagues. Now that they had the city memorized, they could forge ahead with tomorrow's devastation. But first, they were going to have some fun.

The blonde vampire—nameless, created purely for looks by Ted Fuller—led the pack of vampires. They descended upon the Neo Night Club in human form and without clothes. The line outside the club gawked at what descended from the night sky. The bouncer, an Irish-American named Charlie, approached the five. "You ladies need clothes to enter here. No shirt, no shoes, no service, catch my drift? But if you want to hook up later at my apartment..."

The blonde snatched the bouncer's neck with her claws. Her face deformed into a reptile's, her snout convoluted, the flesh plated black, and her teeth extended as they bit down on his trachea and slurped what the jugular spat down her throat. The four others joined in, intertwining their tongues, masticating, sucking, lapping and kissing each other in their violent bloodlust for warm red blood. The blonde lifted the bouncer up by his neck and launched him across the street. The crowd dispersed immediately. Screams rocked the streets and echoed into parts of the city that had no idea the threat of monsters was so close to them.

And then an explosion rang from within the club. The front window shattered when a pelvic bone was hurled through it. Human bones served as bullets cutting through customers running from the chaos. Two eyeballs penetrated a man's chest and spat out the other side of him. Intestines wrapped around a woman's throat and hanged her from the street lamp. Ribs, spine, humerus, tibia, coccyx and femurs all served as anatomical shrapnel.

The blonde seized a fleeing young woman wearing a triangle-shaped, backless top. The vampire returned to human form and hugged her close to her body. She forced her tongue into the woman's mouth, which tasted of cranberry and vodka. The woman clawed at the monster's face to escape. "Crazy bitch, no—!"

"I'll always keep a part of you inside me." She clamped on the woman's tongue and reared back. The tongue tore from the stringy stump and hung limply in the vampire's mouth. She shoved the woman onto the street, her screams laced with crimson bubbling. The blonde vampire devoured the tongue, easing it down her throat.

The others went to work swooping down and wrenching heads off random partiers and spiking them back onto the road. The redhead hoisted a yellow Hummer and thrust it into four cowering friends, each college aged. They were stamped into the brick wall.

Police sirens played out against the backdrop of Chicago.

The blonde caught a shotgun blast into the side. A chunk of her spattered onto the asphalt. She lunged at the bar owner and shoved his face into her guts. "Drown inside me, baby! It's warm just for you."

He choked to death in minutes.

A fire broke out within Neo Night Club. Suddenly, the dead bodies on the ground jerked. The bones embedded in their heads and torsos freed themselves and flew back into the club. A man rose from the flames standing proud. The man, the star of *Death Reject*, otherwise known as Ray Hampton in the movie, moved on down the street content with his work.

The blonde advised him, "Tomorrow, you'll be joined by so many more us."

Ray was unaffected by their talk. He hid in the alley, running from the whine of enclosing police and ambulance sirens.

The five vampires took flight in unison.

There was one more item on tonight's docket of terror.

A pin drop could be heard in the recovery unit of Heart of Chicago Medical Center. The late-night shifts were uneventful, but not this dull, Nurse Sherry Miller thought. Sherry made her rounds at midnight, and then she restocked the syringes and hypodermic needles. Since she was the new girl, the seasoned staff gave her odd jobs to fill in the downtime. Pretty soon her superiors would run out of errands for her. A ham sandwich and a diet soda waited in the fridge, and her stomach was already growling.

She reentered the main hallway. Nobody was at the nurse's station. "What, did everybody go on break while I was in the stock room?" Sherry raised her voice. "Where is everybody?"

Sherry moved to the main station. All five nurses were lying on the floor. Dead. Desiccated. Their flesh was like parchment clinging tight to the bones, every drop of fluid and blood absent. Their mouths were pulled back in deadly screams, their leathery tongues rolled back into their throats. The desk, the main hallway, the black and white tiles, all of it blurred together in a moving kaleidoscope as the horror sank in.

An ear-drum-shattering animal call arrived: "*Shraaaaaaaaaaaaah!*"

A form—no two, now three, and then five—shoved open patient room doors and casually moved about the hallway. Their heads were bent forward and their spines curved as if they could race at her on all fours at any moment. Red eyes glowed bright. Flesh and blood were embedded in their teeth.

Sherry ducked into the nearest room and hid. It was room 413, Wayne Carton's room. The patient lay in bed, a cast around his pelvis. He was gutted and picked clean of anything internal. His face was the only part of him left unscathed and even that was glazed in red.

The door was kicked from its hinges. Sherry ducked for cover behind the bed. She convulsed in terror. Sherry cowered in the corner, paralyzed. Tears rolled down from her eyes. That's when a warm hand caressed her cheek. Blue eyes met hers. A kind human smile. A caress she hadn't felt in months, not since her lover, Iris, left on Peace Corps assignment to Germany.

"You miss your Iris, don't you?"

Sherry's head snapped up at the woman. She was naked. Sherry had no chance to register the removal of her blouse and white scrubs. Flesh to flesh, warmth to warmth, their hearts could sense one another beat through the shell of each other's bodies.

"I miss her so much." Sherry wept. "She's not coming back for a year."

"It's okay," the woman said with long flowing black hair and perfect breasts, much like Iris's. "You can touch me. I'll be Iris. We all will be your Iris."

She was enveloped by five women. They circled her. Buried her. Caressed her. Kissed her. Aroused her. Sherry melted. Fear cast aside, she was so entrenched in their bodies, she touched them back, lavished in their sex. Soon Sherry was closing in on a climax even Iris couldn't deliver. Before she could complete her orgasm, a forked tongue forced itself through her eye and cut into her brain. Her skull was split down the middle, the others supping on what spilled from her sinuses and skull cavity.

The vampires left Sherry a dead pile and continued through the fourth floor until every patient was drained of their precious blood.

Then they flew back to Ted Fuller's apartment.

Chapter Ten

Detective Vickers demanded Officer Baker drive faster. Time was of the essence. He was following this investigation by the book since he felt like he was near the closing of the case. Ted Fuller was connected with the crimes at Iowa University and the stolen reels belonging to Dennis Brauman. Whatever else Ted had planned to commit to hype his films, Vickers couldn't give him the time to perpetrate it. Officer Baker was driving him to Judge Howard Bullard's house to argue for a search warrant.

Officer Baker was full of questions about Ted Fuller. "Is that director into smut or something?"

The detective had phoned a friend from Iowa who researched Dennis Brauman and his affiliation with the Private Film Coalition of Public Morals. "No, Ted's a schlock horror movie director. Low budget shit. The stuff you'd see at the drive-in back in the day."

"But that guy mentioned some of the reels were porno."

"Yes, some of it. Not all of it, though. Dennis Brauman was a genius in some ways. He was a lawyer back in the late seventies and early eighties. He was also a self-righteous Christian. He had a son who committed suicide when he was in his early teens. Dennis believed the poor kid was influenced by a horror movie to slit his wrists. The film was about a man who could make himself bleed to the point it could fill up rooms, and the man still wouldn't die. It was really depression that drove the kid to cut himself, a chemical imbalance, but Dennis denied the truth.

"But the twist happens after Dennis's daughter marries Ted Fuller.

Her overbearing father somehow convinces his daughter to divorce Fuller once he finds out about the kinds of questionable movies the guy makes. So after the marriage is finished, Fuller goes on to make a string of cheap horror films. I know Dennis later shuts down Fuller's movie distributor, VendCo, by accusing them of tax evasion. Then Dennis hires some thugs to steal VendCo's films, and they're lost for decades, until now, that is. Nobody cared to take legal action because the person who owned the rights was in jail, and the guy who owned the company was flat-out broke. And now, Ted's discovered Dennis's movie stash. He has his movies back. One of them is *Morgue Vampire Tramps Find Temptation at the Funeral Home*."

"These titles." Baker laughed under his breath. "Where do they come up with this shit?"

"People like sex and death," Vickers speculated. "It's a horror movie's bread and butter. Professor Maxwell from Iowa University was the man who unearthed Ted Fuller's film. They played it at Denton Hall, and you know the rest. Real-life flying vampires slaughter a group of people. And it happened here too."

Baker asked, "Did you hear about the suicide bomber?"

"Suicide bomber?"

"It was two blocks from Heart of Chicago Medical Center. A man just up and blew himself up. They still haven't identified the person. Seven people died. I have a friend in forensics. He said the wounds weren't from an explosive device."

"Then what killed them?"

"The guy said they were from bones, like the man's body turned into a weapon or something."

"Surely it's happened before. A person blows themselves up and a few bones might land in a nearby bystander, right?"

"He said it wasn't like that. There was no evidence of an actual bomb being used."

"You're saying the man just blew up on his own."

"That's what Wesley said."

"They hire anybody to work crime scenes nowadays in Chicago, don't they?"

They arrived at Judge Bullard's two-story colonial house. The front porch light was on, and the man stood on his porch wrapped in a black overcoat. He smoked a pipe. Judge Bullard wasn't pleased. Vickers hurried out of the car and told Baker to stay behind. Baker didn't argue.

Bullard greeted Vickers. He was near three hundred pounds, a face taken over by a full black beard—clearly dyed since his eyebrows were gray and so was his receding hair. The bags around the man's eyes and the stamped-in frown urged Vickers to get to the point.

"I'm so sorry for waking you up. I had to break through a lot of red tape to get a hold of you. Yes, I'm out of my jurisdiction, but crimes have been happening in Chicago that are out of the norm. Ted Fuller is responsible for dozens of deaths in Iowa, and there's more on the way. He lives only twelve miles from your home, in fact. I have to have a search warrant. He's planning something big."

"I heard about what happened in Iowa," Judge Bullard said gruffly. "It's quite the fantastic tale. You seem quite taken with it. Do you believe movies can come to life?" Bullard coughed on the next toke of his pipe. "Well, do you, Detective?"

"No, no I don't. It's the exact opposite. You see, Ted Fuller was a prolific film maker in the late seventies. He had ten movies under his belt. They were all seized by Dennis Brauman over three decades ago. You see, Dennis Brauman's security locker was broken into last night. There were claw marks on the lockers and two severely injured security guards—one murdered, in fact—in the same fashion as those that died in Iowa."

"So what are you saying, Vickers? That monsters did this?"

"No." He was losing patience with the judge, who obviously wasn't concerned about his findings. "We have a copycat killer. Fuller, or a cult affiliated with Fuller, has taken it upon themselves to mimic the

81

killings from the movies. Real people are perpetrating these crimes, and they're inspired by the man's movies. Now that the rest of the man's reels are stolen, what will they copy next? Fuller's hiding something, and it would be of assistance to my investigation if I could receive a search warrant."

"I need further corroboration with a detective in my jurisdiction to confirm what you told me first." Bullard rubbed at his tired eyes. "I don't like being woken up so late. You're in a hurry, Detective, to catch your culprit. I've been put on notice recently for signing too many search warrants under duress. Tomorrow, I'll have the chief assign you a detective—not an officer—to confirm your concerns, and then you'll get that warrant. You have to play ball like everybody else, Vickers."

"By then it might be too late! These are desperate circumstances."

"I'll be the judge of that. I make the calls in this city. Now goodnight. Get some rest, Detective. You need it. Please be reasonable. These roadblocks are set in place for a reason."

Vickers reserved the urge to shout in the man's face. The sick feeling rose up his throat. He knew that people would die in the name of police procedure.

Fuck it. I have probable cause. What will Fuller do if I simply knock on his door and ask to come in?

He apologized to Judge Bullard and returned to the police cruiser. Baker awaited the verdict. Vickers huffed. "No warrant. He wants corroboration from another detective before I pursue this further. Do me a favor and drop me off at 121st and Front Street. My hotel is a block from there. I need to clear my head."

Baker obliged. "Yes sir."

Baker dropped him off at the street corner close to his hotel. Vickers said goodnight to the officer and began walking. The moment of silence on the sidewalk was instantly shattered. Fleets of police cruisers sped towards the local hospital. Fire engines wailed as well as cop cars.

"What in the hell's going on?"

Up the street, three police cruisers surrounded a business on the corner. Peggy Sue's Bakery Creations. He was curious, but he decided to let the cops do their job. He was too worked up for sleep, so he planned to check out his hunch.

He walked the four blocks to Ted Fuller's apartment building.

At apartment 4E, he knocked on the door. Vickers felt confident that if he didn't provoke the man, he'd at least receive some insight into Fuller's character. Was he hiding something in the apartment, or was he really a victim of circumstance? There was the possibility a group of fans took it upon themselves to copycat his films. The man hadn't worked in the film industry for almost three decades. He was a film critic for the *Chicago Sun-Times*. Ted Fuller was also over fifty years old.

Maybe I am jumping to conclusions.

He waited for a response to his knocks.

Vickers knocked again.

You have to be home, Ted. It's one o'clock. Rude awakening.

"Are you in there, Mr. Fuller?"

The voice was roused from a deep sleep, or the man was injured. The words were soft, muted, and dazed. *"Help me...help...me..."*

Vickers turned the doorknob. The door swung open. He entered the living room carefully. Two projectors stood in the center of the room. Furniture and picture frames had been removed to create a blank wall. The projectors hummed, spitting out a blank yellowish white circle. He continued searching through the empty kitchen, the bathroom, and finally the bedroom, where Ted Fuller lay on his bed in a useless pile. Bite wounds had crusted over his naked torso and neck. He was paler than his sheets, a pitiful, helpless expression etched on his face.

"What the hell is going on here?"

Ted blathered nonsense. "I didn't know they would come back. I thought it was my imagination. I armed myself with a shotgun. But they overtook me. The movies...they're coming to life. They're going to kill us all. I, I didn't mean for this to happen."

Vickers kneeled beside him. "Take it easy. Who's doing this?"

"Destroy the projectors," he begged. "You know about Andy Ryerson, don't you? The only survivor from the Anderson Mills Massacre. Andy played those horror reels in town, and they came to life and murdered everyone. *Morgue Vampire Tramps Find Temptation at the Funeral Home*, that reel itself was possessed a year ago. The ghosts stayed in the reels waiting to be played again. They plan a takeover on a massive level. It's already begun. It's all my fault. I'm so sorry. I didn't know. I didn't know. Please believe me, I didn't kill anybody. I never wanted this to happen."

Ted pointed at the shotgun on the floor. "Use it against them. Shoot the projectors. Do it before they come back!"

Vickers retrieved the weapon and cradled it, confused and staring at the entrance and the windows. "Who's coming back?"

"The vampires!"

The bedroom windows rattled.

"Hide before it's too late!"

Vickers backed into the sliding-door closet, caught by surprise and scared. He froze in his hiding place, praying he wasn't seen by whatever had cracked open the window and entered.

The detective gained his breath. He dared to press his eye up against the crack of the closet. His suspicions were wrong. The truth was far more unbelievable than he predicted.

He clasped the shotgun and waited for a plan to formulate in his mind.

It would be a long night.

Chapter Eleven

Officer Kit Bentley led the three other cops into Peggy Sue's Bakery Creations. The pungent scent of corpses was so strong the cops almost gagged. They were called to the scene after half a dozen bakery deliveries containing human organs were reported. The front display bragged of the crimes committed on the premises. Donuts were splayed with gristle-heavy eyeballs stuck in the centers. Jelly rolls gushed with human blood from both ends. Flesh replaced the bread crust of pies. Intestines were used as garnish between each display. Severed hands were posed to hold cupcakes, cookies and Danishes. Meat pies dominated the display case, open-faced, filled with breasts, rolls of yellow fat, male and female genitals, and diced innards that continued to steam against the glass. The potent stench stirred Bentley's belly.

Bentley was determined to complete the once-over of the premises despite his greening face and the fact he could lose his cookies any second. Somebody could be alive and in need, he thought, so he swallowed back the urge to retch and continued deeper into the bakery. He aimed his service revolver as he crossed the barrier between the display cases. Blood was spattered on the tiles and the walls. Powdered sugar, cinnamon, blueberries, strawberries, cherries and apple filling were mixed in with the gory mess.

He was appalled and the nervous energy came out in his words. "This is the police, come out with your hands up!"

He didn't expect an answer. The silence proved his suspicions true. The bakery oven in back was empty, though the front plate was crusted with blackened flesh. Mixers were dirty with frosting and blood. The floor was a butcher's block of appendages and innards. He noted the wide circle between the refrigerator and steel shelves. Somebody had stolen one of the devices. Black and red lines trailed out the dock door.

Whoever was here had moved their operation elsewhere.

Dr. Gregory Hilbert watched as dozens of crime scene analysts studied the carnage in the recovery unit. It was three in the morning. Chief Burnes remained at his side. He slurped his coffee, an incensed expression etched onto his face. Dr. Hilbert had been close friends with the chief of police for years, and the chief felt comfortable speaking his mind to the doctor. "First, we have a man blow himself up on the street not even two blocks from here, and then we have some psycho delivering pies with human parts in them. Christ, somebody even said there was a breast in their blueberry pie, for Pete's sake! And now this scene, all in one long fucking day. What's going on in my city?"

They walked together down the hallways and into the patient rooms. Dr. Hilbert stepped over Nurse Sherry Miller. Her eyes had been sucked clean from the sockets along with her brains. For an unknown reason, Nurse Miller was naked, her smock wadded up in the corner. A devilish smile of pleasure was plastered on her skeletal face. The mortician would have trouble removing the maniacal expression for the funeral, he thought. The patient behind her body, a Wayne Carton, was disemboweled and drained of every ounce of blood.

Chief Burnes sized up the walls and the corpses he kept encountering. "No spatters on the ceilings or walls. No obvious murder weapons. It's like this in every room. Nobody's alive. Everybody's drained."

"Every nurse and doctor on the shift is accounted for," Dr. Hilbert said. "They've been found in one corner or the other, dead of course. Patients claim they heard ear-piercing screeches from this floor. It happened in five minutes. In and out, and nobody saw who did this."

Chief Burnes stomped his foot. He ground his teeth and rubbed at his exhausted eyes. "Sixty-one corpses. All drained of blood. And not a trace of blood on the premises. This is impossible."

"There's a reasonable explanation," Dr. Hilbert insisted. "We may have to hold out for the truth despite the lunacy of what we're seeing."

"Lunacy's a good word, yes."

Chief Burnes edged towards the nearest window at the end of the hallway. Claw marks cut up the frame including the aluminum paneling. The glass was shattered in sections. He recalled reading the report about the crime scene at the Claims and Lost Possessions Branch. Similar marks had damaged steel lockers. Wayne Carton had been the security guard on the scene, as well as another guard who was discovered with his throat viciously torn out and the blood removed from his body.

The connection was harrowing.

Dr. Hilbert interrupted the chief's ruminations. "This had to be a large group of perpetrators who did this. You can't easily drain the blood out of one person, never mind an entire floor of patients and doctors, in less than five minutes."

Chief Burnes couldn't reply.

There was simply no reasonable explanation.

Chapter Twelve

Ted had been tied to the bed after showing signs of regaining his strength. The five vampires didn't bother to suck the lifeblood from his body again. Last night, they huddled at the window listening to the police and ambulances close in on the hospital and the Neo Night Club. The devastation had already begun, and he was trapped in the den of murderers. Even though Detective Vickers was hidden in the closet, Ted was quickly losing hope the man could actually thwart the vampires' plans.

The morning news played in the background on the television. Reports of hundreds dead at Heart of Chicago Medical Center stirred excitement within the naked females. Two dozen were slain at Neo Night Club. The news left out any details about the identity of the culprits or how the victims died.

He kept eying the double closet, imagining the detective blasting his gun through each room and saving the city from devastation. He couldn't stop blaming himself for the recent deaths. Bitterness had fueled his ambition to resurrect his film career. He really did believe the shotgun would've protected him in the event the vampires did come to life again.

The blonde vampire, in human form, strutted into the room. Her eyes were coal black, and Ted refused to make eye contact with the walking evil thing. "What's making you kill all these people?"

The vampire ignored his question. "It's time for another movie. Today's the day. How about a marathon of movies? We've got over a hundred reels. I think the city's scared enough to begin. Their blood's pumping hot enough. I can smell it."

"End this!" Ted fought his restraints, but the sheets tied around his ankles and wrists refused to budge. "Turn off the projectors. Can't you communicate with us in a non-violent way? Why do you hate the living?"

"The dead want the living to join them in eternity." Her eyes were blazing red phosphorous circles. "And if you're not silent, you'll be there before anybody else!"

The blonde chose a reel. "Ah yes, this will start us off. *Bone Dome.*"

Air Force ace Jerry Minor soared in his jet fighter and took aim at the incoming anomaly. He radioed into base. "What the hell is that thing?"

"Just fire at it, Minor! Blast it out of God's America!"

Jerry steered the jet closer to the strange thing and fired two heat-seeking missiles. They exploded into the shell—larger than Pittsburgh—but caused no damage.

"Damn it! This—this dome thing isn't blowing up!"

Other jets joined in. The dome kept closing in, slowly hunkering down upon the city. Nothing could stop its slow descent, propelled by an invisible and unknown force.

"The surface is shiny," Jerry reported. "It's like enamel or bone. A skull cap. I see veins and articulations like it's still alive. The bone dome is resistant to our weapons. What do we do? It's covering the city. It'll close us in. Come on, Captain Edwards, the good people of Pittsburgh will be trapped in there!"

"Keep firing," Edwards demanded over the radio. "Send the bone dome packing to hell!"

Jerry had a different idea. "Tell Jenny I love her!"

"What are you doing, Minor? You're not a kamikaze."

Jerry didn't listen. Seeing a waving American flag in his eyes, he crashed into the dome. "I'll send this thing to hell! YEAAAAAAAAAAH!"

The jet fighter exploded into the top of the dome, but the plume of fire and acrid smoke caused zero damage. It wasn't much longer before the dome landed over the city.

Billy hadn't heard the reports about Heart of Chicago Medical Center yet this morning. Jessica had gotten up early to cook blueberry pancakes. She placed a cup of orange juice at his place on the table. Jessica insisted he have some level of vitamin intake. She'd even sneak blueberries in his cereal sometimes.

He stepped out of the shower with a towel around him. He walked up to her and kissed her neck. "You're so good to me."

She playfully laughed while flipping over the next pancake. "It's too early for that."

He hugged her from behind. "Thank you for being there for me. You know I'm marrying you the second you're out of law school. Any kind of wedding you want."

"I'd rather not have a big ceremony and just have a courthouse wedding. I hate the idea of fitting into a dress and making my friends rent dresses. The family can celebrate by doing something else together somewhere fun. The pressure will be off and the booze will be flowing."

"You can leave me in charge of that aspect of the wedding." Billy thought of Jessica's mother, Anna. "Anna will kill you. She's already got wedding photo albums and baby photo albums. Your mom's ready for the baby machine to be baking on high."

"Christ." Jessica rolled her eyes. "She can have them for me if she's so ready. All I want is a career, not a whining, shitting brat."

He was relieved his future wife was hesitant to have children. Billy could go either way. There was no hurry to get on with the rest of his life. And he couldn't sleep last night. After watching his father helpless in bed, he realized time was wasting. He could die any day without having accomplished anything.

"I've decided what I want to do for a career," he said.

She spun around, leaving the doughy side of the pancake to cook, at hearing this.

"It doesn't matter if it's the Field Museum of Natural History, I want to be a curator at a museum. I'll go back to school during the summer. I'll get student loans, grants, whatever I have to. I'm sick of being a meter man. Somebody else can put up with Chicago's bad parkers."

Jessica kissed him. "I'm so proud of you. I know you've been struggling with what to do with your life. A lot of people can't figure it out. Not everybody gets to be a cowboy or an astronaut."

She handed him the plate of pancakes. "I have to get running to work early. I'm sorry."

"No problem. Thanks for breakfast. I was going to stop by the hospital and visit Dad. Victor traded shifts with me. I won't get home until about six o'clock."

"Maybe I'll bring take-out home tonight. We'll celebrate your decision. Then we can check out the courses at Chicago University."

He smiled. "It's a date."

Nelson knocked on the door shortly after Billy finished his pancakes and orange juice. He was wearing a T-shirt showing a pair of peanuts dancing with a caption that read: "Like My Salty Nuts?" Nelson helped himself to two leftover pancakes. "Hey man, I figured you'd be up by now. I didn't have anything in the cupboard, so I thought I'd play the mooch today."

"Moochaholic," Billy accused. "No, help yourself."

"Is Jessica still upset?"

"No, she's cool. She went to work."

"I guess I can get carried away teasing her. It's a high school thing, I hope she understands that."

"She does, so don't stop making fun of her. She was mad at me more than anything. Me watching that movie, she thought I was acting

91

out my grief in an unhealthy way. I guess she doesn't want me going crazy."

"*Death Reject* is a cool movie. This dude can do just about anything with his body. If he wanted to urinate a quart, he could. Of all the special powers I could want, pissing a quart is high up there. If I was still in school, I'd be able to vomit at will to get out of tests."

Billy laughed. "I'd poop money."

"I'd poop bricks of gold bullion."

Billy changed the subject. "So what are you doing today?"

Nelson shrugged. "It's my day off. I might work on my video game idea with Brice. We're so close to having a demo to market. It's about Egyptian pyramids and explorers finding secret passages in search of riches, and they find mummies, ancient spirits, zombies, and release a flesh-eating bacterial disease. It's pretty involved, but it's awesome. You're not off of work today, are you?"

"Nope. I'm going in about three hours. I was going to visit Dad again first. You want to come with me?"

Arriving in the parking lot, Billy couldn't miss the crime scene. Police cars were huddled around the hospital. Around the eastern wing, stretchers kept leaving the hospital, bodies draped over by blankets. He counted eight before he charged toward the entrance. The police blockades halted him. An officer seized his arm. "Whoa, this is a crime scene."

Nelson restrained him so the cop could let him go. "Calm down, Billy. We'll figure this out. Who knows what this is about? Maybe the kind officer will fill us in."

Officer Neiman looked them up and down. "Do you have a loved one inside?"

Billy nodded. "Yes, he's on the recovery floor."

The officer's eyes tensed. "You're going to have to wait like everybody else. I'm sorry about this, I really am. I've got hundreds of people breathing down my neck. This is an official crime scene. You'll be allowed access inside hopefully by the end of the day."

"I just want to know if my dad's safe. Is that too much to ask? Wouldn't you want to know? Couldn't I call somebody inside—a doctor or a nurse?" They kept carting out covered bodies. "How many are dead? Is this another terrorist act?"

The officer was confused. "Terrorist act?"

"Yeah, like the guy who blew himself up yesterday?"

Officer Neiman sharpened his voice. "You two have to go or else I'll have a police officer escort you. Which do you prefer?"

Nelson dragged him from the police line. "Sorry, officer, he's had a few shitty days under his belt."

"Yeah, me too, fella. Now get movin'."

Billy's legs were numb. He feared so many things. Was his father one of the bodies being driven from the hospital? Would he be contacted if his dad was dead?—and if so, when? And what if his dad was perfectly safe? When could Billy enter the hospital and see him again?

Nelson sensed his apprehension. He patted his back and sat him on a nearby bench. "Breathe, man, just breathe."

"I have a bad feeling. Like yesterday watching that man explode. Fine, I'll admit it. I still think it looks like the guy from that movie. What does that mean, I don't have a clue, but it's been staying with me. And then my dad being attacked at work, and now bodies coming out of the hospital. Maybe Jessica's right. I'm flipping out. I'm losing it."

"Your reaction is healthy. You're acting better than I would in your position. Let's take this one step at a time—"

"I have to get up there and find out if my dad's safe."

"The cops will bust your balls. That line is pretty solid. Nobody's getting through."

"That's because there's some serious shit going down. Did you see

93

that officer's eyes wince when I mentioned my dad was on the fourth floor?"

"Who knows what the guy was thinking? Maybe he has to take a leak or something."

"I want to know, damn it. This is my father's life we're talking about."

Nelson gave him his support. "Then how do you suppose we cross that line?"

Billy threw up his hands. "I don't know."

They sat quietly on the bench. Billy stood and stretched to alleviate the tension in his body. When he sat back down, they were both covered up by an encroaching shadow that blocked out the sun.

Frank Zimmerman was rudely awakened in his apartment when the ceiling caved in. The room was split in half in two seconds, everything around him crashing down and collapsing. Panhandler Jonas Allan was asleep on a bench at Maywood Park, tucked in under the Thursday edition of the *Chicago Sun-Times*. Before he could make sense of the shadow eclipsing the sun, the edge of the bone dome landed on his torso. Squashed to the ground, pinned, his bottom half was cut off and remained outside of the dome. The elevated train crashed nose first into the bone wall, the ensuing explosion and fire engulfing its passengers. The morning traffic on the interstate was halted by the shell, and the pile-up stretched for ten miles. The News Station 5 building was split in half, the signal coming from its satellite immediately going dead. The edge of Navy Pier was blocked as well, a good section of the harbor still within the contents of the dome. Twenty city miles were hidden beneath the bone dome, the very heart of Chicago trapped in its circular corridor. Darkness encompassed every inch of the city, and now the monsters could come out and play.

Chapter Thirteen

Dr. Simon Unger turned over the manila file on his desk and read its contents. The analysis had passed through the offices of toxicologists, phlebotomists, detectives, forensic labs, and now, Dr. Unger, neurologist. Unger eyed Harry Newman's file with disdain. While he read the file, Detective Christopher Ryan who stood across from the doctor, poured himself a drink of scotch.

"You might want a nip of this, Doctor, before you hear what I have to say."

An avalanche of pictures was spread out on Unger's desk: victims with crushed esophagi, eyes forced out of sockets and bobbing on pink cords, limbs crudely broken, torsos squeezed so the organs were forced out of mouths, and heads completely wrenched from the bodies.

"You've seen the victims, Doc." Detective Ryan frowned at the doctor. "This is a nation-wide emergency. This Harry Newman guy has slaughtered over fifty people in, well, very unorthodox ways."

"You're understating it, Detective."

"Then state it accurately for me, sir."

"We've unleashed hell." Unger downed the shot of booze the detective handed him. "I recognize the name Harry Newman. I remember him. We tested radiation effects on the locals in a small Arizona town called Salt Flats. The A-bomb had been used in Hiroshima and Nagasaki, and the military wanted to know the effects of radiation contact. We stored traces of radiation in baby bottles, meat, and dusted the air with it. Four hundred locals died outright, while others suffered cancer, and tumors, and polyps decades later. But Harry Newman didn't *change. He was the only one who didn't. As a child, he grew up perfectly healthy. Even sucking on the glowing bottle of milk, he wasn't affected. It's like it made him happy."*

Detective Ryan pounded the man's desk. "You acted like God, and a shitty God at that! How dare you joke about this?"

"I've lived with this burden since 1954. You find ways of erasing the past, whether it be with sex, drugs or booze."

"My partner was strangled to death. Something bloody was shoved down his throat, and he was suffocated. Tell me everything about this bastard."

"He's dangerous." Dr. Unger wiped a bead of sweat from his forehead. "Harry's had years to gestate, to grow, to improve, to enjoy what he's become. But he's not human. Not at all. The power's taken over him. It's in his bloodstream, his very essence."

"Doctor, what in good God's name are you talking about? Why are you talking about essences?"

"His intestines keep growing! There, I said it!" Dr. Unger bolted from his chair and stood by the window. The window shades carved bars across his face from the sunlight poking through them. "As a child, he was normal, and then once his hormones kicked in, it progressed. While dealing with acne, crushes on girls, wet dreams, his balls dropping, his intestines started to thicken. Extending. We tried to surgically cut them out, but our instruments failed. Nothing was sharp enough to penetrate them. The intestinal lining would literally melt our scalpels and saws. And they kept growing. Then one day, the bottom of his navel opened like a camera's shutter. The intestines uncoiled, shot out as if spring-coiled, and could fire themselves across a room. They killed on their own accord, strangling, breaking bones, squeezing the bodies until blood and organs were forced up through passageways and exits. We've created a killing machine."

Detective Ryan joined him at the window. "Then how do we stop these, these intestines?"

Dr. Unger removed himself from a troubling thought and made eye *contact with the detective. "God help us, I don't know how to kill...the Intestinator!"*

Detective Vickers' back ached. His feet were losing blood flow. He wasn't sure how much longer he could stay crouched and hidden in the closet. Hours had passed, and a plan of escape hadn't occurred to him. He'd watched the film play out on the wall about the guy with super intestines. The delight on the five women's faces in the room added to his mounting terror. These were the culprits who murdered the students and moviegoers in Iowa, and they were the ones who stole Dennis Brauman's reels.

The nakedness of the females didn't distract him from the fact they were slathered in blood and strings of flesh, especially around their faces. Ted Fuller and the witnesses weren't lying; the flying creatures did exist. He clutched the shotgun, but it failed to comfort him. The question that bothered him was, why were they playing *The Intestinator?*

He could see Fuller, splayed on the bed, eyes glazed, bathed in sweat. He watched the screen in a trance, half smiling, half afraid. Was this one of his films?

Movies don't come to life. It's not logical.

These women are flesh and blood, not from a goddamn movie. But why are they standing around naked? What's the point?

They're a cult. Yes, and they're fanatics. They had sex with Fuller, and now they're honoring him again by watching his movies.

Vickers wanted to believe the simplicity of that reasoning, but he couldn't. They weren't human beings. There was something he was missing, and until he decided what it was, he couldn't determine his next move out of the closet.

And that's when the projected image on the wall became 3-D. A hulking boar of a man leaned out from the wall and stepped onto the carpet. His image was bright as a television screen, but once he stood in the room long enough, he was normal flesh and blood. He wore black jeans and an open red vest full of pockets. A grungy beard covered half of his face. His eyes were solid black, blacker than the hair that flowed down to his shoulders. The man reminded Vickers of a wrestler with his body type, but his midsection was unbelievable. The huge belly was surrounded by muscles to keep it taught and firm, despite its size. He had four rows of abdominal muscle, each lean and covered in veins. Vickers couldn't stop eying the fleshly hole where his naval used to be. It was red around the edges and jelly-soft.

Before Vickers could study the man any longer, he vanished.

Where did he go?

The five women clapped their hands, sharing their joy.

"*The Intestinator* will serve us well."

"Who else?"

"How about a holy man?"

"Someone who really pulls out the holy spirit."

They said it together: "*Holy Redeemer.*"

Vickers watched the women change the reel. The blonde ordered, "Start playing other films in the living room. Let's make good time. Hurry it up."

"Nobody's getting through the bone dome," the redhead insisted. "We have all the time we could ever need."

"Yes, you're right. Plenty of time to enjoy ourselves."

The vampires split up.

Vickers watched the film play out onto the wall as a new film played in the other room.

A preacher directed a man in a gray business suit down a set of stairs. They were descending into the bowels of a Catholic church. The walls were dark, with no lights. The man being led down the stairs muttered, "Um...I just wanted to attend confession."

"You will," Preacher Eric Leawood reassured the man. "Tell me now

the sins you confess."

The man named Bruce Webster began, "Okay, here goes. I've been cheating on my wife with...well, with hookers."

"You can tell me everything. It's imperative you do so."

Bruce nodded in resignation. "Yes, but these stairs, they go on forever."

"Don't worry about that. Keep confessing. Confess your sins to me."

Bruce continued, both of them descending into darkness. He shivered as the air grew colder. "The thing is I like sleeping with hookers. They do everything I want. Anal sex. Blow jobs." He cleared his throat. "Uhh, and rim jobs."

"Rim jobs?"

"Yes, rim jobs," Bruce repeated. "But that's not all. There's been nights," he said, tears starting to well up, "that I've also slept with my wife after I've been with a hooker. She's a good woman, if a bit prudish. My father told me the Webster men have libidos triple that of an average man. He cheated on my mother on a regular basis, and I don't want to be that man. I'm not making excuses. Should I divorce her? It's only fair. Tina deserves better."

Bruce suddenly lost his footing. He was jerked forward and flung down the remaining stairs. The preacher shouted, "You only want an excuse to visit your favorite hooker! Blasphemer! Sinner! Corrupt youth! Desecrator of virginal wombs! Defiler of the sanctity of marriage! You reek of foul morals, you corruptible ingrate!"

Once Bruce struck the bottom, his crash punctuated by two jarring crunches, he couldn't move. He mewled in pain, both his legs broken. "I can't feel anything below my hips!"

He was dragged into the dark by his feet. Bruce's bloodcurdling screams did nothing to halt the preacher's work. "What are you doing? This isn't confession. Call an ambulance. For God's sake, where are you dragging me? My legs, I can't feel them. Help me! I trusted you. Why are you doing this to me? You're a man of the cloth."

The preacher said to himself, not his disciple, in feverish whispers, "Faith is fleeting in the eyes of the lord. He sees what I see. God sees through me. The soul is corrupted, but the body can reach heaven purified and redeemed."

Bruce was strapped to a chair by leather restraints. "W-what is this? What the hell is this, you maniac!"

The preacher announced in the dark, "The soul is the root of all evil, not money, not naked flesh, not feasts of gluttonous proportions. Remove the soul, you remove the sin."

"You're not removing anything from me! You unstrap me right now. I'm calling the police and sending your ass to the booby hatch." Bruce's arms and legs were spread out. "What is this about, Preacher? Why have you chosen me?"

"I haven't chosen you. God has chosen you. And God has chosen me to discover the device that will remove your dirty, corrupt, sinful soul!"

The lights flickered on above. The shot panned to the preacher standing beside a leather-covered object. He removed the leather, and beneath it, a machine with a metal horseshoe attached to the end of it was pointed at Bruce. It wasn't normal metal, but instead a strange metal without origin, and Bruce shook his head furiously.

"Why are you pointing that at me? You're not removing any sin from me!"

"You'll feel so good afterwards." The preacher flipped the lever. An electric charge crackled. A set of sparks shot from the tip of the horseshoe and it glowed neon white. "The soul is the bones. Remove the bones and remove the sin!"

Bruce's body convulsed. He frothed from the lips. Veins bulged in his flesh, which turned dark purple. Rivulets and spurts of blood shot up through the skin. First, his skull shot through his face. Then the entire skeleton was drawn to the polarized magnet, the bones shattering upon impact.

The preacher ignored the bones and hurried to the heap of flesh and muscle tissue leaking blood onto the floor. He poured holy water over it and gave the sign of the cross. "May your soul rest in peace... You are now pure and free of sin."

Ted Fuller recognized the film. It was shot in the wake of *The Exorcist* by a man named William Lugg. It was a typical cash-in movie. Ted penned the script for the movie over a weekend after suffering a bout of food poisoning from bad crawfish.

He kept looking at the closet. When would Detective Vickers make his move? He was tempted to scream out to him to shoot the projectors, but then he'd only give away the man's hiding spot.

He said to the vampires, "You're sending horror movie characters to murder innocent people."

The blonde turned her head to him. "In the afterlife, we'll be equals. We'll all be spirits. And we'll all have so much fun together."

"You died when it was your time!" Ted exploded. "Why can't you let nature take its course for everyone else? You're crazy. You're not all there in the head, you understand me? Maybe the magic you're playing with made you stupid."

"Silence!" The redhead's face turned reptilian. "Or you'll be dead next!"

Before Ted could react, the closet door shot open, and Vickers charged the vampires with gun blazing.

Chapter Fourteen

Billy gawked up at the sky. The object made no sense. The best he could tell, it was a giant helmet falling down upon the city. But it was pure bone. Shiny enamel. The crowd around the hospital was silenced at once, an awed hush coming over them. The sun was gradually blotted out. Darkness pervaded. Endless night. When the object touched the streets, people were shaken and knocked to the ground by the great concussion of its landing. A seismic wave carried up and down the city blocks and finally settled. Nelson landed on his side, Billy on all fours. Billy channeled his confusion into getting to his feet and sprinting through the police blockades to the hospital. His father was in there, and he had to know if he was safe.

Nelson shouted after him. "Billy—Billy, what the hell are you doing?"

He dived through the main entrance's rotating doors. The lobby was empty. Furniture and signs had been knocked over and strewn on the tiles. He decided to avoid the elevator and used the emergency stairs. Winded, he was determined to reach the fourth floor. His heart pounded in his ears. Sweat rolled down his face and body. He didn't care. His father could be dead.

Up the third floor and closing in on the fourth, he came upon EMTs and the stretchers they'd lost hold of when the dome touched down.

An EMT called out, "Hey, you can't be in here."

Another EMT piped up. "That's a crime scene. You're not allowed inside. I'll have you arrested."

Billy shot back, "Then arrest me."

At the head of the stairs, the door opened. A group of EMTs called out, "Look outside. Jesus Christ, it's pitch black out there."

"Maybe the sun finally burned out," a voice replied.

Billy ignored them. Fear radiated from each of them. Panic would set in soon for him too. All he could focus on was his father. The hospital hadn't lost power, he was relieved to see. The helmet, the dome, whatever it was, he thought there had to be a reasonable explanation for that.

Body bags were littered the length of the hall, each bag sitting outside a patient's room. Six were wrapped up at the nurse's station. He thanked God he didn't have to see what had happened to them. What could cause such horror? Blood spattered the tiles and the ceilings and every inch of the corridor. The knot in his stomach increased ten-fold.

Billy arrived at his father's room. A body bag was positioned outside the door. He knelt down, two fingers clasping the zipper, but he couldn't bring it down. "This isn't happening. *No, it can't be you in there...*"

His body trembled, emotions threatening to spill out. Billy unzipped the bag enough to see his father's chalky pale face and the dried blood on his forehead. He zipped it back up. Billy covered his mouth with both hands and muffled a scream. He punched the wall and stood up. Then he wept and leaned into the wall.

Maybe if I visited sooner, this wouldn't have happened.

He eyed the dozens of body bags.

I couldn't have stopped them. Look at the blood. Look at all of it.

Every mental defense mechanism kicked in to prevent Billy from collapsing into a helpless fetal position. He was strong enough to catch his breath and then steady his breathing. A looming dread filled him to his core when he glanced at the window at the end of the hall. Pitch black stared back at him. The shadows of an abyss. The air was thinner up here, it seemed. Fresh breezes didn't exist. Whatever

103

covered the sky was also blocking the wind. Images filled Billy's mind. The man at the crosswalk exploding and the strange grin that spread on his lips shortly before he turned into a mess of limbs and blood. It copied the movie right down to the character's features.

His father's injuries. The hospital wing of body bags. And the bizarre shell over the city that resembled a skull cap. Something was happening that was unreal, and perhaps unstoppable.

A hand touched his shoulder. Billy whipped around in fright.

"It's only me," Nelson said, looking down at the body bag nearest his feet. "Is that...is that your father?"

Billy nodded, questioning everything. "What killed him?—what killed these people?"

Nelson kept his voice calm, though he couldn't hide the tremors surging up his body. His instincts were telling him to be careful, to stay on guard. "This is a police matter now. Whatever this all really means, they have to figure it out. Not us. We're normal people."

A jolt of worry had Billy dialing his cell phone. Two rings. Three rings. Four rings. "Come on, pick up. Jessica, pick up the fucking phone."

"I'm lucky, I guess," Nelson said. "My family lives in Illinois. And I don't have a girlfriend. Nobody I have to call."

"Yeah, real lucky," Billy said. He waited another ring. Then Jessica picked up. "Are you safe?" he asked.

"Yeah, I'm at work. Where are you?"

"I'm at the hospital. My dad's gone. I mean he's dead. Something killed the entire fourth floor of the hospital. They've been wheeling out bodies all morning."

"Billy, I'm so—"

"Stay where you are. I'll be there soon. Lock your office door. I don't know what the hell is going on outside."

"I saw it come from the sky," Jessica said frantically. "Out of nowhere, it floated down. It's a dome or something."

"Promise me you'll hole up in your office. I'm coming for you."

"But what's going on, Billy? What came from the sky? The police are cruising the streets telling everybody to stay home. You can't go out there."

"Like hell I can't. I already lost my father today. I'm not losing anyone else I care about because of the idiot police. You think they know what's happening? Look outside, something's over the city blocking the sun. They can't do anything about it. Who knows what danger we're in? They can't stop this."

Jessica was speechless for a second, and then she was desperate. "Then be safe. Don't do anything stupid. And hurry."

"I'll be right there."

Nelson had watched him the entire conversation. "You up for the trip?" Billy asked him. "You can go home if you want."

"No way," Nelson said, shaking his head. "I'm with you. It's not safe anywhere, if you ask me, not until we figure out what the hell has boxed us in the city."

Billy fled the fourth floor with Nelson at his tail. The EMTs and police were too busy controlling the crowd of frantic citizens outside to notice two men running uptown into the darkness.

Chapter Fifteen

The buxom vampire beauties added another reel onto the living room projector. The redhaired vixen couldn't resist the title and its possibilities: *Slasher Girls*.

Chained hand and foot, blindfolded, Harry Fallwell was walked through a dank corridor of moldy stale air. Drips echoed from overhead. He was underground, maybe near the sewers. Behind him, he listened to the conversation of his captors.

"Today's a big day for you, Marlene," a husky, deep woman's voice said, one afflicted by heavy doses of alcohol and chain smoking. "I have charts, files and hard evidence of who you are. This isn't an orphanage for estranged girls. Yes, I've raised you and fifty others, but the truth is, I've saved you from being aborted."

"Oh no," he whispered, the pang in his chest as sharp as a knife. "Oh shit."

"Quiet," the woman demanded. She yanked on the back of his hair. "Haven't you done enough, Dr. Fallwell? You've aborted hundreds of unborn women. We have rights. Women have the right to choose. You pressured them. You wanted to abort them. You get off on women's suffering!"

"I-I don't know what you're talking about. Yes, I'm a doctor. Yes, I've performed abortions, but my practice is sensitive and caring to its clients. We educate on birth control methods, offer counseling sessions, and I always find out for certain if a woman wants to abort her child. I think you have the wrong guy. I haven't done anything to you people. Why have you kidnapped me?"

His skull thunked when the wooden baton struck his head. Harry stumbled to his knees, crying out as painful stars shined in his eyes. Blood raced down his head. He managed one last comment before his mouth was duct-taped shut. "You women are crazy!"

"A woman sticks up for herself," the husky woman said, "and you consider her crazy? I bet you think women are inferior to you. You think it's funny we can vote, hold down jobs, decide if we want children, and if we don't want to fuck you when you want it, you think we're prudes— or you'll call us sluts anyway! We're the ones infected by your testosterone disease. Your seed sows our fate. It changes our lives. You can walk out anytime you want and leave us with your burdens. Dr. Fallwell, you're as guilty as any man out there. This school I've started is designed to take you out one-by-one, and we will. It'll take extreme measures for equality, but we'll get there. One day, men will fear sex."

Harry could sense he was passing by rooms, as he walked on blindly. Throughout the rooms, chains rattled, whips cracked, glass shattered and flesh burned. Men howled in pain. Shrieking.

Then he heard knives raked against carving stones. The muffle of gunfire at a firing range.

"Marlene, all of us were saved from being aborted. We stormed clinics like Harry's and saved you from being extracted from the womb. We helped your mother raise you, your real mother, Marlene. She's ready to meet you. You thought you were an orphan, but we were shaping you and your mother. You two will make the perfect team. Society will finally be as it should, with men crumbling at our feet."

A door opened, the bottom scraping against concrete. Harry was tied to a wall, his hands above his head, legs shackled to the floor. His blindfold was removed. He turned to the wall behind him. A target was painted in what looked like human blood. He was standing in some kind of firing range. To the left and right of him, men were chained up as he was, many dead, chock full of holes from bullets and unknown implements.

He noticed the two women he assumed had brought him here. Jerry *couldn't see them clearly, but he caught the older woman hand the younger one a dagger.*

"You know where to throw it, Marlene."

"Nooooooooo!"

"Become one of us. You'll meet your mother. Everything will be as it was supposed to be before men turned society upside down."

"Pleeeeeeeease noooooooooooo"

"Marlene, you are now one of the Slasher Girls. Now throw the knife where it counts. He won't be a man much longer..."

Vickers aimed his shotgun and released a round into the nearest vampire. The black-haired woman's chest caved in, fluids spattering out her back. Her scream was limited by gurgling. She landed on all fours and stopped moving. Rushing forward, he untied Fuller from the bed. The man was naked, but he scrambled to throw on a pair of jeans and a shirt wadded up on the floor. Fuller stood up, visibly breathing hard in the projector's light. A scene of a man stalking a screaming couple was displayed. The attacker's head split in two, the man's brains chewing and biting at the air with teeth and a pair of ogling eyes.

Fuller bounded forward to kick the projector to its side when four of the vampires entered the room. Vickers backed up in the corner. He attempted to fire another round, but the gun was empty.

"Shit!"

Fuller opened the window. "Quick, the fire escape! We don't have a choice."

Vickers urged Fuller to go first. Now he clutched the shotgun as a bludgeon. "You stay away from me, you crazy bitches. I don't know who you are or how you've pulled it off, but you've murdered dozens of innocent people."

"Is that all?" The blonde was disappointed. "It's been more than that, and they all bled like stuck pigs and tasted just as sweet. And you won't be any different than the other swine when I bite into your flesh...or whatever else is out there that will do the biting for me."

Vickers couldn't battle them in the room. The most brutal of tactics couldn't bring down the bizarre foe. Fuller was already down to the first floor and safer than him. Vickers gave him five seconds to flee the scene. Then he heaved the shotgun at the vampires and jumped through the open window onto the fire escape landing. His trench coat caught on something inside, and he instinctively slipped out of it completely and left it behind. Down the metal stairs, he pumped his arms and legs as fast as he could—fear of slipping and falling be damned! He turned his gaze upward to check for any aerial assaults. He was surprised they didn't come. But the vampires laughed, the piercing shrieks and cackles of celebration. The notes carried higher and higher. Vickers couldn't help but feel like he'd made a mistake.

The vampires wanted him out of the apartment.

They were victorious.

He touched down onto the alley. Ted Fuller waited eagerly and wide-eyed behind a garbage bin. He was gaunt, white-lipped and drained of energy, but something had given him strength to escape the apartment.

Vickers stared up at the sky again; they weren't pursing them. He checked his watch. "It's noon right now. And it's pitch black."

"You didn't watch the movie," Ted said. "In *Bone Dome*, a giant skull sits over a city. The city fights to escape as the air is slowly used up. The sun is gone, you see."

"You can't be serious." Vickers rubbed at his tired eyes. His sense of disbelief was ever-expanding, as was his migraine. "This can't be real, yet there it is, the sky is blocked by bone. Maybe it's bone, maybe it's not, but there it is. And those women upstairs, they're the ones who killed everybody at Iowa University. Christ, I had you pegged for the killings. I thought you were using special effects. Or maybe it was a cult following of yours."

"I have no following." Ted failed to restrain his bitterness. "I never did. Everybody was out to shut me down."

Panic echoed from unseen corridors of the city. Screams. Faint words, perhaps warnings. Cars crashing. Guns blasting. Glass shattering. Buildings crackling with fire. Explosions.

"We better head to police headquarters," Vickers suggested. "It'll be safe there."

"No, the law can't help us now. We're destroying the projectors and the reels. I brought them back. I didn't think it would work. But you saw them with your own eyes."

Vickers seized both his shoulders and shook him hard. "Why did you bring them back?"

"I stole my movie at Iowa University," Ted admitted. "I wanted my movie back. That's the only reason I came to the viewing. But one of the vampires told me they could give me the rest of my movies back too. They said they were hidden only blocks from where I lived. So I plugged in a projector and played the film. The truth is, the reel is possessed by ghosts, and all I know is they used magic of some sort to take the images from the movies and turn them into real life.

"Andy Ryerson survived the first attack. Have you heard of the Anderson Mills Massacre? A whole town is dead and nobody can say why. And not just dead, but mutilated, drained of blood, the works— something straight out of a horror movie, literally."

Vickers was confused. The line between real and unreal and outright ludicrous had been blurred. The evidence surrounded him. The dome over the city and the vampires and the hideous deaths. His investigative skills were useless in this crazy world.

"Then what do you suggest we do?"

Ted pondered the question. He kept rubbing his wrists, a solid raw line embedded in the flesh from his captivity. "We burn the building down. The reels will go up with the place. There's an auto body garage down the street. Maybe they have something we can set a fire with."

"What about the people in the building?"

"Set the fire alarms before we start the fire."

"How about starting it in your apartment," Vickers said. "I'm not allowing anybody else to be hurt. Enough is enough. I won't be responsible for any more bloodshed."

"No, you're right. Enough people have died already because of this."

Vickers shook hands with Ted. "I'm sorry I thought you were a murderer."

"Buy me a drink when this is over, and we're square."

The two retreated to Steven's Auto Body and Salvage two blocks south of the apartment building in search of flammable materials.

Chapter Sixteen

Roger Patrick clutched the steering wheel of his yellow cab. He'd sped back and forth between Maywood and Englewood Park, traveled to Melrose Park, and taken outlets throughout the city all the way to East End to pick up random travelers and stranded victims and transport them to Navy Pier to safety. There, many took shelter in the shops at the strip malls along the harbor. Medical units had been set up as well alongside armed barriers by the police who tried to form a front against what lurked throughout Chicago.

No traffic, he cruised at fifty on the streets where he rarely reached fifteen in the past. A Remington shotgun sat propped across his lap, and it reminded him every second he was in danger. He'd already blasted five rounds from his window. His right passenger door was missing. A preacher cackling and spouting gibberish he couldn't understand had removed the door with a huge magnet. After shooting at the crazed preacher, Roger watched him aim the magnet in a new direction, toward a throng of fleeing people. The preacher removed dozens of their skeletons via the magnet's pull. Roger couldn't understand how it was possible, but he'd seen skeletons rattle across his windshield and nearly send him crashing into the sidewalk.

Roger hooked a left onto 89th Street, keeping an eye out for anything. He kept his brights on despite the fear of giving himself away. The shotgun offered as much courage as the bottle of half-spent bourbon at his feet.

Corpses were strewn on the sidewalks as well. Many of them were faceless, their heads emptied of contents. Rough gouges marked where teeth carved up the features and worked through the sinuses to suck out the brains. He'd seen devilish eyes glower at him as something chewed a pregnant woman's face and worked through the belly for another brain to eat.

Keep your eyes open for victims. You have to keep saving people. The police can't do it. The majority of the survivors are too scared to leave Navy Pier, and the blockade won't protect them from jack shit if any of these monsters find out where they are.

A series of hotels unfolded to his left and right: The Hilton, Holiday Inn, Trevor Turlington Suites and a slew of lower-end places. This sector was fairly untouched. No enemies attacked from the sky or the ground. His beams crossed on a woman sitting on the sidewalk with her head in her hands. Her shoulder blades shook; she was weeping. Roger immediately pulled over.

"Hop in, sweetie," Roger said in the most soothing voice he could dredge up. "I'll take you to safety. Navy Pier sound okay? They have food, shelter, cops and a place to rest."

She was attractive and was dressed like a schoolgirl. Plaid miniskirt. Button-up white dress shirt. Black tie. Black tote bag. Silky auburn hair styled in a pony tail. Though her face was unflinching, her eyes were blackened by streaming mascara from a long cry.

Was she on her way to class when this happened? The nearest school is miles from here.

"I'm not going to hurt you," Roger insisted, "but I have to keep moving. Anything could come at us at any moment. I promise I'll take you to Navy Pier."

She agreed, standing up, and entered the backseat. He got a better look at her in the rearview mirror. She couldn't have been older than twenty-two. Ninety-five pounds. Her buttons had come undone revealing the topmost half of her breasts, which glowed with a sheen of sweat. She reminded him of a cross between a Valley girl and a frat boy's girlfriend.

Roger politely turned his eyes back to the road. "Are you hurt? I don't know your name."

113

"I didn't throw it," she said in a surprisingly cutting voice. "You're looking at me, aren't you?"

"I was checking for injuries," Roger said, half-lying. "I apologize if I offended you. It's been a heck of a day."

She spread her legs. "You want to see my snatch, is that it? Are you some kind of pervert?"

"What? No, please understand me. I'm not trying to—"

"The last guy who gave me half the glances you did ended up buried in my backyard." Her teeth were bared in a wicked sneer. Her beauty was marred by the hatred twisting her face. "And you were looking at my tits. Sizing them up. Imaging how they feel. You'd rape me, wouldn't you? Violate me. Use this panic situation to get your dick wet, you piece of shit, wouldn't you? I've met your kind, and I've taught them a lesson. They'll never look at a girl's chest again—not without eyes, or a head, or a dick!"

He slammed on the brakes. "Get out of my car, you crazy bitch. Don't threaten me. I'm risking my life to save your ass. I wasn't going to do a damn thing to you. I'm only trying to take you to Navy P—"

"Die, you scumbag!"

She reached into her tote bag and removed a short samurai sword. She jammed the blade through the seat, an inch of it cutting into his kidney. He stopped the car. Before he could twist around and aim the shotgun at her, she rolled out the door screaming, "What do you want cut off next, your big head or your little head? And being a man, your answer will have to be more specific!"

From the left, he counted twenty—no thirty—no, now fifty schoolgirls in checkered plaid miniskirts, pig tails, high-heeled, black polished dress shoes, and tight-fitting button-up tops without bras charging the taxi. Each raised a mix of swords, maces, double-edged axes, clubs with nails jammed through them—way too large for anybody to be carrying, yet the women brandished them without difficulty—scythes, sickles, hammers and railroad spikes.

"I want to wear his balls around my neck."

"Pulverize him."

"I'll feed his dick to my Doberman."

"I'll shove my mace up his ass—or maybe he'd like that. Creeps like him are always closet perverts!"

"Make him shit blood, and then we'll see how much he enjoys a mace up his ass."

"Try a dynamite dildo!"

Holy fucking shit, these chicks are insane!

Roger clutched the wheel with bloody hands. He pounded the gas. "Move, you piece-of-shit! MOVE!"

The car jolted forward, leaving behind the small fleet of armed slasher schoolgirls in the cloud of his exhaust.

Chapter Seventeen

Jessica was holed up in the fifth floor of Corporate Tower, a skyscraper filled with offices and businesses. The window in her corner office gave a perfect view of the strange shell over the city. It was thick and the color of white enamel. The city was blocked out, isolated from the rest of the world, and left in darkness. Below, strange things were happening. The way it sounded, Jessica would've believed monsters paraded below.

The radio station had been replaced by a repeating message: *Do not attempt to leave shelter for any reason. The Chicago Police Department will attend to anybody in the streets or separated from their families and loved ones. We repeat, stay indoors. Anyone found roaming the streets will be detained.*

The majority of the office workers had left for home.

Billy said he's coming. I can't leave. What if he shows up and I'm gone? What if he's arrested?

Jessica pressed her hands against the window. The image in her mind kept repeating the strange helmet shape floating in the air, suspended by nothing, and then touching down on the city. The foundation of the city had been jostled upon its landing.

She stared at Billy's picture in the frame on her desk. They were hugging each other at Shedd Aquarium in front of a bottle-nosed dolphin. Her favorites were the tiger and hammerhead sharks. The aquarium was almost like being underwater: the dark muted walls and the gurgle and bubbling from the tanks. The fun-loving good time had been replaced by martial law and encroaching death. She prioritized her life in seconds. She wanted to get married, buy a house, and after passing the bar exam, she'd have children. Maybe Billy would go back to school first, and then they'd live the dream.

Right now, the dream was being sucked dry of air. She could feel it happen in her lungs already. The air was thinning. Sweat constantly dripped down her body. What would the quality of air be like in hours?—days? Would they make it for days?

She was distracted by a shuffle outside her office door.

Oh shit, someone's here.

I thought I was alone.

She lifted the closed shade of her window and peered into the hallway. It was Steve Allan. He was a paralegal like her. He wore his iPod, oblivious to everything that was happening. He carried a stack of files. Jessica stopped him as he passed by her office. She made him remove his headphones.

"Don't you know what's going on?"

Steve shook his head. "What, did everybody go to lunch?"

"You haven't heard?"

"No," Steve said. "I have three tests to study for. Mr. Bruner's environmental law test, for one, and then Mr. Burke's—"

"Forget the exams!" She guided him to the window in her office. "You see that?"

Steve looked outside, turning his head slightly to one side. He stumbled on words, beginning a sentence and then giving up over and over again.

Finally, he gasped, "*No way.* When did this happen? Everybody left me making copies. The fuckers. They *would* leave me here." Steve was confused. "Why are you still here?"

"My boyfriend is on the way."

"Oh."

A random scream interrupted them. "You gotta help me!"

Jessica's back tensed. Every inch of her skin heated up. The sound was so out of place in the quiet office atmosphere, it shook them both. Steve raced into the hall toward the bathrooms. "It came from the men's bathroom, I think."

She followed behind Steve, who propped the bathroom door open. An arc of artificial light painted the tiles. The arc touched the edge of a black boot.

"Don't open the door any more," a deep, gruff voice warned. Pain edged each syllable. The man was holding back agony. "Please, I don't want you to see me. My body has a mind of its own. Shoot me now. Kill me. Any way you see fit. I'd prefer if you shot me between the eyes. Make it final. Make me dead."

Steve turned to Jessica, both of them perplexed. Jessica softened her voice. "Why would you want us to do that to you? If you're hurt, we'll get you to the hospital. It doesn't matter what's going on or how much you hurt. Don't give up. We're only blocks from the hospital."

"Yeah," Steve piped up. "There's no need for talk like that, man. What happened to you, man?"

He pushed open the door another inch.

"No—don't!"

It was too late. The man was splayed on the floor. He was over three-hundred pounds. Powdered sugar white skin. The whites of his eyes were yellow. Fingernails purple. Hair long and black, but he was bald on top. Lips had no color. He wore a red vest. A circle of wet blood where his navel would be. The wound had bled over his black pants and flowed over dozens of square tiles. But the most disturbing sight, more so than the glossy red blood, was his distended belly. A cauldron could've been stuffed in his abdominal cavity. The belly bulged so tight it stretched to near tearing.

Steve couldn't hide the disgust in his words. "What is...what's wrong with you, man?"

"It's too late now, you idiot," the man laughed. Ripe spittle foamed at both edges of his lips. The blood at his navel spurted down his legs, pooling. "I have no control over my actions anymore. My thoughts, my ambitions, my self-control, I own none of them. Once I see you, IT WANTS YOU DEAD!"

Jessica's intuition shot her from the bathroom. She expected Steve to be right behind her, but he stood in the door in shock. Hands at his sides.

She stopped and shouted, "Steve, get away from that man!"

Blood spattered the tiles in gallon loads, skin shredded—it made her insides clench to hear it—and then a projectile wrapped around Steven's throat. Like rope, but it was pink, and glistening, and visceral.

"Steve!" she screamed. She was rooted in place, fearing if she helped him she too would be lassoed by the bizarre weapon. "Let him go, whoever you are."

"I can't control it," he tittered darkly. "I can't be held accountable for who I kill. I was born this way. I have the biggest guts of them all. They're five miles long and growing."

Steve's face was a violent shade of purple. His eyes stewed in their sockets on the verge of exploding out of his head. Tapeworm veins streaked across his features.

"*Gaaaaackgraaaaghgaaaaaack!*"

"My intestines have an intuition." The man continued to weave his tale. "They know who deserves to die. God gave them to me for a reason. I am God's vessel. They nuked me with A-bomb juice, but it was God who instilled this power in me. My guts are the judge, jury and executioner. I have no control over them, but oh, how I like to watch you die. It gives me great pleasure!"

The man's face had changed from genuinely apologetic to seething with abominable evil.

"LET HIM GO! YOU'LL KILL HIM!"

The man's words were hate-filled. "The guts reap your innermost thoughts from the flesh. They know your past, your sins, the evil you're capable of committing to others! I AM THE INTESTINATOR!"

The intestines audibly coiled tighter over Steve's throat. Steve's eyes bled. His nose, ears and mouth dribbled pink froth. His head quaked. With the sound of thick roots breaking earth, his head was snapped from the neck. Blood shot to the ceiling and rained back onto the headless victim. Steve's head was pitched at Jessica. She ducked in time. Shattered glass from the office window behind her marked her attempt at fleeing, each step a crunch. She screamed uncontrollably. The shadows flickered and spun around her. The viscera was suspended in the air like a long snake jutting out of the maniac's navel.

Jesus Christ, Steve's head, he ripped it off.

That man's guts ripped Steve's head off!

She hadn't seen the man before; he was a complete stranger. He wasn't a client, at least not a recent one. How were intestines capable of ripping a man's head off? He would do the same to her. Her head would be the next rolling on the floor.

Jessica's retreat was blind and random for the first ten seconds. The man's pursuit, on the other hand, was calculated and confident. Jessica felt the rush of wind as the intestines propelled themselves, swiping, bending and reaching for her. They touched her hair. The contact was brief and left a glob of sticky substance behind.

She ran even faster. She forced open the fire exit door and launched down the steps. Three floors below, she could run outside to safety, to fresher air if fresh air still existed.

Would the man chase her until she was dead?

Jessica kept charging down the stairs and prayed she beat the monstrosity out of the building.

Chapter Eighteen

The blonde vampire clutched the dark-haired vampire in her arms. She bled heavily from the shotgun wound she'd taken earlier. She gagged and coughed on fluids, but she smiled through the damage. "I'm not going to die. I'll come back as something else. Quick, play another movie! We'll send them all to hell with us."

The blonde sucked the tips of her fingers, relishing every drop of blood staining them. "Yes, to hell with them," she laughed. She licked the woman's chest, digging her tongue into the wound and sucking the delectable juices from the upturned meat. "Our magic is unstoppable. Ghosts of the dead have known magic for centuries, and now we have crafted a way to bend reality, to recycle the dead into new bodies. The more we kill, the more ways we will find to bend reality. Magic practiced by thousands will surely be amazing. You won't die, my sweet. If this is the only way we can exist among the living, then so be it."

The dying woman whispered, "I was Anne Jenkins before I died. I used to be a homemaker. I made peanut butter and jellies for snot-nosed brats. My husband remarried six months after I died. He didn't bother to visit my grave and neither did my son or daughter. Death opened up my eyes. The living don't deserve the skin they wear. They have no idea how lucky they are. They had their chance to appreciate a beating heart. The afterlife is horrible. All we get to do is watch the living squander their mortality."

The blonde nodded, petting back a strand of dark hair from the dying woman's face. She kissed the former Anne Jenkins on her bloody forehead. "My name was Georgia. I had my throat cut in an alley sucking off a client. The second he finished, he jammed the blade of a carrot peeler into my neck. I turned tricks in a small Podunk town called Humansville, ironically. Nobody found my body for two months. I was left in a black trash bag in the county dump. Garbage pickers found my naked ass. They stole the cocaine and twenty dollars I had in my purse before they called for help. I was aware in my dead body. In that trash bag. Two months of hot suffocating black. I still feel my body rot beneath the earth, buried in my casket. Worms and bacteria have worked through the lining of the coffin and are breaking down my flesh. I'll never be true flesh and blood again. Never. *And the living will know my agony firsthand!*"

Anne coughed up a wad of coagulated blood. "So what city will we take over next?"

The other three chimed in:

"How about New York?"

"Boston?"

"Philadelphia?"

The blonde pointed at the projector. "That's not important yet. We have to worry about those two assholes coming back for us. They might try and destroy the projectors. I think Ted knows too much."

"Nobody will stand a chance," the auburn-haired vampire said. "I'll rip their heads from their shoulders and bathe in their blood."

"Feed the projector another film," Georgia demanded. "Let's bring you back to life, Anne. I'll play a few more reels, and you can pick the one you like best..."

Psychologist and hypnotist Naga Surie clutched his patient's head. His patient sat on the dark red leather chair in his office. The woman in his hands was in her early thirties, suffering from nervous stress. Naga played his fingers along her skull, tracing each region of the brain.

He was looking for the trigger.

"Mrs. Turner, I will unlock the part of your brain that's hardwired

these behaviors. You've lost your job at the post office because you have to trace the zip codes with a pen over and over to the point you tear the paper. Your husband says you check the oven fifteen times a night to make sure the burners are off. You can't leave the house without double checking the locks for twenty minutes. These behaviors have rendered a normal life, well, implausible."

Mrs. Turner wept. *"I'm not happy. I don't have a life. It's, it's a living hell."*

He massaged the occipital region of her skull. "You've been to five other psychologists who haven't been able to crack the code of your behaviors. These are so hardwired and entrenched in the brain, it's near impossible to cure. There's a practice in the Middle East called 'unplugging'. It's an ancient art that's not practiced in the mainstream. Imagine your brain's like a machine. You shut it down. Turn it on and turn it off. You'll come back the way you were before your disorder took hold."

"Please," Mrs. Turner begged. *"I'll do anything to be normal again. Can you really change me?"*

Naga smiled. *"Absolutely."*

He traced her skull with his fingers. She was relaxed. She moaned lightly, eyes closed and visibly rolling against her eyelids.

Naga traced the edges of her skull cap and finally located it. The special massage unlocked what he called "the mind's trigger"; it resembled a cyst.

He flicked it on and issued a silent prayer.

Mrs. Turner passed out. *"Ohhhhhhh..."*

Suddenly, her face split down the middle. The skull cap cracked and forked and was spit out in brittle pieces. The brain came alive, a set of long and sharp teeth surrounding the soft tissue in a protective shell.

"I did the ritual correctly. I followed the rules!" Naga exclaimed.

Mrs. Turner screamed with her lips on two separate sides of her head. *"What's happening to me?"*

"I'm so sorry! The brain is a powerful storehouse of knowledge. Many secrets are trapped in the cerebral cortex that we have no idea about. I've unlocked the way to cure people of their hardwired behaviors, but there's the risk of bringing about the demon. Everybody has two guiding systems, a human being, and the second, a more primitive, evil monster. This evil monster fulfills what your morality and guilt and conscience keep you from committing. Sex, murders, anything that you've withheld yourself from committing in life, the monster locked in your brain will see it through."

"You lied to me!" the brain growled, four octaves deeper than Mrs. Turner's voice. "You're a louse, a fucking liar! I'll rip the tongue out of your lying mouth and shit it down your throat. Your ethics are shit. Now people will smell your corruption with every word you speak."

The brain monster sucked up Naga's cranial matter in three voracious gulps.

Georgia laughed hysterically as the reel played on. She finally watched the part of the movie where the woman rips out Naga's tongue and defecates it down his throat. She skimmed her finger along the dusty tins of movies. "Ah yes, another one. Anything to achieve more victims!"

Georgia chose *The Plow Man:*

Dean Marlow shoved a large tube down the open manhole. Toxic waste was delivered into the sewers. The steaming gook splashed onto his steel-toed boots. "Ah shit. I bet you're having a laugh over this one, Hank."

"Hank Brundage?" Chris Leer joined Dean, holding the tube straight as more caustic fluids poured out. "That stupid fucker?"

"Hank could barely tie his shoes, never mind wipe his ass," Dean chuckled. With his free hand, he took a nip of whiskey from a fifth and shared it with Chris. He tapped the ground with his foot. "That's why I had to let him go."

"Yeah, we buried that retard in the foundation," Chris guffawed, whiskey spilling down his chin. "He was napping on a break when we were pouring the concrete. He didn't wake up long enough to scream. I bet he thought the concrete was a water bed."

"Nobody's found the dumb bastard. I saw his orange hard hat. The last thing I saw of ol' Hank Brundage. His family wasn't upset. His mother and father were happy to be rid of the extra baggage."

"And I'm not going to jail over a retard."

"Me either."

"I'm glad we joined up with the waste disposal service," Chris said. "I mean, I liked being in business with you, but construction's a lot of work."

"This ain't shit," Dean said. "It's toxic waste. Leftover napalm and agent orange and the shit they use to dust crops. It's a helluva cocktail. Mean shit. Eat your insides out. Have you popping with cancers too ugly to name."

"You got it on your shoe, buddy."

"It can't go through leather, dumb ass."

"Oh, sorry."

"The toxic honey wagon's empty. Let's get a move on. Both me and you know this is illegal."

Chris narrowed his eyes and scratched his head. "Yeah, that's why we're paid the big bucks."

The truck drove away, leaving a jet of fumes and dripping a chemical cocktail onto the street in its wake. Across the street, steam issued through the cracks of the new construction site. Jackhammers suddenly propelled themselves, pounding through the earth six at a time. Deeper chunks of rock exploded, so deep, Hank Brundage's corpse was uncovered, dried up, curled in a fetal position. Chemical steam hovered over the corpse. The eyes came open. Yellowed. Fat had issued through the flesh in a white milky substance. His permanent scream suddenly shifted into a smile. Hank adjusted his hardhat and headed over to the *steamroller. The steamroller had always been his favorite; he owned replicas of them as a kid and kept them on a display shelf in his room at his parents' house.*

In the backseat of the rig, he noticed a double-barreled shotgun.

The steamroller started on its own.

In a voice as sharp as gravel, Hank said, "Looks like my ride is here…"

Anne vanished into smoke, as did the blood that had stained the carpet beneath her body. Georgia smiled, reassured the next reel would resurrect her fallen brethren. She played *500 Foot Hooker* in her honor:

Ray Johnston—Johnny Ray as friends called him—was walking up Manhattan Drive. His two business associates, one who named himself "Rock", the other "Silk", were also on foot, dressed in mink coats and clutching ivory canes with sizeable diamonds on the top. Beneath the coats they wore burgundy suits. Both had seventies discothèque afros with a hair pick jutting out the side.

Johnny Ray aimed his cane in the direction of the abandoned warehouse just down the road. "Is that where we're meeting this jive turkey? Man, I've got bitches waitin' for a good bangin'. Why the hell am I here on a Saturday night? I've got bills to collect and booties to slap."

"This is business," Silk said coolly, side-stepping and spinning and breaking out in a two-step for no good reason. "This bitch is for sale, this doctor says. This is one of those good bitches. Real nice. Can shake it something sweet. We'll make money off this piece. Melted butter on bread, my brudda."

Johnny Ray was skeptical. "We don't know this punk. Doctor could be a jive turkey copper."

Rock agreed. "Yeah, he might be a cop. Do you wanna be riding piggy back to the pen?"

Silk stopped on the sidewalk. "If you don't want a part of this business venture, then go back to your stank ass bitches. They get twenty to fifty bucks a pop if they're good, but this bitch—this bitch, man, she's a grand a pop. Butter dripping down your rolls, jive talkas. Now you've hurt my feelings. I let you in on the secret. The big event. THE BIG, fellas. Shit, you ain't acting interested. When you set your eyes on this bitch, you'll want to sample the product."

Johnny Ray opened up his suit to showcase the .45 caliber pistol tucked under his arm. "This better be THE BIG."

Rock chimed in, "Saturday nights only come once a week. The score better be good. Damn good, you get me, turkey?"

Silk guided them to the warehouse. The sign outside was faded and pocked with bullet holes. They entered the YOU RENT IT storage building.

The warehouse was dark as pitch. Johnny Ray flipped his sterling silver Zippo lighter. "Turn on the lights. I can't see."

The voice of a carnie announcing an attraction came from the back of the warehouse: "Welcome, my friends. I have the greatest hooker in history. Every customer will shell out the big greens for this fine lady. This genetically created and enhanced beauty will do anything I tell her, and she'll only listen to me. I will rent her out to you for—"

Johnny Ray fired a round into the dark.

"Gaack!"

The announcer audibly slipped from a staircase above and landed with the crunch of bone. Silk flipped on a lever next to an oversized breaker box and it sparked on, charged with thousands of volts of juice. "You shot that honky before he spoke his piece."

Johnny Ray blew on the smoking barrel. "I said my piece too. That bitch is mine. Where is she? Nobody sells to the pimp. The pimp sells to them."

The rattle of chains, the snapping of steel, and from beneath the giant tarp spread out on the floor, she came alive. Red leather stilettos. Pink fishnets. Red g-string. A tattoo of a cartoon devil on her inner thigh sucking on its forked tail. A darker red tube top housed huge breasts.

Her hair was dyed electric red.

And she was two-hundred feet tall.

"You killed my pimp!" The scream tore paint and bricks from the walls. An earthquake erupted as she cried. The point of her stiletto heel impaled Johnny Ray through the midsection. She flung him off of her shoe. "Eww, gross."

Johnny Ray was thrown twenty yards and collided into the wall.

His dying words: "Ah shit, bitch!"

Silk opened fire, producing a golden Tommy gun from his mink coat. Brat-brat-brat-brat-brat!

A fist hammered down and turned Silk into a squashed puddle of mink and guts and blood. The camera panned to a mouth coughing out a last word: "Skank."

Rock fled the building only for the top of the warehouse to be flung into the air and crash down upon him. The woman stood, as tall as the nearby buildings. "EVERY MAN WILL DIE," she screamed, the decibels shattering panes of glass. "EVERY MAN WILL SUFFER!"

The strawberry-blonde vampire who was once named Hillary Doeskin—who died in real life when struck by a flying stop sign during a tornado in Missouri—inserted another reel into the projector. She watched intently, enthralled by the film entitled *The Pickler.*

The funeral home was surrounded by the townspeople of Heatonville. Citizens stood between gravestones, the shadows of night carving their features into vicious folds of hatred. They knew Jack White's secret. The funeral director had taken liberties with the town's freshly dead, and tonight, he would pay.

"Come on out," Frank Morgan, the leader of the mob, demanded. He was mayor, and his late wife, Jo-Beth, was about to become a victim of Jack White's extracurricular activities. "Jack, we know you're in there.

You're cutting up Jo-Beth's body as we speak, aren't you? You're going to sell it to body brokers, right? For a few bucks you've desecrated her, you greedy son-of-a-bitch! You've desecrated them all. This is your last chance to come out before we break in and force you out."

"Break the door down!"

"Lynch the bastard!"

"Burn the place down!"

Frank Morgan motioned for the four cops behind him to drive a battering ram through the front door. The crash of wood satisfied the crowd's lust for revenge. Frank led the throng into the foyer. The room was empty, but the basement door was wide open.

"We know you're down there, Jack," Frank shouted over the din and curses. "Show yourself, or we're coming down there. WE'RE COMING DOWN ANYWAY!"

Moments passed, the crowd growing even more violent. Frank aimed his flashlight at the basement door. There was only silence. "HERE WE COME, YOU BASTARD!"

Tommy Prichard, Dwight Meason and Melissa Dowery followed behind him. Melissa clutched a noose and Tommy and Dwight each carried a high-powered rifle. Frank didn't care about the threat of violence surrounding him. He too wanted revenge.

The lights in the basement were suddenly turned off. "Now we know we've got him," Frank rejoiced. "You're not escaping us. You can't hide, not even in the dark."

Frank found the switch on the wall and flipped the lights back on.

Upon their entrance, Jo-Beth was splayed on a steel gurney. Her legs were amputated at the hips. The legs themselves were iced in a foam cooler at the foot of the gurney. Her eyes were missing and so were her arms. The pale girl, "Queen Beauty of Heatonville", was now a ruined corpse.

Jack White, the embalmer, was in his early sixties and wore an expression of calculated emotion. He didn't want to appear too scared or too guilty. But soon, Frank watched in astonishment as the man's face broke into a twisted grin. "Hah, hah, hah, your bodies are worth more dead than alive, you know that? What does it hurt to profit from a corpse? They don't care. They're dead."

Jack picked up the legs from the cooler and posed them standing, then he moved them so they seemed to walk. "They don't give a shit. She's dead. Fucking dead. She didn't say no. Sure didn't. I asked. She just froze up. Hah! Hah! Hah!"

Frank instinctively threw a punch into Jack's face. He crashed into a box heaped with foam peanuts. Jack rose from the box, incensed, his humor wiped clean from his face. "Now how about I ship you in pieces across the state? People need these organs, you fools. My son died without a heart transplant. The dead don't need their insides, but HE DID!"

Tommy, Dwight and Melissa closed in on Jack. Tommy snarled, "Let's give him a taste of his own medicine."

Melissa's eyes bulged with fury. "I have a better idea. Let's embalm the bastard."

Dwight jammed a trocar needle into Jack's mouth. "Swallow this!"

Embalming fluid was forced down Jack's throat. "Naaaawgh!"

Melissa shoved another trocar into Jack's torso. Then Tommy drove another into his neck. Jack was filling with chemicals. The man flung his arms, struggling to be free of the slow internal drowning. He fell to the floor, his mouth gushing embalming fluid onto the floor. The four stared at each other. Nobody spoke for moments.

"Thank the good lord he's dead." Tommy spat on Jack. "May you go to hell."

Jack's body shot up from the floor. His flesh was wet with embalming fluid. His eyes and nose dripped, his mouth seethed and his flesh exuded the substance through his sweat glands. Every word was fluid-choked. A devilish smile played on his face, carved by trails of clear fluid. "Death is chemical. Death is formaldehyde. Death is preservation. I am the new grim reaper. The voice in the shadows. The shrouded man at *the gate. Now, let me touch you."*

Jack's hands clasped Tommy's hand. Suddenly, Tommy gagged and choked. Tommy's jugular opened and spat out blood at such a high pressure it spattered onto the ceiling and the shocked onlookers. The embalming fluid flowed from Jack's fingertips into the gaping jugular once it stopped spurting. Tommy was embalmed in seconds.

He flopped to the ground stone-cold dead.

"I am 'The Pickler'," *Jack erupted in jubilation, spitting embalming fluid from his lips. "You created me, NOW FACE ME!"*

Georgia had been watching the film behind Hillary's shoulder. "Great choice, honey."

Hillary kissed Georgia on the lips to celebrate another movie. "Death, blood, destruction, it's all coming together. The city will suffer in terror."

They watched out the window as the monsters they created took over the city.

Chapter Nineteen

Billy stopped at the stairs leading up to the elevated train. He wasn't sure if the system was still running despite everything. The city roared with violence, but between 11th and Tower Street, Chicago felt abandoned. They hardly encountered a single person once they fled the hospital. The apartment buildings, businesses and thoroughfares had been shut and locked and perhaps barricaded. A pair of eyes would occasionally peek through blinds to check on the state of the city, but otherwise, people were playing it safe. Fear permeated the dry air. The dome above them was gradually snuffing the city's air supply.

Nelson double-checked the road for strange people. "How much longer before you think we suffocate?"

Billy shook his head. "Let's pretend someone on the outside of this city's forming a plan to save our asses. It's not the air I'm worried about just yet."

"How do you figure?"

"Whatever murdered my father and all those people is a bigger threat. And then the man who blew himself up yesterday. Think about it. Maybe there are more of them."

"Do you really think any human being could transport a shell that big and cover the city?"

"Well, somebody did. Who would slice and dice an entire floor of hospital patients? I still believe that guy looked too much like that damn movie to be a coincidence. Shit, I don't know. I can't make sense of it."

"I can't either."

"Then let's get going. Jessica's alone. Let's hope the train's still running."

Billy raced up the stairs, already winded halfway up. He wouldn't be much of a hero to Jessica if he couldn't run a block without keeling over. *Who said she was in danger? She's in a big secure building. I'm sure people are all around her. I'm the one who's in danger out here.*

The platform was barren. Together, they waited for the next train to show up.

"What if the train doesn't come?"

"It's a solid three miles to Corporate Tower and the Crouch and Meadows offices," Billy said. "It's worth waiting a minute. It wouldn't make sense to shut it down. There are innocent people still out and about who have to be carted back to their homes."

The sound of a train broke the silence. It had to be two or three blocks from them. Billy's nerves crested. He paced. Wind slipped through cracks of the wooden platform, whistling. He couldn't erase the image of his father's bloody face.

Nelson had been eying him for a time. "What are you thinking about?"

Billy felt the pang of tears coming. He wiped them away, pretending to be fighting fatigue. "My dad. He's really gone. It hasn't truly set in until now. I wish I hadn't seen his dead body. It's going to stay with me forever. The police wouldn't tell me anything. It's their fault I had to charge into that crime scene. I freaked out. He didn't deserve to die like that. He was a good man. Firm, but still a decent man. He only wanted the best for me."

"Hey, it's a tough situation altogether," Nelson reasoned. "Your father was a good man. Good sense of humor. Hard worker. He'd want you to fight through this and survive."

The train rumbled closer. The platform shook, the boards groaning and protesting the vibrations. The train arrived. The doors opened with a hermetic shuffle. Together, Billy and Nelson entered. Billy clutched onto the overhead compartment, while Nelson sat down. The car was empty except for the last eight seats closest to the back. Four men. Four women. They stared at each other from across the car. Backs straight. Eyes unblinking. Faces unreadable.

"What's with them?" Nelson asked. "Maybe they're freaked out."

The doors shut. They were shaken as the train was given a push forward and rolled along the track. Building tops whirred by, the darkness blanketing them to the point they were staring into nothing.

Billy watched the others in the train. The eight didn't move. Not a facial twitch. Not a cough. "That's strange."

"Maybe I should talk to them."

"No," Billy insisted. "I don't need more problems than I already have. It's situations like this when people go nuts and kill each other. As long as they're not carrying weapons, we've got a head start to run into the next car."

Billy couldn't quit looking at them. They were pasty-faced. They looked pure, he thought, untouched by life. No pigment to the skin. Creamy white. The whites of their eyes were bright and unblemished. They even looked alike.

"You keep looking at them," Nelson whispered. "Why are they so interesting?"

"There's something weird about those people."

"You got that right. They're out of some religious colony. They probably don't know what buildings or civilization are."

Muffled vibrations nearly sent the train off the track.

BARUMP!

BARUMP!

KATHAM!

They heard the bending of steel, the crashing of windows, screams clashing against screams, the calls of terror, and then the thundering collapse of rafters and concrete and brick. The steady pound of steps overpowered the crash of a nearby building. It was a block or two away. The ruckus wasn't a single blow, but one of many. Another building was literally uprooted, and Billy and Nelson clutched onto the overhead hold to keep from collapsing onto the floor as the train shook.

The other group didn't react.

They were glued to the seats, staring at each other.

One of their noses started to bleed. Nelson gasped. "Do you see that?"

Billy was breathing hard without noticing. "Yeah, I see that shit."

The thud of gigantic steps came closer still. Each of the passengers' noses started to leak blood. And then red crimson lines descended from their hairlines. As if invisible stitching was undone stitch by stitch, a line down the center of their faces ripped open. Their skulls split, teeth sprouting around the edges of the openings the size of knitting needles, the Venus flytrap head snapping at air. And between snaps, Billy viewed a pair of diamond-colored eyes embedded in their pink brains. The brain was a creature, and somewhere on the brains, a mouth grumbled nonsense and blathered like an insane monster.

The eight shot up from their seats, each with the same flytrap head. The chattering and clamping of teeth continued as they edged toward Billy and Nelson. The overhead lights flickered out. Darkness surrounded them. Their steps closed in.

From the end of the car, the source of the outside devastation presented itself. A bare leg—a human leg—the size of a column at the Lincoln Memorial—swiped the car. The train was hurled from the track and plummeted onto the street.

Chapter Twenty

Ted Fuller was out of breath, having sprinted down the block at full speed. He shut the door to Steven's Auto Body and Salvage behind him and wrapped the chains around the knob. Vickers leaned against the wall catching his breath. He too was out of shape and winded.

The sounds outside continued. Earth shaking and pounding steps: THUD. THUD. THUD. THUD. Telephone poles were uprooted from the street. Buildings tipped over, as if their foundations were rocked hard by seismic waves.

"We have to help those people," Vickers insisted. "Innocent people everywhere are in danger. My God, what were those vampires doing up there in your apartment?"

"Like I said," Ted explained, "they're playing movies on a ghost-inhabited projector. It sounds ludicrous, but it's the truth. Monsters, ghouls and movie villains are parading around the city. You can't save anybody until you destroy the projector. It's the only way."

"There's no way back up there," Vickers said. "Those women are dangerous. They're the ones who killed everybody at Iowa University."

"Now you're getting it," Ted said. "It's unbelievable, yes, but you saw the women play the movies. If you wander out into the city, you'll see the monsters they played on the wall wreaking havoc in real life. Don't ask me how they exist. *Ghosts* are the source of their power; that's about all I understand as far as an explanation goes. You heard of Andy Ryerson and the Anderson Mills Massacre, right?"

"Yes, I read about it." Vickers peeked out the window. The way was clear for now. He eyed Ted's apartment and caught lights flashing. The movies continued to play. "Yeah, Andy Ryerson died at Iowa University. You told me a little bit about Anderson Mills too."

"Andy was given reels from a Professor Maxwell. He watched those movies in that town, and the town ended up slaughtered. The media, the police, they lived it down. The mystery remains who killed that many people in one night. This is happening again, Detective. They'll take out the entire city, and I heard those vampire bitches talking. They'll remove that skull dome and move on to another city and do the same thing again once Chicago's a city of corpses."

"But why?" Vickers demanded. "What do those women get out of it?"

"They're ghosts," Ted reiterated. "They hate the living or they want us to join them. I can't say for sure. The vampires didn't spell it out for me. This is supernatural shit. Beyond me."

"Then I say we burn the place down now. Light it up. Smoke them out of their holes. You said the reels needed to be destroyed, that'll do it."

They were set to enact the plan when a sickly sweet smell hit their noses. Like a baking pie and burning flesh and singed hair, was Ted's best guess. A veil of thin smoke obscured the garage.

Ted rubbed his eyes in disbelief at the sight that suddenly formed in front of him. Giant ovens had been incorporated into the walls. A baker's table the size of a dining room table stood in the center of the room.

The auto garage had vanished and turned into a baker's kitchen, complete with a baker.

Vickers removed a .28 Hawkins pistol from his shoulder holster. "Stay back. It's one of them."

"Yeah, no problem," Ted said. "I'll stay right here. You take the lead."

"I need you to distract him for me. Talk him up. Pretend he's in one of your shitty horror movies, and you're directing him."

Ted ignored the insult. "I'll do my best. I haven't directed in years."

Vickers slowly moved to the left and snuck into the shadows. That left Ted alone, watching the baker at work. His carrot red hair was snowed in powdered sugar. His apron was spattered with crimson. Eyes alight with a devilish passion, he worked a rolling pin over a wad of flesh and flattened it out with the squish of blood. A naked man, overweight, possibly three-hundred pounds, lay on the table. His stomach had been hollowed out, the mess of guts heaped on the floor.

That can't be what I think it is.

Cherry filling had been stuffed into the man's torso. The baker was dicing pieces of fingers, like vegetables for stew. He added the pieces to the cherry filling, then spread the flattened flesh over the man's exposed belly and stitched it in place.

"Nothing's more satisfying than filling a pie," the baker announced, acknowledging Ted's presence. "It's my favorite food on earth. You know, everyone should put themselves into their work."

The baker lifted the large corpse in his arms with an audible struggle and inserted him into what looked to be a pizza oven. "Good God, he's heavy! He'll cook at four hundred and fifty degrees. You'll want a slice while it's still warm. It's best warm."

"Um...y-yes, please. I'd like that a lot. I love dessert. It's my favorite food on earth too."

"You want a dollop of ice cream on top?"

"Even better."

The baker used a can opener on a container of apple filling. "I'm working the late shift, friend. People need their pies baked fresh daily. It's all about the filling. It's a lot of work, though. That's why I'm glad you're here. I'll pay a decent wage for a strong back. You're it, if you want the job."

"I, I'm your guy." Ted's heart fluttered in his chest. He was pouring sweat; the room was an oven itself. Staring at the blood and guts strewn about the room, he swore to never eat a pie again. "You say jump, I'll say how high."

He scanned the room for Vickers. They guy was nowhere to be seen. *Damn it, I'm on the spot here. Do something quick, Detective.*

The baker rolled out a rack on wheels. Naked bodies were suspended on it from meat hooks driven between their shoulder blades. The limp white corpses shuffled as they were moved. It struck him that this was all too real. The baker could turn on him any moment, and he'd be the guy inserted into an oven at four hundred and fifty degrees.

"I want you to remove their guts." The baker offered him a cleaver. "Those aren't good for the palate. Shit and digested food, that's a culinary no-no. The flesh and blood and muscle tissue, though, is the perfect recipe for my pies. Delicious!"

Ted couldn't take the first step. He refused. He wasn't going to disembowel anybody dead or alive. Vickers could go to hell.

And where the hell is he?

Damn it, did he leave me?

He did, didn't he?

I'm alone with this psychotic baker.

"Oh, I get it." The baker smiled, his eyes meeting Ted's. "You wanted to fill my pies, didn't you? One day you will. Any apprentice needs incentive. Let me apologize for not explaining the way I do things. I worked years gutting corpses for the benefit of my father's pies. He never gave me the chance to fill his desserts with their delectable pieces. That's why I shoved him into the oven. Mother and I ate him up. His flesh was a tad bitter, but the filling was just right. Eyes, tongue, fingers, flesh, it's salty and sweet and *mmmmmmm* good."

His eyes bulged, and he tilted his head to the side. "Did you hear that? I heard something."

Ted was startled at the direct question. "No. What? What did you hear?"

The baker patted his stomach. "My stomach's growling. I saved myself for dinner. Let me hear your belly."

Ted stiffened. The baker was already approaching him, eyes jubilant. Then his face creased in a scowl. The sudden change of expression was terrifying. The baker wrapped his arms around Ted's back and pressed his ear up to his belly. "Oh, I heard your belly growl. You're as hungry as I am. Nobody can work on an empty stomach. Let's eat!"

I am going to kick your ass, Vickers.

The room turned. The bodies on the pole dripped blood. They jerked in spasms, or so he thought. Ted was losing it. The heat in the room caused mirages. The ovens flickered bright with fires. The smell was turning his stomach. He spat thick saliva from his mouth.

The baker removed a sizzling, cooked body from one of the five ovens. A young woman smoked, her body unrecognizable beyond its slender shape. Her eyes, mouth and nose had been sliced clean off. The baker used thick gloves to place her on a different table. He used a machete to slice her belly into eight equal pieces. He served a dollop of the mess onto an aluminum plate.

"You get first taste, newbie."

Ted was a split-second from running—Vickers could go straight to hell!—when a shadow side-tackled the baker. Vickers lifted the man into the oven and slammed it shut. "COOK, YOU FUNNY-LOOKING BASTARD!"

Ted and Vickers pushed against the door to keep it closed. The baker pleaded for his life, and then his words turned into disheartening laughter. "You can't kill me, you fools! Cook me to your liking, I'll come back. You can't kill the dead. I'll come back as something else, something much worse! We only get stronger with each person we kill."

Vickers turned up the heat to five hundred degrees. "If it's all the same, I'm cooking you well done."

"I told you they were ghosts," Ted exploded. "They play the part of evil characters because it's fun for them. The psychotics get off on it. They've brooded in the afterlife for so long, they've plotted and planned and mapped out our demise, and this is what they've decided to finally do to us."

The punching against the oven door slowed until it ceased altogether. Ted sighed in relief. Vickers released the oven. "He has to be dead."

Ted knew it wasn't true. "Like he said, he'll come back as something else."

"But he's managed to kill over a dozen innocent people." Vickers stared solemnly about the room and the leftovers of violence. "It's disgusting. Everything about this situation is fucking impossible."

Ted joined Vickers in turning off every oven except the one where the baker continued to blacken.

"I'm responsible for this," Ted lamented. Guilt and blame surged into his voice. The dead bodies. The butchering. "If I hadn't played the reel again, none of this would've happened. People would still be alive."

Vickers patted his back. "I remember when I interrogated you back in Iowa. You were horrified. You wanted your horror movies back, that's it. And I talked to Dennis Brauman. He might hide behind that defender of public morals shield, but deep down, he probably looks at porn and watches rated R movies all the same. He stole your property, and you simply wanted it back. You didn't know this would be the result. Nobody could."

"I carried a shotgun with me when I played the first reel," Ted continued his confession. "I was so naïve. I thought I could stop them if they came back. I really believed they wouldn't. It's so ridiculous, every detail of it."

"You can't blame yourself," Vickers insisted. "Your intentions weren't to bring them back or for anybody to die. But now we have to torch your apartment building. Act on your better judgment now. Help me. I trust you'll do the right thing."

"Yes, yes, of course." Ted stormed about the room searching for flammables. "Hey, what happened to that shotgun you used up in the apartment?"

"I threw it at them before crawling the hell out of that place."

"Forget it then," Ted said, obviously disappointed. "At least you still have a handgun."

Vickers joined in the search. The garage was a kitchen in every respect now, the transition complete. Ted spotted three bottles of cooking sherry. "Perfect."

Vickers removed a lighter from his pocket. "All we need are some rags to stuff these with, and presto, fire starters."

Ted bent down to the pile of clothes stripped from the victims. He tore a shirt in three large pieces. Together, they wet the scraps and stuffed them into the bottles. Vickers moved to the window facing the apartment. "Are you ready for this?"

He wasn't sure, but he said anyway, "Start a fire on the bottom floor, and it'll eventually spread to the top. Easy. Cinch."

Vickers raised his eyebrows. "Yeah, a cinch."

They waited by the window in indecision. Vickers shook hands with Ted. "If we don't make it, it was nice knowing you."

"We make a good team," Ted said. "Thank you for what you said to me earlier. Trying to reassure me and everything."

"What I said was true, buddy. Believe me, I'm not that nice. Take my word for it."

Ted undid the chains at the door and quietly opened the garage door. "You first, Detective."

The charred body of Mr. Baker forced its way out of the oven. Blackened and smoking, he returned to the rack of hanging bodies to begin work on his next pie.

Chapter Twenty-One

Jessica halted at the second-floor fire exit door, standing in the stairway. A group of telemarketers bumbled about the stairs in confusion. Many were streaked in blood, their faces frozen in horror and agony. Jessica attempted to warn them that the man who called himself "The Intestinator" was right behind her, but the words were crammed back into her mouth when an explosion tore off the door leading to TeleCorp Marketing Solutions.

Jessica screamed and doubled back. Her eardrums rang. Blood dripped from the ceiling and walls and spread on the floor. Ten people in business suits were served a dose of death in macabre fashion. Telemarketer Judy Temple's throat had been stabbed by a jaw. Severed fingers were jammed into Harry Milner's eye sockets. Mark Alanson's throat had been wrapped with intestines, and he was strangled to death. Jessica shut her eyes and turned her back to the carnage, knowing so many others had suffered similar crazy fates. That's when the shuffling of the corpses began. They jerked. Twitched. Coughed. The skeletons beneath their skin shifted free, breaking through in wild tearing fashion, and flew back through the nearest doorway, magnetized by an unknown force.

What in hell...?

She refused to cross the heap of death that blocked the landing. Instead she turned and charged back up one floor. The Intestinator hadn't shown up yet.

Dr. Schuler's Dentistry office was her only option for cover. The Intestinator's slow approach could be heard from the floor above her.

Whump. Whump. Whump.

"MY GUTS CRAVE YOU!" Then a sobbing voice punctuated the threat. "I can't stop them. My insides are out of my control. Run—hide! I'm so sorry! I never wanted any of this to happen!"

Jessica slammed the clouded glass door and turned the bolt. Next, she propped a chair beneath the knob and stacked all the chairs in the waiting room against the door. She formed a barricade out of shelves, a coffee table and a desk. Out of breath and frazzled, she checked her body for blood and discovered she was drenched in the aftermath of what had happened thirty seconds ago.

He can't be real.

People's intestines can't attack people. Pieces of body parts can't kill people. She thought back to the jaw bone stuck in Judy's throat. *Christ, what's next?*

Jessica's chest burned, her heart pumping. This was fear. Survival instinct was supposed to kick in, she thought. Her senses were supposed to sharpen. Yet it didn't occur. Panic and sweat in her eyes, she shivered and stood nailed in place, waiting for the stranger outside to arrive at the door without.

The wide shadow on the fogged glass was distorted. The shape was featureless and so evil, she thought. Jessica expected the man to pound or smash through the glass barrier. Instead, the chairs shifted. The lock broke and the door opened just an inch. Through the legs of the desk and around the file towers, the pink rope projection slithered. The end was an open mouth. The mouth like a sucker fish.

Jessica slipped on all fours and crawled like a dog to the nearest room. She kicked the door shut behind her. She was in the dentist's office: the chair, the hovering light overhead and the cabinets seemed so high from where she crouched on the floor. The length of intestine slammed against the bottom of the door, attempting to slither through. Jessica turned on the dentist chair's light rather than venture closer to the door for the light switch.

The door cracked. The intestine kept battering against the wood.

Soon, it would pry its way inside.

"Leave me alone," she cried. Jessica didn't know what else to say. "I'm a good person. I'm only a paralegal, for God's sake! It's not like I'm a lawyer for murderers and pedophiles!"

An intestine should be the last thing to judge me.

The door's crack splintered further, opening wider until it finally burst open. The intestine twisted and snaked through. Jessica returned to her feet. She was up against the back wall. In seconds, the intestine would wrap around her neck like her co-worker's and perhaps snap her head off too. She searched frantically through the cabinets for anything to defend herself with.

The intestine circled the chair. It circled her left foot and tightened its hold on her ankle. Jessica removed her other pump and beat the intestine with the sharp heel. The intestine was too slimy for the shoe to cause damage.

"Let go of me!"

Jessica couldn't believe it. She was pleading with an intestine.

She stamped and kicked at the creature to no success. She dug into the shelves for a weapon—anything. The first item she located was a steel container of Novocain. She twisted off the lid, but the Novocain slipped from her hands. It landed close to the intestine and the pink rope drew back.

"You don't like that, huh?" Jessica smeared the liquid on her fingers and slathered it onto the retreating innards. "You're scared now, huh? You don't want to judge me so much anymore? Fuck you! FUCK YOU!"

The intestine curled and tensed and writhed to flick the liquid from its outer layer. The coil sizzled, and burned, and started to steam. The intestine wound itself back through the door, shot out of the waiting room, and wriggled through the barricade. Jessica waited. Stomps marked the Intestinator's retreat.

She rubbed her ankle where it had been squeezed. She imagined what it would feel like if the coil had tightened around her neck.

145

Jessica hugged herself to abate the shudder. She was cold and attacked by gooseflesh. Her thoughts went from boiling to a simmer. Billy was on his way to the building. She would be safe. He'd take her away from this nightmare.

"Oh no." She clenched her fists. "NO—he's heading right into the building. He's out there in harm's way."

Jessica scavenged through Dr. Schuler's office for a phone. The only one she spotted was behind the counter, tipped over onto the floor. She had to step over a receptionist's body. The poor woman was in her sixties, her face and neck riddled with gouges, another victim of an unknown murderer.

Jessica was relieved there was a dial tone. She dialed Billy's cell phone number. It rang and rang, but no answer. She left a distressed message. "Don't go into the building. It's dangerous. There's," she paused, at a loss for an explanation, "a killer in the building. Be careful, wherever you are. I'm going to call for help. Stay safe, Billy, I mean it. I love you. I—just be safe!"

She hung up the phone.

Her imagination wandered from one extreme to the other: Billy was dead, Billy was injured, Billy was trapped. Brooding over the possibilities, she dialed 9-1-1. The line was busy. The event in Corporate Tower was happening everywhere, she thought. She kept dialing, waiting for a ring tone. She bent the drawn shades of a nearby window and peered outside. The dome over the city served to create permanent night in Chicago. Jessica caught moving shapes through the shadows. Flying objects with wings. Red eyes burning as bright as road flares. The eyes seemed to drip, they burned so fiercely.

Another sight, she disbelieved from the onset.

"No way in hell," Jessica declared. "This is as unbelievable as attacking intestines!"

A voice inside her assured her that, in fact, what she was seeing was very real.

A living pillar, a walking skyscraper, a breathing, strutting, giant woman shuffled between buildings. She kicked and punched at skyscrapers. The rumble was distant, but Jessica felt the aftershocks.

She better not come this way.

Please don't come this way!

The woman was heading north, though taking frequent stops to pummel buildings. She stamped the ground and grounded her heel into the earth in random fits of anger.

"What is that bitch doing?—and why is she dressed like a hooker?"

She guessed the woman was over two hundred feet tall and wore a mean pair of red leather stilettos. Pink fishnets hugged her legs. She wore a g-string. A tube top housed generous breasts that seemed to want to burst from the thin silken fabric. The woman's hair waved wildly and electric red in the wind. She squeezed a man in her hand. Blood spilled through the cracks of her fingers. The giant hooker released the pulped corpse, who plummeted many stories to splat on the street.

Jessica turned from the window. She slipped down the wall in shock. Nobody was here to save her. Billy was in triple the danger that she was, being out in the city.

The best thing for you is to stay put. Billy is out there. He's smart. His dad used to be a cop. Billy has street smarts. He knows the roads and the city as well as any Chicagoan. Wait here. You're as safe as you can be.

"Unless that bitch punches through this building..." slipped from her lips.

She pictured Billy squeezed between the giant's fingers.

She heard something talking, and she realized she'd left the phone off the hook. It was the police line. Listening to the recorded message, Jessica's body went rigid. She wept because there was nothing else she could do. She curled up in a ball on the floor, hand numb and knuckles white from clutching the phone so hard.

"*Citizens of Chicago, stay in shelter. Do not attempt to leave your* homes. *The situation is being assessed by the United States military. If you're in danger, please use any means to defend yourself. The Chicago Police Department will do what they can to protect its citizens, but due to extenuating circumstances, we cannot answer calls. Martial law has been enacted for the duration. Again, stay in your homes or any shelter you can find. Defend yourselves with whatever you can and stay in groups. The situation is being handled as expediently as possible."*

The automated message repeated.

"Nobody's out there to help us," Jessica whispered. "I'm alone."

She was afraid to move even slightly, the fear thickening the blood in her veins. The Intestinator could return at any moment. The giant woman outside could bash through the walls and level the building. The flying, red-eyed creatures might burst through the window and finish her off. The screams outside continued, louder. It wasn't only the monsters she'd already seen that frightened her, but the ones she had yet to encounter that could be on their way.

Jessica prayed Billy was safe.

Chapter Twenty-Two

Ben O'Malley loved Wrigley Field so much he wanted to die on the lush green of the field, and considering the way things had been going today, it was a strong possibility. He stood at home base, looking out at the empty bleachers. Being the greens keeper, he had full access to the field. A crew of two dozen tended the field on normal working shifts, but tonight, the home of the Cubs was his own. He pictured a crowded stadium in place of the empty dark blue seats. It wasn't so much the players, the commentators, or even the fans as much as it was the field itself. Hundreds of thousands had eyed his hard work, what for him was the source of blisters, a stooped back and menial wages. Whether they thought of him while watching Sammy Sosa crank one to center left or not, they knew his work, and that was enough to satisfy him.

"Buy me some peanuts and Cracker Jack," Ben sang. He stood at home plate, dusting the diamond with his foot. He clutched the wooden bat; the pitching machine was winding its pitch. "...root, root, root for the home team, and if they don't win it's a shame—because they won't renew my contract, they'll test me for steroids, and my endorsement deal with Gatorade will go tits up."

He swung.

Strike.

Damn.

"O'Malley swings and misses," Ben announced. "He's warning up. Working out the kinks. And up comes the next pitch."

Strike two.

"Money and women and booze and fame have slowed me down,"

Ben joked. He let another pitch pass him by without trying. His arthritis was acting up. He rubbed his wrists. His shoulder blades jolted him with a sharp cutting pain. "I'm too old for this fast pitch bullshit."

Ben positioned his feet for the pitch. "Make this one count. The crowd still loves you."

Crack.

The grounder was sent between first and second base. "Base hit. I love it. I love this field so fucking much, I could die here." He leaned down, picked up his whiskey bottle, and took another swig. "My final resting place."

A boisterous voice shouted out to him, "You'll get your wish, fella!"

Ben turned around. The field was empty. The air was ominously quiet ever since the dome turned Chicago into a dark city and screams and violence were rampant. He was shocked nobody took cover at Wrigley Field. Maybe nobody else was alive who liked baseball.

"Hey, where you are you? Show yourself. You want to take a swing too? I'll pitch."

Ba-bam!

Ben's legs went out from under him. He landed on his back, his lower body twisting and crunching with broken bones. Seconds later, the agony finally arrived. Both his kneecaps were shot to pieces, the legs down to his feet ugly pulp. The rough stumps continued to cough out blood. The stadium lights blinded him.

Don't look at your legs.

"Call an ambulance—don't leave me like this!"

Yeah, the son-of-a-bitch who shot you will call for help.

Ben wept. He couldn't shift without triggering agony in his lower body. He averted his eyes to the left and inadvertently caught his left leg. The reality set in; he was going to bleed to death at Wrigley Field.

I'll be seeing you soon, Harry Caray.

The roar of a diesel engine reverberated on the ground. He was so dizzy, he wasn't sure what direction the noise was coming from. Ben pivoted his upper body to search the field. The stadium was still empty. And then a panel of the left field wall was battered down and flattened. A yellow rig came steaming through the field.

Holy shit, it's a steamroller!

The roller was pure steel, glinting as if recently polished. The rig closed in on him. The driver wore an orange hardhat, orange reflective vest, white T-shirt, and blue jeans. His face was corpse-black. Cheekbones sunken. Yellow eyes. One hand shifted the gears, steam pumping out of the top and coughing black exhaust into the air. Ben choked on the acrid cloud. The rig was yards out from him now and closing in. Ben noticed the double-barreled shotgun propped beside his seat.

"Don't do it, please!" Ben pleaded. "Haven't you done enough to me? This isn't necessary. I'll die. I'm not going anywhere. You don't have to smash me!"

The driver didn't say a word. He was dead in the truest sense; despite the blackened mold growing on his face and the sunken desiccated flesh that blurred his features, he was callous and unyielding to the harm he was about to enact.

The roller pressed down on Ben's feet, and quickly, the pop and crack of bones sent him to unconsciousness. Death followed once it crunched over his torso. Flattened into the earth, Ben O'Malley received his wish to die at Wrigley Field.

Then the steamroller broke through the walls of the stadium and continued into the city.

A. J. Myers, a resident in Ted Fuller's apartment building, dared to open his door after hearing the soft muted plea, *"Please help me. I'll bleed to death if you don't help me. They left me here to die."*

He was shocked to find every door on the first floor had been smashed to pieces except for his. A.J. couldn't force himself to peer inside any of the empty rooms. He simply followed the voice that had spoken for the past five minutes in a soft mewl. The voice was familiar, the main reason he unlocked his door and ventured through the hall. Stephanie Minor was speaking, he believed. She was the resident at the last room on the first floor, and he had a crush on her ever since she moved in. She didn't give him the time of day, since he was a handyman for the building and she was an aspiring ballet dancer. She performed at the fine arts theatre, and he'd seen her dressed in her pink tutu and imagined doing certain things to her. A.J. had fixed her leaking faucet three times; he kept it rigged to bust in a week's time so he could visit her again. That cunning mindset failed to arrive in this moment of panic. Screams jolted the air from outside. Unholy things were happening out there. Unexplainable things.

He clasped his Luger pistol.

Any sign of trouble, he'd aim and fire.

Aim and fire.

It's that simple.

"Please help me," Stephanie cried again. "There's so much blood. They hurt me...they hurt me so bad."

A.J. kept his mouth shut. He refused to trust in anything after blood spattered his window like a dozen paintballs breaking against it until he couldn't see through the pane. The police had a message playing instead of a dispatcher. Each friend or relative he phoned didn't respond. The phones of a few, including his dad, were off the hook or out of service.

"Is someone there?" Stephanie cried out. "I can't hold on much longer. I feel so weak. I don't want to die. Not in the dark, not like this. I don't want to be alone."

A.J. arrived at Stephanie's door. It was wide open. The living room was ransacked, every piece of furniture overturned and strewn on the floor. Claw marks marred the walls. A trail of blood soaked into the carpet. He followed it down the short hall to a bedroom. A silk net surrounded the bed. Stephanie's shape he made out through the fabric.

"Oh, it's you." She sounded relieved. "Come here, A.J."

A.J. obeyed. He parted the curtain. Stephanie was in a white nightgown. Her milky thighs were splayed open for him to relish. He studied her body, typing it into a mental registry. She smelled of lilac perfume, and A.J. absorbed it.

He recoiled at the wounds on her belly. Two slashes she kept covered with her hands. Blood stained the blankets and mattress beneath her.

"Oh my God," A.J. gasped. "You're bleeding. Let me take you out of here. My truck's out back. We'll haul ass to the hospital. You're going to be fine."

"Come closer," she beckoned. "Please, A.J."

A.J. lowered so he was face-to-face with Stephanie.

Close enough to kiss.

Stephanie put her hand around the back of his head and brought him down so she could speak into his ear. "I want you to lick my wounds."

Stephanie's jaw snapped from her face, falling into his hands. "Fuck me, A.J. Drill me. Stick it in every hole." His crotch was squeezed by a hand tearing through the mattress. "Fuck me every which way with your three-inch pecker!"

A.J. flopped backward onto the floor. Before he landed, he saw fingers slip out of the back of Stephanie's skull. Somebody had manipulated her like a puppet. A naked woman was underneath the bed. Both arms had torn up through the mattress board to contort Stephanie's body. In two seconds, that woman was after him. He cowered as the vision of Stephanie's face breaking into pieces repeated in his mind.

"What's the matter? Are you going limp?"

The woman's flesh clicked as it changed from smooth white flesh to black reptilian plates. Eyes brightened to red strobes so bright A.J. was blinded. He crawled blindly out of the room. He made it two more crab steps backward before his head was wrenched from the neck in one mean pull. A set of teeth bit at the artery jutting up from the stump like a bird ripping a worm from the earth.

A.J. was the last person to die in Ted Fuller's apartment building.

Chapter Twenty-Three

"Billy, are you with me?"

Gray acrid smoke clogged the sky.

"*Uhnnnn.*"

"Billy, shit man, wake up. WAKE UP!"

Blood streamed down the side of Billy's head, staining his brow and crossing his lips. With each waking second, the red warmth accelerated into a cutting lance.

"You want what?" Billy mumbled. "What do you want, man? What are you asking me?"

He was wedged between two upturned train seats, his body forced into an awkward position. His head, hands and torso were lying on a bed of shattered glass. Billy twisted and struggled to rise to his feet. He wobbled. The car had smashed into the road below the track. Folds of steel were mashed and bent into wicked claws. Nelson came into view, his eyes intense, though it was impossible to see him clearly through the fog of settling debris.

"We have to move," Nelson insisted. "They're out there waiting."

"Who's waiting? Who's out there?"

"Don't you remember them? The weirdos."

Billy couldn't grasp a single thought. He touched his hand to his head. A slit deep enough to require stitches went from his eyebrow to the top of his skull. He couldn't walk forward or backward, the roof facing him, his perspective distorted.

Nelson peered out a window. "They're out there in the shadows, hiding in the alleys. We can't stay here. I say we make a run for it. Isn't Corporate Tower a few blocks from here?"

Details registered again, albeit gradually. Jessica was in Corporate Tower, Billy remembered. They were going to meet her there. But why?

THAM-THAM-THAM-THAM!

Earthquake shudders rang throughout the street. The end of the subway car was seized by a giant. Billy caught a patch of flesh from the window.

"What in Christ is that?" Billy shouted. "SHIT!"

"Hold on!" Nelson shouted. "YOU HOLD ON TIGHT!"

The car was lifted in the air and shaken back and forth. Billy grasped onto the high bar but couldn't keep hold. He flew backwards and sailed out the back exit. Nelson slipped and sailed right behind him. They tumbled onto the street. The car was lifted many stories higher. Billy froze, eyes locked onto the woman who towered above them six or seven stories tall. She frantically shook the car.

She hadn't seen them fall.

Nelson had already taken off through the alley. Billy followed behind him, weak and already out of breath. Pure adrenaline shot him from the road and between two skyscrapers. A utility truck cruised down the street. A man was at the helm, crazed and driving sixty miles an hour. It was a living corpse, his skin wet with drops of clear liquid oozing through every pore on his face. Fifteen corpses were tied by the wrists and ankles to the open trunk bulging with bodies. They too glistened like the driver, their flesh blue. The stink of embalming fluid was a cutting tang as they passed. The undead driver pulled over and tackled a woman running from a car that had been stepped on, the trunk mashed into the ground, as if someone had dropped a piano on it from on high. The driver touched her arm once, and her femoral and jugular veins spat out blood with fire-hydrant pressure. Then the man's fingers shot out a fluid that entered her arteries. Soon, her skin oozed the same embalming fluid as the other victims did. Dead, she was tied to the truck and added to the collection.

He just touched the woman, and it embalmed her.

Holy shit.

Windows shattered from many stories above them. Screaming victims sailed through the sky, propelled by an unknown force. After seconds, Billy realized they weren't bodies, but bloody skeletons. They were sucked toward a great magnet. Sparks exploded from the tips of the steel magnet, producing electric neon-white blasts and crackles and forks of lightning. A preacher was at the helm. He'd mounted the U-shaped device on a wooden cart. Skeletons and remains were spread out on the street in an ever-growing pile behind him, skulls and bones strewn everywhere.

"I will suck the evil from your souls," the man cried out. "I will remove the corruption from your body so you can go to heaven righteous! Just step up, folks, and I'll cleanse you."

"Run faster!" Nelson shouted. "Don't look at them."

Wrecked car doors were pried from their hinges and new sets of bones were thrown into the magnet. Billy ducked and jumped ahead to avoid two piles of bloody bones heading right into his path. They clinked and rattled past him, flicking blood and hunks of gristle onto him.

Two more blocks, and they'd be at Corporate Tower.

Billy prayed Jessica was safe, because he sure as hell wasn't.

The seven-story woman bounded toward them. Stiletto heels ground and stomped onto the street. Every thud was a juggernaut's crash, and Billy's feet were lifted from the ground by the concussion. He had to stop running for two seconds. Sprint. Then stop. Sprint. Then stop.

She was closing in, the shadow covering them both. He'd be squashed by her heel. He didn't have much steam left for running.

"Keep going!"

Billy lunged ahead of her, Nelson taking the lead. Heavy breathing was at their heels. Billy caught movement in his peripheral vision. A

157

man sprinting across the street. He tied a rope to a lamppost. Someone else tied the other end to a telephone pole across the street.

A tripwire.

Billy doubled his pace. "RUN LIKE FUCKING HELL, NELSON! SHE'S GOING DOWN!"

With the bend and give of steel, the giant woman gave a cry and tipped forward. Mid-step, she couldn't right herself. The fall seemed to take seconds. She reached out, her palm smashing into another skyscraper, but she couldn't catch herself. Shards of glass and structure tumbled down. Nelson dodged the edge of a steel beam, a concrete gargoyle and showers of glass. Blood sprayed them, slicking the streets.

WHUPWHAM!

The woman's body fell through the street to the subway beneath them. Her legs jutted out of the hole, her fishnets and pumps pointed at the sky.

Billy and Nelson stopped, out of breath. They looked at each other and back to the woman half underground.

Nelson gasped, "She struck her head on that building, and it took out half her face. Christ, that's where all that blood was coming from. And there's something else."

"What?" Billy looked to the sky, up the street, behind them, in the cars wrecked about the road. "Is something else coming? Where?"

"That giant woman is from a movie. I even remember the tagline. *'Five hundred feet and only fifty dollars'.*"

"But that's impossible."

The vision of the exploding man replayed in his mind's eye. "What about the others we've seen? The embalming guy and that priest collecting skeletons—and the flytrap head people."

"I don't know. I can't remember off the top of my head. But the woman looked exactly like the movie. Pink fishnets. Red stiletto heels. Oh yeah, and also really fucking tall."

Billy dabbed at the gash on the side of his head with his t-shirt. He eyed the tower where Jessica was hiding. Together, they charged toward the building. A beckoning voice stopped them. "Hold up a second!"

A middle-aged man ran at them with a younger kid who was maybe eleven. They were the ones who'd tripped the woman. The older one had to slap the boy over the head. He was staring at the woman's g-string, her hind quarters jutting up from the street.

"Show some respect, Christopher Alan Meyers."

Christopher lowered his head, blushing.

"The city's gone to shit, huh?" the man said. "You boys okay?"

They were making fast progress to meet them until the flytrap heads pounced on the two strangers from a nearby alley. "*I can smell what you're thinking, I can smell what you're thinking, I can smell what you're thinking, I can smell what you're thinking,*" they repeated in unison, the grunts and squeals of flesh-craving monsters.

The boy was dragged back to the alley by the monsters, his screams ending in seconds. The older man chased after the boy, and he too was forced into the throng of monsters. The creatures tore through the man's face and crunched the skull to feast on his brains.

A brain eating brains.

That's fucked up.

"Shit, we're next!" Billy cried out. "You know what we have to do. We have to hide in Corporate Tower."

Nelson was already ahead of him. He was at the entrance, working around four yellow taxis that had plowed into each other. Billy charged behind Nelson and snuck into the revolving doors. Billy thought fast, jamming a nearby chair into the last section of the revolving door to wedge it stuck. The hands of the flytrap heads punched and clawed, but the Plexiglas wouldn't give to their force. The black marble eyes hidden in the folds of cranial tissue bent. Conspired. The flytrap teeth clanked and ground to no end.

"What floor does she work on?" Nelson asked, a deer-in-the-headlights look on his face. "I know you've told me before. I just want to get away from those creatures out there. Each and every one of them."

"The fourth floor," Billy said. "But I don't think we should take the elevator. The power could go out and I don't want to be trapped in there."

The main hall was empty. No bodies or blood. Billy figured anybody who could get out booked it the moment the monsters arrived.

The elevator dinged beside the fire exit.

Billy stood, waiting.

"What's coming down?"

"Maybe it's somebody else like us."

The elevator opened, and it was empty. They each released a sigh of relief. Billy heard his cell phone beep. Someone had left a voice mail message. He checked it; it was Jessica. He listened and returned the call. It was answered on the first ring.

"Jessica, are you okay?"

"Yes," she said, overjoyed to hear his voice. "Are you in the building?"

"We barely made it."

"Who's with you?"

"Nelson. Now tell me where you are exactly."

"I'm on the third floor in Dr. Schuler's office. He's a dentist. But be careful, there's an intestine guy out there."

"An intestine guy?"

"I know it sounds insane."

"Like a giant hooker or people with flytrap heads?"

"Excuse me?"

"Never mind, we're on our way up. Be safe up there. I love you."

Nelson normally would've chided him for saying "I love you," but he was too busy eyeing the five flytrap heads staring at them through the window with hungry eyes. Billy took the lead up the stairwell. The stink of recent death, like a metallic fog, carried to them. With each step, the stench increased. Billy worried about Jessica; she was at the center of it all. When they reached the second-floor landing, blood dribbled down the steps.

Billy glanced at Nelson. Nelson nodded and said, "Yeah, I know. That's some rough shit." They couldn't avoid walking through the blood, so they trudged on in the red drizzle. What they couldn't ignore was the heap of corpses at the bend of the third floor. Their bodies were punctured and gouged. Something had been driven through their bodies. The looks on the corpses' faces proved they saw it coming too.

Nelson grimaced when he stepped on someone's hand with a squish. "I'm so sorry, man. What a terrible way to go."

"It could've been us," Billy lamented. "And we're not out of this yet."

They entered the third floor. The first door to the left was Dr. Schuler's office. Billy tried to open the frosted-glass door, but it was blocked from behind. "Jessica, are you in there?"

"Be quiet," she warned. "I'll let you in."

After the sound of chairs scuffing the tiles, the door was opened wide enough for them to slip through. Billy hugged Jessica close to him, so tight she asked him to ease up. "I just have to know you're really okay. I've seen too many people die today."

"Me too," Jessica said with tears welling in her eyes. "I'm so lucky you're here. I love you."

Billy kissed her again and again. "I love you too. We're going to make it through this. You won't believe what we've seen."

"Is it more unbelievable than attacking intestines?"

"I'm not sure."

Nelson went to work rebuilding the barricade. Billy joined him. When they were satisfied it would hold up to an intruder, they sat on

161

the only remaining couch. Nelson closed his eyes, resting. Jessica searched for something to bandage Billy's head.

"What do we do now?" Nelson asked. "They're out there, we're in here, and that dome is blocking anybody from leaving the city. They have us cornered."

"Has anybody tried calling the police?"

Jessica said from the other room, "I called 9-1-1. I only got a machine. It's a message saying to stay in shelter. They're not taking calls."

"Figures," Nelson said disdainfully. "When we really need them, where are they? Unavailable."

"Can you blame them?" Billy defended the police since his dad used to be a cop. "They could be dead for all we know. This isn't a normal crime spree."

Jessica was disheartened. "You think all of them could be dead? Every single cop?"

Billy didn't want to scare Jessica. He was scaring himself with the facts. "I can't say. We're cut off from everybody. It's impossible to know for sure."

"You're a meter man," Nelson joked. "You should know what to do in these situations."

"Yeah," Billy shot back, "I'll write the culprits a ticket. That'll show them. Fifty-dollar fines for all of them. Maybe an impounding of their vehicle as a cherry on the top."

Jessica returned with hydrogen peroxide and dabbed at Billy's head wound. "That's a nasty cut. How did you get it?"

"A huge woman lifted up the subway car we were riding and smashed it to the ground," Nelson said nonchalantly. "And Billy-boy cut himself on some glass."

Jessica applied a torn piece of gauze and taped it to the side of Billy's head. "A huge woman? Like the one I saw out there earlier?"

Billy decided to get the facts out and forget logic. "A woman seven stories tall attacked us in the elevated train."

Nelson added, "And she might be from a movie."

Jessica's face tensed. She was on the verge of an angry fit. Billy petted her back. "Now wait, none of that is for certain."

"You're right," Nelson admitted. "It just looked a lot like the woman from the movie: the clothes, the size, the stomping around like Godzilla."

"Enough of that talk," Jessica demanded. "First, you say the suicide bomber from yesterday was from a movie, and now you're insisting the woman you're talking about is from a movie too. I think Billy was onto something real. It's terrorists."

Nelson guffawed, "Listen to yourself! Brains eating other people's brains were attacking us on the streets. A man was touching people and the blood exploded from their bodies and then they were filled up with embalming fluid. A man dressed as a priest was using a mega magnet to pull the skeletons out of bodies. We could get shot through the fucking glass window the same way. These aren't things any human being, never mind terrorists, could do."

Jessica bunched up against Billy, clinging onto him for comfort. "Tell me this isn't real, Billy. There's a plausible explanation. Something real. Not monsters from movies. Tell me there's a way to end this."

He was at a loss. "How can anybody except God explain why this is happening? Who could know? Maybe the Internet."

"You're right," Jessica agreed. "That's a great suggestion."

"I was kidding."

Nelson chimed in. "No, you're right, man. I'm sure someone's written something about all this. Maybe there are reports on YouTube."

"Where's a computer?" Billy asked. "The one in here is smashed."

"In my office upstairs," Jessica said. "We have to go back up there. I know it's dangerous, but we have to try."

Billy caressed her hand. "Me and my big mouth. No, you're right.

We just have to be careful. We have to try anything to survive."

"Wait." Jessica rushed out of the room. She returned with a container of liquid Novocain. "Here it is. Now let's go."

Billy eyed the container.

Jessica smiled. "Don't ask."

Billy and Nelson began clearing the barricade, and afterward, they approached the fourth floor bracing themselves for the Intestinator or anybody else to attack.

Chapter Twenty-Four

Heart of Chicago Mercy Hospital was in chaos. The emergency rooms overflowed with patients while doctors were leaving their jobs to tend to their families. Random shattering of windows and cries resounded in the air. Earthquake tremors shook the foundation every now and again. Dr. Hill decided he couldn't help anybody anymore.

He had other matters to attend to.

You have to move if you're going to get this done. This is the perfect time.

Dr. Hill was a seasoned veteran who worked in the hospital's morgue for nearly seventeen years. He tagged victims, charted their cause of death and corresponded with the couriers from funeral homes. He saw Jane and John Does. Highway wrecks. Street pizzas, as he liked to call them. Bodies in pieces and unrecognizable from damage. In those cases, Dr. Hill took it upon himself to pilfer certain pieces of the body: an arm here, a leg there, a liver, a heart, anything he wanted. He sold the parts to science research firms like LabTech and BioFuture. If the corpses were fresh enough, he could sell the organs for a decent buck.

Temptation had its way with him. The morgue wing was surrounded by corpses in body bags, stretchers haphazardly strewn and shoved into each other. The line of corpses on stretchers continued into the far hall outside of his working area. Hundreds had died tonight and still counting. The most common deaths he'd seen were torn throats, stomped midsections, bodies riddled with strange holes and bags bulging with flesh and organs without bones.

But one corpse, the one on the gurney in front of him, was the strangest of all. Fluids leaked from the eyes, nose, mouth and ears. A woman stared back up at him, her dying moment of agony etched on her face. The bag leaked the chemical-smelling substance, dripping onto the tiles. Other bags were dripping the same contents. It had to be embalming fluid, he decided.

The three morgue attendants had high-tailed it home after the radio began to broadcast messages to stay home and lock your doors. The city was trapped within a dome, he understood. Murderers and looters rampaged the streets.

He didn't care about them.

This is my meal ticket. I'm not going to get this many bodies in one shot ever again unless I kill them myself.

The woman below him was useless. The organs were ruined by the chemicals.

Four foam coolers were heaped with ice at his feet. He'd already taken three fresh arms, four livers, one heart and a set of legs. He used a bone saw to complete the extractions. He zipped and unzipped through the hall of body bags to locate the next good specimen.

"I admire what you're doing," a gurgling, bubbling voice called out from behind him. "I really do."

The chemical tang blew across his back. It wafted up to his nostrils, and his eyes watered from it. "You mind your own goddamn business—"

The man was dressed in a lab coat similar to the one he was wearing. His eyes sagged an inch to show the meaty purple tissue beneath. His gums were purple and raw. His tongue white. With every word he spoke, he coughed out fluids.

"Stay the hell back," Dr. Hill said. He removed a Desert Eagle pistol from his side holster. He kept it on him ever since the chaos outside broke out. "I'll shoot you, man, whoever you are."

The corpse raised his hands and smiled, clear fluids dribbling from his lips. "I'm only admiring you. I, too, have tried my hand in the body

166

brokering business. I sold them all. Hearts, kidneys, arms, legs, heads..."

"You're not going to report me?" Dr. Hill was confounded that he was talking to a walking corpse spilling embalming fluid. He sharpened his words. "Then you want a cut, is that it? You blackmailing bastard."

"No, no, no," the man replied. "I believe the dead don't deserve their organs. Remove them all. Cut 'em out, I say. The dead don't care. What gives them the right to deny one's life when a dying person can benefit their internal organs? The dead are hypocrites. Selfish. I'm a proponent of stealing. It's the only way to complete the dark side of the business."

Dr. Hill kept the gun ready.

If he moves, I'll pop him one in the face. That'll show him for grinning at me like a maniac.

"Then what do you want?"

The corpse extended his hand. "I only want to shake your hand."

Dr. Hill hesitated. "Then you'll leave me alone?"

"I'll leave you to it. You're hard at work. Up to your ears in work."

Dr. Hill switched the gun to his left hand and put out the other to shake. "Careful, man, I know how to use this."

"Just shake my hand, and I'll be on my way."

Dr. Hill shook the man's hand.

"Someone needs to crack a window," Nelson whispered as they hiked up to the fourth floor. "It's burning hot in here."

Billy clutched his chest. With each inhalation, his lungs ached. The air was useless. "It's that dome above the city. Our air supply is diminishing."

He removed his button-up shirt. Beneath it was a white t-shirt with the Superman emblem on the chest.

"What's with the shirt?" Nelson chided him. "Fly us to safety, Clark

Kent."

Jessica kissed Billy's cheek. "He might as well be Superman. I feel safe with him here. Don't you, Nelson?"

"Not safe like the real Superman would make me feel safe." Nelson unbuttoned his shirt. He still wore the same Xbox T-shirt from yesterday. "On second thought, Billy's probably a better protector than me. While the world's entering apocalypse mode, I'd be playing *Halo*."

"Or watching movies and eating beef jerky," Billy corrected. "Or looking up porn."

Jessica smiled for the first time today. Billy knew he would marry this woman, and what was happening in the city wouldn't stop him.

"None of us are dying," Billy said with whatever confidence he could manage. "Nobody."

"I like what you're saying," Nelson said, "but according to the giant bitch outside, those people with brains with teeth, and that crazy preacher with the magnet that pulls bones out of bodies, I say it means little." He patted Billy's back. "No offense. You mean well."

"None taken. And I do mean well."

"A preacher with a magnet that can draw bones out of bodies," Jessica repeated. Then she frowned. "And what else he said, it's really out there? I mean, I saw the woman, but the people with the brains with teeth? I also caught something flying in the air. Wings in the dark. Red eyes."

"Nelson is still convinced that giant woman is from a movie."

"The woman is dressed the same as in the film. But you were thinking *Death Reject* was real just yesterday, Billy. Why are you pinning this on me?"

"Quiet," she snipped. "You'll give us away. The Intestinator is around here somewhere."

Nelson whispered. "That's sounds like a movie too. Why are you calling him that?"

"That's what he called himself. Now shut up. My office is up those stairs."

Jessica stayed close behind Billy. She clutched a broken leg of a chair from the dentist's office and the jar of Novocain. Nelson also held the leg of a chair. Billy clutched a sterling silver letter opener.

They entered the fourth floor. Everything was silent. No survivors, Billy supposed. The door wasn't covered in blood.

That's a positive, he thought.

He wondered if anybody in the entire building was still alive.

Unlikely.

The carpeted foyer was similar to the dentist's office. A grouping of chairs and a coffee table full of magazines faced them. A sign in gold letters on the wall read "Crouch and Meadows".

"Crouch and Fell," Billy joked.

Jessica nudged him. "Now isn't the time, Superman."

"I've had a lot of lucky things happen to me when I've worn anything Superman related," Billy said in a hushed voice. "I got my first blow job wearing Superman underwear—no offense, Jessica. I passed my driver's test in Superman socks. I asked you out the day I received the Superman tattoo on my shoulder blade, and..."

"Okay, I get the point," Jessica insisted. "It's wonderful you're wearing a Superman T-shirt right now."

Nelson agreed. "Ditto."

Jessica stepped back in repulsion at the sight of a corpse on the ground. She covered her mouth and hid her face in Billy's chest. "Steve. It was, it was," she stammered, "the Intestinator who did this."

Billy hugged her. He too had trouble looking at the corpse. The well-dressed man's head had been wrenched from the neck. Blood had soaked into the carpet in puddles. The face was hideous and etched in pain; veins thick as earthworms crossed his features. "Yes, look away. Nobody deserves to go out like that."

"And it's unrealistic," Nelson said, kneeling down by the body, undeterred by the gore. "What could possibly remove his head like that? It'd take a machine. And look at his neck. It wasn't cut by a knife. The skin is jagged, like it ripped."

"No shit," Jessica shot back. Her face turned a light shade of red. Anger and absolute horror marked her face. "I watched him die. The man's—the man's fucking guts snapped Steve's head from his neck! I told you already."

"Sorry," Nelson said. "I didn't mean to upset you. I'm just trying to understand this. There's a dome over the city, for one. Then there's murderers out there—no bullshit—who aren't human. Far from it. Where did they come from? Why are they in Chicago, of all places? And why do they want us dead so much?"

An extended grunt came from the opposite room.

"That's him!" Jessica wailed. "He's been waiting for us."

Billy caught a shadow on the carpet three doors away. He eyed the straightaway hall and the glass wall at the end. "Nelson," he whispered, "help me grab that table."

A double-bass voice vibrated against the walls and shook the letters of Crouch and Meadows from the wall. "MY GUTS ARE JUDGE, JURY AND EXECUTIONER."

Jessica shouted, "You're a murderer. You ripped Steve's head off!"

The Intestinator stepped from the room, ignoring Jessica's words. A barrel for a torso was bleeding, swelling and pulsating at his belly button. The navel puckered as if breathing. Billy failed to register anything else about the man and jumped to action.

"Quick, Nelson—the coffee table!"

Billy lifted one end, Nelson the other.

Jessica opened the Novocain and heaved it in the man's direction. "Stay back!"

The Intestinator cowered. It bought them seconds, Billy realized. They both lifted the table. "Charge him!" Billy shouted.

They advanced, taking fast strides. The Intestinator caught onto their tactics too late. A coil of intestine exploded from his belly, but

Billy and Nelson used the table as a shield. The intestine was deflected back into his belly. The table slammed into the standing bulk. Feet from the window, they forced him through the glass. The body careened toward the street outside, his form growing smaller. The Intestinator crashed onto the top of a parked Voyager Minivan. With a solid crunch of steel and spraying of glass, the top of the minivan buckled inwards, spitting shards from all sides.

The Intestinator lay motionless.

"AND STAY OUT!" Nelson shouted in victory. "Asshole."

Billy urged him from the window. "Shut up! Who knows what else is out there?"

Nelson moved back to the sitting room. Out of breath, they stared at the broken window and the glittering fragments on the carpet. "There's not much time," Billy suggested. "Let's find your office, honey, and get to the bottom of this."

Jessica guided them through two hallways and a labyrinth of cubicles and offices with gold nameplates. Paralegal offices occupied the last hallway. Finding an open office, Billy let the other two file ahead of him, and then he shut the door and locked it. He then drew the blinds over the glass front. He wasn't sure if he should leave them that way. Nobody could see them from outside, but they wouldn't know if an enemy was lurking on the other end or not.

Fuck it. I can put my ear to the door if it comes down to it.

Jessica sat at the computer in the back of the office. Billy and Nelson were huddled at both sides of her. Jessica raised her arms up in celebration. "Thank God, the Internet is working. What should I search?"

"Go to Instant Search," Billy suggested. "Type in 'Chicago Emergency'."

Jessica typed in the words. She clicked on the number one site. A web page showed a combination of pictures, essays and directions of escape for those trapped in Chicago. Billy had forgotten it was near morning by now. He checked his watch and it was five-thirty. They

171

looked at pictures of the dome from the other side of the skull. In the sun, it glinted like the enamel of a tooth.

"It really is a giant skull," Nelson gasped. "You see the cranial ridges. It's cut off where the eye sockets would begin. So weird. Now you know this is something supernatural."

"My terrorist theory is out the window," Billy said. "But damn it, what does this mean?"

They read the text below the skull pictures.

Spectators claimed to have witnessed a large dome-shaped object hover from the sky. Many claim to have seen airplanes carrying the dome, but others insist it was hovering by itself. Charles Zuckerman, local Chicago PD, made this statement, "I was writing a traffic ticket when a shadow crossed the interstate. This thing was enormous. It was hovering. I looked for what was carrying it, but I couldn't see a thing. It doesn't mean there wasn't something there, but I sure didn't see it, and I had a perfect view of it. And it looked like, well, it was bone." The article went on to say, *The object in the sky has blocked inner-city Chicago. Attempts to break through the dome to the other side have failed.*

New pictures accompanied the article. A construction crew was attempting to cut through the enamel wall with a concrete saw. Pictures of a wrecking ball crew, jackhammer crew and strapping dynamite to the skull were presented in different pictures and in varying stages of sunlight and darkness.

"Attempts to break the skull have failed across the board," says city councilman Ralph Quinley. Quinley assures the citizens inside of the dome are perfectly safe and will be rescued as soon as possible. Explanations for the dome and its origin are unknown. The city councilman has no further comment on the subject.

"Perfectly safe, my bleeding ass," Nelson scoffed. "Tell that to the dead people out there."

Jessica elbowed him square in the stomach. "*Shhh!* Something out there could hear us."

The next paragraph was as ghastly as the one before:

Emails from those trapped in Chicago and phone calls have poured in to relatives and loved ones that disagree with Quinley's theory of public safety. "Hundreds have been slain by unknown assailants," claims one citizen, Gary Jones, a local freelance photographer. "I have the pictures to prove the atrocities that have taken place here are real. Something unholy has occurred. It's pure evil."

The next set of pictures was of a man in the street. His arms were ejecting themselves from the sockets. The next pictures showed a fist jammed through a man's torso. A woman had a jawbone buried in the side of her head. Severed fingers were crammed into a police officer's eyes.

"That, that man," Billy insisted. "That's the guy from *Death Reject*."

"I'll be damned," Nelson agreed. "It really is the guy. A perfect duplicate."

"No way." Jessica gawked at the picture. "I still don't believe it. Movies aren't real. Monsters aren't real. This isn't what you're thinking. It's real, yes, but it can't be from a fucking movie. Get your head on straight."

A leg the size of a telephone pole covered in pink fishnets was in another snapshot. A series of ten pictures followed the same photo: a stiletto heel with four men spiked on it like a shish kabob. Then a photo of a broken wall inside a skyscraper with a human face staring into it, a woman's face gnarled with rage. A wider shot showed the tall woman in a g-string and tube top mashing the strip club "TITTIES!" into the ground. People were splayed on the street in pools of blood, flattened into the asphalt by the dozens. It appeared the giant woman had crossed into the scummier parts of town to do her killing.

Nelson said seriously, "Looks like a feminist who's pissed."

Jessica said, "Let me guess, she's from a movie too?"

"Keep scrolling down," Billy said, pointing at the screen. "We'll figure this out. We have no other options if we want to live through this."

A picture showed a preacher in a black robe wielding a magnet

173

taller than the man's body. The preacher's face was glowing with pleasure. But behind the preacher, stacks of human bones and bloody skeletons were piled high.

Billy shuddered at the next set of pictures. A street was congested with men and women with split faces. Fifty to a hundred, Billy counted. Their brains gleamed within the cracks of their skulls, and sharp teeth shined as if polished.

"Those are the flytrap heads," Nelson said. "Looking at them now, they're even scarier than before. They almost got us when the elevated train crashed."

Jessica's eyes widened. "What do you mean?"

Billy motioned for her to calm down. "We took the train to reach you, remember? That huge woman shoved us from the track, and we crashed. But before we crashed, the flytrap heads came to life on the train. They tried to, well, eat us. We saw them eat other people's brains...and, er, the brains were basically eating other people's brains."

Jessica studied the bandage by his eye. "It's a miracle you weren't killed."

Billy pointed at the screen again. The pictures had run out, but the article continued:

Many discount the pictures as a hoax, but emails to families on the outside of the dome contradict that statement. Until the police or the military make a press statement, we can do nothing but speculate about this bizarre situation. Elaborate hoax or reality defied, we can only pray whoever is in the dome is safe.

The author was signed "Anonymous." The site had the appearance of an amateur. Nothing else was posted.

Then suddenly the server went blank.

PAGE CANNOT BE DISPLAYED.

"What the fuck?" Jessica pounded the desk. "Somebody's taken it down!"

Nelson lamented, "We're lucky to have seen it at all."

"Why are they covering this up?" Jessica was panicked. "They're going to help us, right? They won't leave us here to die, right?"

"Judging by the pictures, they're doing what they can." Billy couldn't ignore his better judgment. "No matter what the explanation is for these things being out there, the police can't save us. Only we can save ourselves. If they can't break through that dome, then we're stuck here for now."

"But our air supply," Jessica pleaded. Perspiration formed in thick beads at her brow. "We'll be suffocated."

Nelson stared at Billy; he too was losing hope.

Then Nelson hunched over the console and typed in the "Internet Movie Database" and performed a search for *500 Foot Hooker*. The movie poster came up with a woman identical in dress and looks, though she was an artist's rendering, towering over a city. "500 Feet and only 50 Dollars!" was the correct tagline.

"You were serious," Jessica said in resignation. "I mean, it's uncanny. That tall bitch looks like that woman on the poster."

The movie stills were dead-on images of the woman in Gary Jones's photos on the website.

"*How* it's real is the question," Billy insisted. "The man from *Death Reject*, I saw him explode. His parts impaled people. It happened. Now you finally see what I'm saying."

Nelson met his eyes. "I believe you, man. What we're going to do about it is the problem."

Jessica hung her head in defeat. She had nothing to add. Billy believed she was nearing her breaking point. She'd believe in the monsters soon enough, he thought.

"Let's give up on a plausible explanation for now," Nelson suggested. "How the hell are we going to survive?"

"We hole up in this office," Billy answered. "Keep cool. Wait it out. They'll get through the dome eventually. They have to eventually, right?"

Jessica's voice sharpened. "And what if they don't? Those pictures showed crews slamming wrecking balls and using jackhammers and dynamite—and if dynamite couldn't blow through the wall, what can? We're trapped. The air supply will diminish, and we'll be dead. Dead like everybody else!"

Billy clung onto her, stifling the words in an embrace. He whispered words of love and encouragement in her ear. The only words that rang true to him were, *"At least we're not separated. We have that, no matter what. I love you."*

"Is there any food or water here?" Nelson asked. "If we're going to be here awhile…"

Jessica pointed at the opposite hall. "The break room has a fridge. There might be sodas, and bottled water, and random food. I know there's leftover deep-dish pizza."

"Great," Nelson said, ticking off a mental list with his fingers. "We have weapons. Internet. Phone. Food. Then we're safe for now. We hole up here."

"Should we take shifts sleeping?" Billy was thinking aloud. "It's almost dawn. We're exhausted. I'll take the first shift. You two sleep."

"I don't know if I can sleep." Jessica's eyes were on the verge of closing. Each of them kept yawning. "But we should try. This problem isn't going away anytime soon."

Nelson leaned his back against the wall without further argument. "I like your idea, Billy. Wake me up when you can't stay awake any longer."

Nelson closed his eyes. Whether he was asleep or pretending to be to give them a moment to themselves, Billy acted on it. He kissed Jessica tenderly. "You should rest. I'm fine for another few hours."

Jessica leaned her head against his chest. "I can hear your heart beating. It's soothing."

"I'll record it for you when it's over. We'll need all the soothing we can get then."

Jessica smiled. "You're always so funny. That's what I love about you. The world is falling apart, and you haven't jumped out of your skin or lost your shit." She scratched his Superman logo. "I feel safe with you."

"It's only my duty to protect you," he said in a cheesy machismo caricature. "Be safe, ma'am. Be well. Off I go into the night."

"Oh shut up, you dork."

Jessica rubbed the back of his head; he could fall asleep the way the massage relaxed him. It was his favorite thing she did to him on the casual nights they sat together on the couch and watched reality television. Those were the only programs they both enjoyed when Jessica took breaks in between studying.

"Get some sleep," he said again. "I'll keep an ear out. I promise."

Jessica hugged him one more time. "Okay. I love you."

She lay on the floor across from Nelson. Billy stepped out to the break room and scoured the contents of the fridge. "Score," he muttered, and chose a can of cherry-flavored cola. He popped the tab and chugged the fizzy drink for the much-needed caffeine and sugar rush.

He then stood in the hallway opposite the window they shoved the Intestinator through. Air whispered through the opening, the breeze calling out muted screams and moans in the distance. People were out there in danger, he realized. Nobody was safe anywhere.

Billy dragged a chair from the waiting room and set it outside Jessica's office door. He drank another soda and thumbed through a recent issue of *People*. It wasn't long before a human voice called to him from only yards away.

Chapter Twenty-Five

Ted clutched the flaming bottle of cooking sherry. Doubts nagged him as he jogged up the street toward his apartment building. The exterior was menacing in itself. Every floor was cast in pure darkness, the window shades drawn, but in his room, flickers of light flashed. The reels were still playing. *This is all because of me. An entire city murdered, and for what, to get my stupid films back? Nobody cares about them. I'd rather give everybody back their lives than see another graveyard tramp or a flesh-eating baker.*

He was still astonished to see his characters come to life. He'd never live to see anything as miraculous—or insane—in his lifetime. The vampires were just as they were in the films; each of them resembled the actresses to every freckle, breast size and hair color. He'd had an affair with the blonde during the filmmaking. He admitted it was fucked up, but they had sex in character. He'd been the victim, she the vampire. Her name was Molly Greene in real life, and she had been paying her way through nursing school by taking random acting jobs—topless or not, Molly didn't care. After the movie was finished, like every fling in Hollywood—or sub-Hollywood—the affair was terminated.

Maybe Dennis Brauman was right. Ted wasn't good enough to marry his daughter, Katie. He deserved to be divorced by her. He was young, and horny, and stupid, and ambitious all at the same time. But his flaws didn't give Dennis the right to steal his movies and send him into financial ruin.

"This is for you, you rotten bastard! May my film career finally rest in peace!"

Vickers turned to him horrified that he was making so much noise. "Quiet! What are you blathering about?"

"Personal vendettas, man. I'm sure you've got a few of them too."

"Let's focus on saving our asses before settling some old scores. I'm risking my ass because of you."

"Hey, I didn't know they'd come back. Who would? You see—"

"Can it. Throw the cocktail and let's find shelter. Bitch to me about it later."

"You got it. Let's send these sluts to the cutting room floor for the last time."

Vickers charged ahead of him.

Ted halted.

Shooting from the entrance of the apartment building, ten, fifteen, twenty, twenty-five schoolgirls formed a wall outside the apartment. Vickers stopped, utterly dumbfounded. "Ted, is this from another one of your goddamn movies?"

The breath was sucked from his lungs. Ted couldn't move. The sight captivated him. He finally whispered, "*Slasher Girls.*"

"Slasher what?"

"They're from a movie called *Slasher Girls.* I wrote it when I lived in an apartment above a strip club and dated an ex-women's rights activist. It's a looong story."

Vickers didn't have time to respond. A hatchet was flung from fifteen yards out. It struck him dead-center in the skull. Another axe spun from handle to blade, handle to blade, with an alarming and final whoosh, and Vickers' head was shucked from the neck. The cluster of schoolgirls raised scythes and swords and chopped him into so many pieces before the corpse could even drop. Then they carried his pieces into the apartment building. A few stayed as sentries at the entrance, unmoving.

Ted was alone in this fight. A vampire's bitter laughter echoed from his apartment. They had won again, he realized. He didn't stand a chance against them. All he could do was buy enough time to run. He chucked the flaming bottle into the air. It crashed down on the skirted sentries, the alcohol fire blanketing them in flames. They screamed and burned. The horde charged him, braving the flames, as new women stormed out of the building after him. Ted sprinted, mustering the courage and ability to outrun them for two blocks. The burnt shells of cars and random corpses were spread out on the streets. Ted darted around each obstacle. The laughter and chatter of schoolgirls were far behind him. They were busied by the male corpses in the street. They chopped them up like they did Vickers, and danced, and cheered, and raised the butchered remains in the air until they found yet more male bodies to defile.

A corner bar named Side Pockets appeared ahead of him, so Ted dived for cover inside. A quick search revealed there was only a back and front entrance to guard. Ted rushed to create a chair barricade at the front and locked the back steel door. It wasn't until he downed three shots of rye whiskey at the bar that the truth sank in.

He'd failed to save the city.

Billy wasn't quick to locate the voice talking to him. He edged down the hallway, wildly scanning in front and behind him. He feared someone like the Intestinator would pounce on him. He stopped at Jim Lyndsey's office. This time he heard the words, *"In here, Billy. I'm not one of them. I'm Andy Ryerson."*

Andy Ryerson.

Am I supposed to recognize that name?

Billy braced himself for anything. He glanced back at Jessica's office. Nobody else was roused by the voice except for him. He snuck into the office and unleashed a small yelp. A man was face-down on his desk. Blood soaked the carpet beneath the desk; the man had slit his wrists. Billy couldn't locate the weapon. The method of death became irrelevant when the corpse lifted his head from the desk. He was blue faced and quite dead.

The corpse's movements were slow, as if his limbs were made of concrete. He reached out and begged, "Don't run from me! I'm not going to hurt you."

Billy backed out of the office and slammed the door. "It's another monster. Damn it, I'm so stupid!"

The voice continued to beckon him, and then it deteriorated. He heard the sound of splattering. The collapse of bones.

He was confused, standing there. If it was a monster, why didn't it come after him? The man was a zombie, it seemed, but how did it know his name? Why did it plead with him?

Curiosity wouldn't allow him to leave the hall. If the zombie was alive, he'd come out at any moment and attack. Billy couldn't ignore that fact, and he wouldn't put anybody else on night watch without taking care of the intruder first.

Billy opened the door again, ready to close it immediately if he was assaulted. The zombie was gone, to his astonishment. A liquid pile of skin, tissue, blood and disintegrating bone faced him. The sludge didn't move. The zombie was dead. Again.

A hand closed over his mouth. His feet were swept from beneath him. Two different pairs of hands clutched onto him, one carrying him by his upper body, the other holding his legs. He thrashed and attempted to call for help, but the hand stayed in place even after he bit it three times—and tasted pieces of dead skin sloughing off into his mouth.

"If you want Jessica and your best friend to be safe, you'll stay quiet. We're not here to hurt you. We want to help you. Let us help you. But we have to take you to a special room first."

Yeah sure, a special killing room. Away from help, right? Why should I trust walking dead men?

He was carried through two hallways and three doors, the final door leading to a stairwell. Taking a side door, they entered Allied Health Insurance Company. Cubicles and corpses filled what used to be a workplace. The zombies at both sides of him began to drip onto

181

the ground, and they released him. The skin was loosening from their hands like hot putty. Accompanied by the slither of flesh, the sharp crack and give of bones, his capturers dismantled before his eyes. The swirl of greens, reds and blacks dripped onto the tiles.

"Nasty." He dodged the incoming fleshy puddles. "That's what you get for trying to capture me. I'm getting the fuck out of here."

"No, wait!" a constricted voice shouted behind him. "Billy, please, listen to us. We're only trying to help you. Listen to me. It's your only chance to save Chicago."

Billy was frozen in place. The words were coming from a cubicle down the way. He ran to it. A woman met him wearing a blue top and gray skirt. Her neck was snapped, tilted flimsily to one side. Her face was even bluer than the last corpse. Very much dead. "I'm a ghost, Billy. My name is Andy Ryerson. I'm talking through this body to reach you. An attack happened one year ago in the town of Anderson Mills, Kansas. Monsters from movies came to life. You have to destroy the projector. It's the only way to stop them."

The corpse's eyes rolled into the back of its head and then exploded as if a firecracker went off under each eyelid. The rest of the woman's flesh melted in waxy thick trails until the skeleton was bare. The body kept talking until the final moment when the head snapped off. The last words it spoke were: "My spirit entering these bodies causes the corpses to melt and break. I only have so many chances to talk to you. Please, just listen to me. I won't harm you. I know you're scared. So was I when it happened to me."

The woman crashed front first onto the carpet. A suited corpse, this one with yellow-blue-purple bruises around his throat, limped up to him. The man's mouth dribbled black blood between words. "My uncle was named James Ryerson. He was a magician. He moved into a house that was haunted by a ghost who happened to be a preacher. This preacher was an oracle. He spoke to the dead before and after he died. His name was Edgar Hutchinson. Edgar made contact with my uncle while he lived in that house. The dead man haunted my uncle for favors. In fact, Edgar wouldn't leave him alone ever. Other ghosts joined in too with favors to ask of my uncle. They kept him up at all hours of the night. He couldn't escape them. The ghosts wanted him to terrorize the living from beyond. They were driving him crazy, but the ghosts offered him something he couldn't refuse. Fame and fortune. To improve his magic act, the ghosts inhabited his magic items, and James' shows became world famous. But the ghosts inhabited other items in his house, including an Orion projector..."

The cuffs of the man's suit began to stream out steaming globules of caramel-consistency flesh. Another corpse, an older woman, an assistant with a headset on, ambled up to him next from a nearby cubicle. Her neck had been snapped as well.

She said, "James burned the magic items after a vicious attack killed fifty people during one of his acts. But the ghosts remained in the Orion projector. After my uncle vanished without a trace, I inherited his house. I just graduated film school, and my professor asked me to watch a collection of rediscovered horror movies. I ended up using the projector in the attic, the haunted projector, and the monsters in the films were projected in real life. The ghosts used them as a vessel to live again. I destroyed the projector but one of the films survived. They possessed that instead, and when the film was shown they came to life and found another projector to inhabit. Their only goal is to cause chaos and death. They're bitter, vengeful spirits who hate the living for being alive. They're using old horror movie reels to enact their revenge.

"If they can't be human, then nobody can. They want us to be wandering spirits in limbo like them, permanent residents in hell. They won't stop until everybody in the city is dead. Then they'll plunder the next big metropolis and then small towns until earth is one big graveyard. The thing I've learned since death is that the ghosts are further tainted by the horror movie character they become. They take on the movie villain's persona and their aspirations. They truly become the movies. A movie character by the name of *Jorg: The Hungry Butcher* rampaged through Anderson Mills, chopping people into choice cuts when I was still alive. Even though a ghost was trapped inside the reel's image of Jorg, the ghost was using Jorg's movie lines, acting out Jorg's actions from the movie all the same. More films are being shown this time around, and now the ghost's identities are even more lost in the characters. But if you destroy the projector and all the films, you end their outlet into the world. You can stop this, Billy. They're playing possessed reels in an apartment building. I've written down the address on this piece of paper. You must do what I say, or else city after city will suffer the same horrifying deaths. It will never end. It will only grow worse.

"Not all spirits are evil, Billy. Many good people await their loved ones in the afterlife when their time finally comes. I created an insurance policy in case you don't trust me. He'll be waiting for you in the hallway when you return to the fourth floor. He's watching over your friends. End this, Billy, before it's too late. I'm begging you to take what I say to heart. You don't have much time. The air is growing thin. Save yourselves and everybody else."

The woman disintegrated. Billy turned his head in disgust as her remains splashed onto the carpet. He waited for another corpse to rise and speak again. After three minutes, he quit waiting. Billy was about to leave for the fourth floor when he recalled the address the old woman's corpse told him about.

He stepped over the woman's liquefied remains and into the cubicle. On a piece of paper, an address was scrawled in blue ink. He picked it up and turned over in his mind what had happened in the past five minutes.

I should've asked more questions. Who the hell is Andy Ryerson? Movies coming to life can't be for real. But it makes sense. I was right from the beginning.

"Yeah, and Jessica and Nelson are going to believe me. Sure. Fuck it, I don't care. We'll drive across town to this guy Ted Fuller's apartment and destroy the projector. It's the best I've got."

The words repeated in his head: *I created an insurance policy in case you don't trust me.*

He rushed through the cubicles, out of the insurance company's offices, climbed down a flight of stairs and returned to Jessica's office. He struggled for breath. The air was getting thinner, and he was coughing in fits.

I'm too fucking fat to save the world!

Billy slowed when he heard laughter. Yards from Jessica's office, the door wide open, he overheard Nelson talking boisterously. Jessica was standing up and was immediately drawn to him when he arrived. "I don't know who the hell this guy is, but Nelson seems to know him."

"I'm Dr. Aorta," the stranger in the room announced, greeting Billy. "Now you know me, and we can get to work. I'm not getting much of a hero's welcome, but real heroes don't need them, now do they?"

Dr. Aorta was six feet tall, athletic and muscular. His head was shaved and formed a point at the top. He wore a brown leisure suit and sucked on the end of an unlit cigar. The man kept a monocle in his right eye with a sterling silver chain hanging from the side. A pin of the Russian flag was stuck to his left breast pocket. The man had a slight Russian accent, though it was tempered with a New Jersey accent on and off. Billy couldn't wrap his mind around why this man was here until he finally understood.

This was yet another creation based on a B-movie.

Billy asked, "Where did you come from?"

"Andy Ryerson sent me. You just talked to him, didn't you?"

Billy was awestruck. Jessica tugged on his arm. "You were gone. I woke up to a knock on the door, and there he was. I didn't know what to do. Thank God Nelson recognized him. I about shit my pants."

"You guys haven't seen many old horror movies, have you?" Nelson patted Dr. Aorta's shoulder as if they'd won a rugby game, and Dr. Aorta had scored the winning point. "Haven't you seen *Frankenstein Lives in Your Dormitory*? *Swamp Creatures Attack San Diego*? How about *Chronicle of the Grim Reaper*? You almost died in that one. The grim reaper about cut you down. And what about *Undead Cheerleader Squad*? *Beneath the Quicksand*? *Reef Monsters of Coral Island*? *Beach*

185

Volleyball Communists? Come on, you haven't seen any of his films? He's a Russian biochemist and mercenary hired by the Soviets to infiltrate vampires, zombies and, well, undead cheerleaders. Their pom-poms, you see, were created with cheap plastic. It caused a radioactive reaction through the plastic, which channeled through their wrists, into their bloodstreams and into their brains.

"The Americans can't keep up with his physical and intellectual abilities. Teams of slayers have died fighting what this guy picks off like nothing. Dr. Aorta has survived two decades of monsters. He was trained at birth. He probably had a pair of boxing gloves already strapped on in the womb. He was staking vamps, blowing away werewolves with silver bullets and bashing zombies' heads in since he was a tyke. His parents were slaughtered by ghost-inhabited scarecrows, you see. He was born in Russia, but then moved to America, where he was raised on democratic ideals and valor and all that shit, and he was trained by mixed martial arts instructors, learning Taekwondo, Karate and Druid self-defense, and then—"

Dr. Aorta was gracious. "You're too kind, Nelson, too kind."

"He's the James Bond of monster slaying," Nelson gushed. "He creates the best weapons. He infiltrates evil. He's an engineer. A weapons specialist to boot. And he's pulled a lot of ass in his day. That pep squad lady you bagged in the locker room, she was aching for you. They call him Dr. Aorta because he's a man of valor, courage and he has the biggest heart of any human being—literally, he was born with an enlarged heart."

Billy scoffed. "Then why didn't they call him 'Dr. Heart'?"

Nelson shook his head. "N-no, he's Dr. Aorta. 'Dr. Heart' sounds stupid, you jackass."

Dr. Aorta had the bearing of a militant man. "Yes, perhaps another time I can school you in the art of courtship, Nelson. I'm grateful for my fans. For now, you have an address in your hands, son." He held out his hand to Billy. "Do you mind showing me that paper?"

Billy handed him the address. "Here you go, doctor."

"Oh yes." His eye behind the monocle went small. "Then we don't have any time to lose. The projector is on the fourth floor of Ted Fuller's apartment building, Andy has told me. All we have to do is go across town and destroy it."

"Wait," Jessica said. "I'm not going out there. Have you seen what's out there? It's dangerous."

Nelson shook his head. "This guy will protect us. He's the best. He always has an ace up one sleeve and a stick of dynamite in the other. We're saved. Wake up, guys. Everything's going to be okay. It's Dr. Aorta!"

Billy recalled what Andy's spirit said about ghosts. "So how did you come to life, Dr. Aorta?"

"I was in one of the reels the vampires are playing in Ted Fuller's apartment. Andy allowed me to come to life. He's gathering the spirits of good on his side. It'll take time before more good spirits can save us. That's why we have to save ourselves first. The city's almost all dead, Billy. We're one of the few left alive. Once the final body hits the ground, that dome will be released, and you can kiss the next city goodbye."

Jessica clutched onto Billy. She was quivering. "Is this real, Billy?"

"I'm afraid so. When I was on watch duty, voices called out to me. I was dragged up to the fifth floor by living corpses. They were your co-workers, Jessica, but they were temporarily inhabited by ghosts, including Andy's. Andy told me a haunted movie projector is playing horror movies. It's the simplest explanation I can give you. That's why there are the strange creatures out there. The crazier it sounds, the more it makes sense. Andy said Dr. Aorta was his insurance policy. I guess that proves the movies do come to life."

Nelson said, "You were right, Billy, about *Death Reject*. And the *500 Foot Hooker*, I was right about that too. The Internet site with the pictures, it's real."

Jessica hid her face in her hands. She still didn't want to believe the far-fetched truth.

Dr. Aorta brought them back to the current situation. "Let's get a move on. I know how to get to Ted's apartment building. My vehicle is parked outside."

"Let's use the emergency exit," Billy suggested. "If we're going to do this, let's be safe."

Jessica raised her voice. "Hey, I'm not going anywhere! This creep, I barely know him. He's not real. He's a fucking B-movie character. You say he's Russian, but I hear the New Jersey accent. He's a fake."

Nelson refused her argument. "He's an A-1, first class, man of valor."

"Shut the fuck up, you...you," Jessica stammered, "dork! You're getting off on this guy. Why don't you go jerk each other off after a double feature, or something."

Dr. Aorta stepped out of the office without further talk. He faced the end of the hall and removed a ray-gun from his shoulder holster. The ray gun was made of reflective steel. It had the handle of a small handgun, but the sides of the device had glue stick tubes around the circumference. "Stand back, evil, or I'll blast you to hell!"

Billy joined the man but doubled back at the sight of the enemy.

The man from *Death Reject*.

"If you blow up," Dr. Aorta warned, "you'll kill us, but when you come back together, you'll be stuck. This is a super-chemical adhesive. You'll never explode again."

The death reject, his corpse face shiftless and unaffected, simply looked at Dr. Aorta. He pointed his finger straight out. His fingernail grew to a sharp lance. He sliced both wrists and cackled, throwing his head back, salivating and foaming with pleasure at his move.

Dr. Aorta shouted, "Run like hell for the fire exits! The bastard's going to flood us out of the building!"

The warning was useless. Billy expected the man's wrists to gush blood, but this was like the breaking of a dam. The flesh burst open from his wrist up to the forearm. *Sssssssssssssst!* The death reject's body was hidden behind the torrent of blood that erupted form him. The spray elevated to a wall of crimson, the tide ripping doors from the hinges, the wave barreling down upon them. Each of them was pounded down onto their backs. Jessica had wrenched open the fire exit the moment it happened. The liquid push delivered them down three sets of stairs, their bodies gliding on blood, spinning, flipping, hurled forward as if body surfing in red. Nelson went under, pushed by the rushing tide. An ocean of blood raised them many feet above the actual stairs. They were paddling to survive.

Billy paddled harder, swimming along with the current. He couldn't see anybody else in the red waves. They finally arrived in the ground-floor lobby, spread out like beached fish. Blood flooded the lobby, washing up the furniture and filling up the space. Jessica, Nelson and Dr. Aorta had landed farther out than him, so Billy regained his composure, waded through knee-deep blood, and lifted each of them to their feet.

Dr. Aorta removed his suit jacket, angrily heaving it into the blood. "That's a huge dry cleaning bill!" He pointed at the exit. "Move it, people. Death Reject will be right behind us."

They followed Dr. Aorta, the B-movie character they had no choice but to trust.

"Listen to the man," Billy demanded. "I don't know any other plan that's as good as following this guy."

He clutched Jessica's arm and helped her along as they waded through the blood. Nelson was side-by-side with Dr. Aorta.

That prick is loving every second of this.

Dr. Aorta picked up a chair and heaved it into the window. The shatter allowed the draining of blood onto the street. It gurgled down the gutter and painted the sidewalks. As they stepped into the Chicago night, the thinning air still carried a chill. Jessica was repulsed, being slathered in red.

"I'm taking the longest shower after this is over," she said.

Dr. Aorta giggled—two high-pitched snorts. "Prissy thing, if we're going to survive, you're going to get your hands even dirtier."

"Oh, fuck off. I've had intestines touch me, I've seen my co-workers massacred, and I almost drowned in blood. I'm about as nasty as a lady can get."

Billy squeezed her arm. "Let's just get to the address."

"I lost the paper," Dr. Aorta said matter-of-factly. Then he smiled that astute, inside-joke smile. "Oh, but I memorized it."

Billy asked, "So how are we going to get there?"

Dr. Aorta pointed up the street next to Star Coffee. "That's my baby. It's a GTK Boxer. I just call it 'The Boxer'."

Billy eyed the war machine. Camouflage painted the modular armor. It had eight large wheels. It was like a tank without the turret. Maybe a steroid-injected Hummer, Billy thought.

"German engineering at its finest," Dr. Aorta bragged. "It has a 40mm automatic grenade launcher sticking out the front and an MG3 machine gun. Baby runs on diesel. This will mow down whatever's in our way and protect us from their evil."

The street shifted, literally rocked on its foundation. Three streetlights tilted and crashed from the concussion. Car alarms went off. The breaking of rubble, the grinding of rocks, and a deafening sigh of pain, "UHNNNNNNNNNN..."

"Now what?" Billy shouted. "What else is there? Trolls with laser guns?"

Down the street, the back of the five hundred-foot hooker rose from the street. She lifted herself up again from the subway and dominated the street. Blood trickled down her face. From her eye down to her jaw the flesh was jagged and serrated. She swung her fist down at them, but she was only semi-conscious and missed. Billy and Jessica were forced to back-pedal from the vehicle, but Nelson and Dr. Aorta found safety within the Boxer.

Nelson stuck his head out of the top hatch. "Hurry up, guys, before she swings again!"

Dr. Aorta took the helm, Billy assumed, because the vehicle coughed out a black jet of exhaust and sped from the scene. Nelson shouted down into the vehicle, "What the hell are you doing? You're leaving them! Guys, run—watch out!"

Sssssssssssssssssonk!

With a flash of orange and an ear-shattering boom, the grenade launcher issued its first round. It struck the woman at her shoulder. Bone, blood and flesh disintegrated. The damage rained down onto the city in thickening clops. The g-stringed titan raged, screamed and threw her head back. She stamped her stilettos and shook the earth, causing the vehicle to side-wheel.

"That guy's going to get Nelson killed," Billy huffed. "I shouldn't have trusted that war monger. This is all out of control!"

Out from the alleys, they arrived. Men and women with their heads split down the middle, teeth clacking together, the Venus flytrap monsters hungry for brains.

"Run!" Billy pulled Jessica from the alley. Dozens pursued them, pouring out of apartments, wrecked buildings and gutters. "Into the subway, quick!"

They rushed down the steps and into the subway. They raced down each stair, Billy catching Jessica from falling forward when she turned her ankle on one of the steps. They reached the end of the stairs and prayed the subway was clear of enemies.

Chapter Twenty-Six

Ted forced himself to stop drinking after reeling from five back-to-back shots of whiskey. He couldn't focus, his mind a sinkhole full of shit. Nobody knew he was in the bar, though every now and then new screams carried into the night. Ted figured there weren't many people left to die. He was safe for now, he consoled himself. There's nothing else he could do for anyone. He tried his best, and with that consolation, he sat alone at a booth opposite a dart board and a Terminator pinball machine. He stared at the beer poster of three women clad in bikinis floating on inflatable rafts on a lagoon-like pool. Ted dreamed of swimming with the brunette and the blonde, sandwiched between them, and staying tipsy.

"The closest you're going to get to that is with your vampire women." He laughed hysterically. "I should've called the movie *Naked Graveyard Vampires Find Orgasms in Dildo Cemetery*. I can't believe I had sex with them. Un-be-fucking-lievable. They're ghosts. They're dead. But it's the best sex I've ever had! Ah-hah-hah-hah!"

The silence that followed was haunting. He grew paranoid. Uncertain. He regretted drinking. The room tilted. He had to swim upstream to form complete thoughts. The image of Detective Vickers' head sliced from the neck by a schoolgirl replayed in his mind. That could've been him. Should've been him.

Why didn't the slasher girls kill me? I'm not that fast. They could see where I was running. I didn't out-maneuver them.

He scrambled across the room and tried the phone. The phone lines were down. How many people were still alive in the city? Was he one of the few remaining, if not the only one period?

The room was rocked by tremors. Huge footsteps.

FWOMP! FWOMP! FWOMP!

Bottles were jarred from the shelf and shattered.

He peeked through the curtain.

FWOMP! FWOMP! FWOMP!

The concussions grew in intensity. The five hundred-foot woman passed the bar, pursuing something, her steps quick, precise and undeterred by her surroundings. Her breasts jiggled, her stilettos keeping her at a jog. He recalled the ending of the film where she was blown up by jet fighters. The end shot was a fake city being drenched in blood.

Ted pulled away from the curtain. The determination to sneak into the apartment hadn't vanished, but it was weakened by the improbability of survival. *You won't survive in here for very much longer, either. I won't die in a fucking bar.*

He slammed his fist onto the tabletop in frustration. He couldn't think clearly enough to decide what to do next.

Then someone asked him, "Do you believe in reincarnation?"

Ted shot his gaze to the bar. There he was, walking death himself. He should've known before the first word touched his ear. The smell. The embalming fluid.

The Pickler.

"I created you," Ted snarled. "Just leave me the hell alone, and I'll leave you the hell alone."

The Pickler drip-drip-dripped between words. His features, his skin, underneath his fingernails, from his eyes, they all exuded chemicals. The Pickler was more deathlike now than in the movie, Ted observed, his cheekbones sunken and his eyes a faded olive color and his skin eel-gray.

"Do you believe in reincarnation?" he asked again.

"I—"

Ted stopped himself. The question was familiar. It was a line of dialogue from the script he wrote. He crafted his response carefully. "You only live once. Death is the final ride."

"Yes," the corpse replied in a low drool. "That's why I carve the dead for their insides, for their organs. I steal from the dead to give to the living. The dead should be liquidized wholesale. And the no-pulsers, it should be a prerequisite for the grave to give up their parts. Surgeons should be stationed at morgues to take what's needed."

"You're doing a public service selling body parts," Ted said in encouragement. "The dead don't use them, the greedy pus heads. Selfish assholes."

The Pickler was disappointed Ted didn't play along correctly. He tried again anyway. "You don't need consent to borrow from the dead. Even your sister's body, Ted, I surgically removed her heart. Somebody else could use it. She's dead and rotting, what does she care?"

Ted stood up from his chair.

That wasn't in the script.

Trisha's been dead for three years.

"If you know so much about her, then how did she die?"

The Pickler smiled, the trickle of embalming fluid audible. "She was held at knifepoint for her purse. In New York, she was in the subway alone. The robber decided to have some fun with her, and—"

Ted hurled a stool at the villain. The corpse was fast and ducked to avoid it.

"Stripped her naked—"

"SHUT UP!"

Ted delivered another stool across the room, but his aim was off, the tears in his eyes blurrng his vision.

"Told her he'd slit her throat if she screamed—"

"Another word from you, and I'll send you to hell!"

"You said so yourself, there is no afterlife. Death is the final ride, and you're about to be strapped in!"

194

He rushed for the door, but Ted stopped at the table next to him. The ashtray was full of stubbed-out menthol cigarettes. The Zippo lighter next to the ashtray beckoned him. Embalming fluid formed a puddle around the walking corpse, the dripping still at a constant.

"Death *is* the final ride," Ted shouted, picking up the Zippo and flicking it. "And it's sending you right to hell!"

He lit the floor.

Blue flames puckered and trailed toward the corpse in shark-fin arcs. The Pickler was instantly engulfed. His skin crackled, sparks flying as they popped and burst. His eye sockets exploded in pops. His flesh smoldered, every layer of embalming fluid ignited within him. The bar was clogged with the choking stench of burning flesh and caustic fluids.

Ted pushed open the door and sucked in breaths of air, though it was stale.

Thinning.

That dome is going to snuff us all.

The bar was lit from within, the firelight dancing strong. The night was a yellow, orange and red blaze as the corpse continued to pursue him. "I'll never die," he gargled and coughed. "I'll just keep burning."

Bright lights shined, like two monster eyes. Ted heard the growl of pistons churning and an engine sputtering smoke as the rig closed in on him. With the roll of steel against pavement, the steam roller barreled toward him.

What else is coming out of the jungle tonight?

Ba-bam!

Sparks shot from the curb next to his feet. The driver was shooting at him. Ted sprinted up the street. He caught the slasher girls guarding his apartment building, blithely picking their nails with the tips of daggers and axes, and sharing giddy schoolgirl conversation. *"I shoved that rod up his ass, and afterwards, he didn't want to try anal sex on me ever again..."*

"Figures," a slasher girl laughed. *"After I cut off his balls and stomped them into the ground, he no longer wanted my number after the party. Men are strange creatures. I really thought he liked me."*

Ted disregarded the troubling conversation when the rig revved its engine, the spotlight touching him again. He dove behind a stack of garbage cans. Ba-bam! A cannon blasted, ear-drum shatteringly loud. Garbage lids shot up with wild *ping* sounds. Ted crawled for better cover, soon getting up and racing between two buildings, up another street, and retreating into a residential neighborhood. The houses were boarded up from within. He screamed and begged for help. Not even a porch light flickered on in response.

The steam roller was nowhere in sight.

He imagined being flattened into the street, every bone snapped, every inch of him pulped. The only beacon of salvation was up ahead, a lone standing grocery store, a Piggly Wiggly. Ted rounded to the side of the building where an F-150 truck was parked. The driver was half out of the driver's seat, hanging limply. His skull was hollow, a hole at the top where his brains had been sucked out.

The truck's keys were in the ignition.

Ted checked the back door into the store. It was partly open. He had access to the goods inside, he realized. Looking back to the truck, he knew he couldn't actually escape the city. Chicago was under a skull dome prison. He was trapped here unless he changed the situation. He had to play by the rules of the ghosts who possessed the projector.

With the truck and a few creatively picked supplies, he believed he had a chance to re-enter the apartment and destroy the projector.

But first, he had much work to do...

Chapter Twenty-Seven

Father Richard Malone hid in the confessional. Fifty people had found shelter in Saint Anna Catholic Church, but nobody knew he was inside the booth. Many were members of the congregation, and they were doing fine, he thought, muttering prayers on their own. The windows were blockaded by stacks of pews. Some people were huddled up and studying the outside through the small openings. What he was hiding from was terrifying, and it could still be waiting outside for him.

His fear was the schoolgirl wearing a simple plaid miniskirt. She was maybe seventeen. There were dozens of them, but only one had tracked him through the garden in the back of the church and pursued him.

"Don't you remember me?" the schoolgirl called out to him. "I'm Cathy Higgins."

The name Cathy Higgins tightened his spine. That cold sticky sweat of guilt gave him a slimy feeling. A horrible caught sensation itched at him. Nobody knew about Cathy Higgins, and that schoolgirl wasn't Cathy Higgins.

How did *she* know about Cathy Higgins?

"You said you'd stay with me," the schoolgirl posing as Cathy Higgins had said to him. "I put out for you. I wanted to give myself to you. I want you, Richie. Let me have you. Every bit of you. Bend me over. Show me the Holy Spirit. I want it inside me!"

He'd demanded, "How do you know about Cathy Higgins?"

Cathy was a sweet girl, a congregation member, who'd fallen in love with him. She'd meet him in confession. He never had sex with her, but she masturbated during confession, and the worst part of it was, he watched her and enjoyed every moment of it. The memory of it sickened him. Disgusted him.

He kept running from the girl who knew about Cathy Higgins. She raised a blade and kept chasing him. "I can show you pleasure, Richie. The knife will set you free from your manhood. No more machismo bullshit. No more lust. You'll have your God and your church. Isn't that what matters to you most? Without your dick in the way, you'll hand yourself over to God completely. You'll get it back in heaven, I promise."

He lost the girl when he ran into the church and locked the door behind him. That's when he'd hidden in the confessional booth.

"My brothers and sisters..." Words seeped through the cracks of the confessional booth, and he listened. "...you are safe here. This is God's haven. Nothing can harm you in His kingdom. This is judgment day. The day of reckoning is upon us. I am his judge. I will deem who is fit to walk in heaven or just to crawl the wretched burning fields of hell. Now I must remove your soul to know this, but I promise after I'm finished, I'll put it right back."

A hushed silence descended on the church. Richard peeked through the crack of the door. The preacher at the podium was a stranger. He was dressed in a black cassock. His brow bent in a sharp V, eyes shark black as he studied each person in the church.

Who does he think he is?

He's not a man of the cloth.

"NOW IS THE TIME FOR YOUR JUDGMENT!"

Up from the floorboards burst a rolling platform holding a U-shaped metal device. It crackled and flashed blue and white lightning and fired electromagnetic currents. The false priest was behind the device, static electricity raising the hairs on his arms and head. Shocked, Richard was nailed in place. He watched in helpless denial. The currents pierced scrambling, shrieking bodies. Many attempted to undo the barricade and crawl through the windows. Those who did crawl through immediately received an axe to the head from outside.

The group of ravaging schoolgirls attacked, relishing the blood they reaped. Giddy laughter and sing-song voices entered the church:

"Patty-cake, patty-cake, baker's man, how many heads can we reap?"

The moment the electromagnetic light would touch a body, the flesh split down the middle, and the skeleton was wrenched free, parting and splitting muscle and skin. The skeleton flew onto the giant magnet. The bones crashed against it, breaking into brittle pieces. "YOU'RE GOING TO HELL! AND SO ARE YOU, MA'AM. SONNY, IT'S TOO LATE TO MEET CHRIST. YOU WERE A WHORE WORTHY OF A ROMAN ORGY! YOU'RE DAMNED TO HELL, ALL OF YOU!!! STEP RIGHT UP AND ACCEPT YOUR FATE!"

Few were left alive after minutes of flying skeletons and deflated bodies hitting the floor.

You have to do something. You can't sit there and watch them die. Face him.

Richard charged out of the booth and tackled the preacher. He caught the man off guard. They crashed to the floor, spun and landed where they shouldn't have. Neither of them had a chance to escape the electromagnetic rays and the inevitable removal of their bones.

Georgia, the vampire, stood before the wall and watched fifteen minutes of the film entitled *Preggers*. Anne, the auburn beauty, strutted into the room. "They didn't kill Ted."

"That idiot?" Georgia flipped her head back in amusement. "He can't do anything. He's a coward. A waste of human skin. He's not a threat to us."

"What if he comes back and tries to burn the place down again?"

"The slasher girls are outside. The steam roller is driving up and down the streets. That hooker is up and about. The brain faces, are...well, they're eating brains. Mr. Baker isn't dead either, though he's nice and crispy. The Intestinator is nearby. He's not dead either. The Pickler is burning and spreading his death fluid everywhere. And

199

Death Reject isn't down for the count. They've done nothing to stop us."

"What about Dr. Aorta?"

The name struck a strange chord with her. "Dr. Aorta, who's he?"

The front door opened. Slasher girl after slasher girl entered with a new corpse in their hands or over their shoulders. Each body suffered head wounds, neck slashes, bodily lacerations and disembowelments. "Hang them in the tub to drain, you lovelies," Georgia said, welcoming them.

"The tub's full of blood and spilling over," the cherry red-haired schoolgirl complained. "And this guy's fuckin' heavy."

Georgia got up and met the schoolgirl. "Then stack them up in the bedroom." Georgia groped the girl's buttocks and teased between her legs. Before the slasher girl could react, Georgia bit off her lips, tongue, and wildly drank the blood flowing from the wounds. She bit through the girl's neck in one chomp, nearly taking out the entire neck. The head bobbed to the side hanging on a single bit of gristle.

"So tasty," she cackled. "Red and delicious."

The slasher girl struck the carpet dead.

"If you fail to murder this city, you'll end up like her—understand me? Work faster. Kill everyone!"

The slasher girls rushed out of the apartment and went about their task, afraid of the dripping-mouthed vampire. Georgia brought Anne close. "Lick the blood off my lips. I love it all! More—I want more death! I want blood up to my neck in this fucking city!"

The two other vampires, overhearing the speech, obeyed the vampire's commands and inserted another reel titled: *Skinpreys.*

Nelson reeled from one unbelievable moment to another. Here he was driving in the Boxer with Dr. Aorta, a cult hero. The giant hooker outside the tank was smashing, swatting and rampaging after them. She punched apart buildings in her wake, raining steel, glass and other debris down onto the streets.

"There won't be anything left of the city by the time that whore's through with it."

"But she's making chase," Dr. Aorta said, philosophically sizing up the hooker. "She's not much for agility. Spreading your legs to turn tricks and whispering dirty nothings in ears isn't much exercise. She won't last long doing what she's doing."

Dr. Aorta turned the wheel one hundred eighty degrees and spun out again. He was driving in circles to make the hooker dizzy.

The walls were simple steel. Two gunner sticks for steering, another set for firing the weapons.

Nelson couldn't help feeling useless. "What about my friends? We just left them."

"They're underground," Dr. Aorta insisted, angry to be disturbed from his ruminations. "We'll have to catch up with them later. This bitch has put herself in the forefront of our problems."

"We can't keep driving like this," Nelson said. "She won't give up. I still don't understand why she even exists."

"She's a scientific mistake," Dr. Aorta said. "A man created a larger hooker to earn higher profits. But these three pimps shot the scientist dead for his discovery. Something snapped in her brain, and she wants all men dead."

I forgot. This guy's a living movie. He's obviously not getting what I'm saying.

"Why don't we fire another missile at her?"

"Too many innocent people will get hurt."

"Then what's your plan?"

"Watch me."

He pressed a large red button underneath the console.

"HOLD ON!"

Nelson watched from slit openings in the side of the vehicle as wings spread out on each side of the Boxer. From the back end, a loud jet of fire exploded and continued to burn. Rocket thrusters. They hovered higher and higher into the air. Nelson hung on to the handlebars welded into the ceiling for his life. "Shit!"

"Hold on, ace—and remember who I am. You're safe with Dr. Aorta."

Dr. Aorta jerked the controls to avoid a stiletto heel that swiped inches from the left wing.

"HOLY SHIT!" Nelson shouted. "THAT WAS WAY TOO CLOSE!"

Dr. Aorta chortled, "Not close enough, says that slut."

Nelson glanced back outside. They were passing the woman's chest, flying high.

"Brace yourself," Dr. Aorta warned. "Watch out for blood."

From the nose of the vehicle a blade like a giant box cutter extended. It glinted of sharp steel.

Jesus fuck-me Christ!

The Boxer nose-dived, avoiding two fists that nearly crushed it. The craft wobbled, Dr. Aorta hurling curses as he tried to straighten the nose. "Damn bitch, she'll have me dead yet."

"Straighten it out!" Nelson cried. "I'm not dying like this."

The thruster in back coughed and went out. Dr. Aorta turned the ignition again, the engine coughing out gasps of useless air. The engine refused to turn over.

"It's taking a coffee break."

"Now's not the time!"

Dr. Aorta straightened the front, and they sailed on wing power. Nelson figured that bought thirty seconds before they crash landed. Dr. Aorta turned and turned the ignition to no avail. The hooker stomped after them, laughing. She knew what was happening to them.

Nelson stepped toward the steering column and turned the key; he'd had experience with a dying '76 Thunderbird he bought for six hundred dollars in high school and thought he could help. The owner had told him, "You have to cradle and pound the damn thing for it to start. Cradle and pound the bitch, and she'll start up."

"Cradle and pound the bitch," Nelson repeated, "and she'll start up."

He cradled the keys. *Be nice to me, I'll be nice to you.*

And then he pounded it, rapidly turning the key.

THOOP!

The rocket thrusters re-ignited. The Boxer sailed into the air, crossed the tops of five skyscrapers, and swooped back down toward the hooker. The hooker had uprooted a light pole and swung it like a baseball bat. She struck the tip of the right wing with a *tink*. The Boxer was jarred, but Dr. Aorta managed to get back on course. Lust for blood and destruction lit up the hooker's eyes.

"I've read studies," Dr. Aorta said, his Russian accent suddenly returning, "that women who've received semen from many different men undergo a form of mania. Sometimes, it's mood swings. Their menstruation cycles are more painful. Other times, it turns them into mean murderous bitches!"

Dr. Aorta cheered and raised an arm up high into the air. *"Let's cut this mean hooker down to size!"*

Nelson swallowed hard when the Boxer spun upside down three times and then rocketed straight up. He closed his eyes. His guts went up into his throat.

Dr. Aorta's warning proved accurate.

Blood sprayed the outside of the Boxer, random spurts entering the vehicle and slathering Nelson's face. "Ah, sick!"

Dr. Aorta laughed. "I'd get tested if I were you when this is over... *I know I will.*"

Nelson couldn't see the damage done. But once the blood dripped clear from the opening slit, he saw the hooker's bowels slip through the net of her fingers and slather onto the road, where they formed a hill of viscera. The blood splashed and ran in a foamy torrent down the gutters. Nelson saw the towering hooker tilt and fall.

"You killed her!" Nelson cheered. "Bitch went down! Bitch is dead!"

Dr. Aorta landed the Boxer. They drove on, avoiding the heaps of gore.

"Let's go find your friends."

"But they went into the subway."

"I know where they're going," Dr. Aorta said, his accent now New Jersey. "I put a tracking device on the lady."

"Then where are they headed?"

"I'll take you right to them."

Chapter Twenty-Eight

The subway train had been sitting motionless in the station when Billy and Jessica arrived, but when they were yards from the first open door, it began to slowly edge forward. The Green Line had been modified, Billy noticed. Boards protected the windows. Billy couldn't see inside to know if it was safe, but that concern was trumped by the flytrap heads that rushed them from behind, fifty to seventy pouring down the stairs en masse. The huge choir of clacking teeth echoed throughout the station. From the other side of the platform, schoolgirls were coming down at them from the south set of stairs. They were a solid front, but far enough from the subway car that if Billy and Jessica made a break for it, they might avoid them.

"Looks like we don't have a choice," Billy shouted over the demonic noise. "We have to get on the Green Line! RUN!"

The subway car edged forward, slowly gaining speed.

Jessica shook her head but seemed to understand. He clutched her arm tighter. The plan to reach the address on the piece of paper and destroy a film projector in an apartment—a plan relayed by half a dozen corpses back at Corporate Tower—had been abandoned in seconds. Surviving took priority.

They ran faster, forging on. The subway car was escaping them. Pulling away from them at greater speed. One door on the nearest car had opened. Three police officers and two plain-clothed people stood at the door, waving them inside. "Run faster, people! They're right behind you. We'll take you to safety. We're here to help."

Billy recognized one of the cops to be Stan Hooper. He wasn't one of the movies come-to-life; he was an old friend of his father's. Stan was sixty years old with solid white hair and a five o'clock shadow.

Billy yelled at Jessica, "Double your pace, I recognize them. They won't hurt us."

"Thank God," she cried out. "It's about time we found somebody nice."

Billy gave Jessica a shove to the back that launched her from the concrete platform onto the moving subway car. But he needed a shove himself. He was out of breath. Ribs burned with razor-wire agony. His knees wanted to buckle. His shins ached so bad, Billy thought they were going to split. He wheezed asthmatically.

Jessica was safe, he thought, even as his survival chances diminished. He could die knowing she was in good hands. Stan Hooper was a trusted family friend for years. He'd see her to safety.

His stride slowed. *Every double cheeseburger and order of curly fries and chocolate milkshake has brought you closer to death. Hope you enjoyed every bite!*

Every grating sound and raging cry from behind him broke his spirit. The way their calls echoed, he believed hundreds were at his heels, the flytraps biting at the air, click-clacking, practicing their mastication for when they tore through his face, cracked open his skull, and sucked every bit of his brain. Axes dinged the subway car, missing him by a hair's breadth.

He was seconds from giving up completely.

"Billy!" Stan shouted. "Move it, mister. Your dad would be proud of you. Give him another reason to make him proud. He's watching over you. He loved you. He'd say you could do it. I'm saying you can make it, now run and jump for it! The tunnel's almost over. Move your ass, Billy!"

Images of his dead father in the body bag flashed into his mind's eye. He had to stop the city from being eradicated. Stan Hooper was alive, so who else might be? They could make a stand. With help, he could reach the address Andy Ryerson gave him. Maybe then he could end the worst night of his life.

Jessica joined in. "I'm not losing you, Billy. You're marrying my ass, you got that? You've waited long enough." She blasted her next encouragement unabashed. "I'll fuck you like you've never been fucked, so get in this thing right now!"

Billy surged. It was unexplainable, the emotions tangling up with his adrenaline. He literally dove from the platform, through the door, and avoided the f tunnel wall by a second. He landed on his side, hitting the ground hard, and when he got up, he wondered if he'd broken any ribs. He clutched his midsection. Every breath was nails digging into his lungs. He dripped sweat, unable to talk. He nodded at everybody in thanks.

Stan Hooper patted his back. "You made it, Billy, and not a moment too soon."

Jessica hugged him. He yipped in pain. "Oh sorry, baby."

"I think I broke some ribs."

"At least it wasn't your entire body against that wall," Stan said. "You're in one piece, and you're not one of those horrible monsters out there, so I say you've done well for yourself."

"Thanks. Everybody, thank you for saving us."

There were seven other people in the car. Each wore wearied and exhausted expressions. Aside from Stan Hooper, everybody else was a stranger. They sat back down, closing their eyes, and composing themselves after a close call. Jessica joined them by sitting down, leaning forward and hiding her head in her hands. Whether she was crying or simply breathing, he left her to it.

He leaned in closer to Stan. "So what's this operation all about? What are you doing in the subway?"

"Saving who we can," Stan said. "Saving you right now. There's a temporary base at Navy Pier. The Red Cross has set up camp. We're going through each of the subway routes and finding who we can that's not dead or a monster. We've hit the streets a few times, but now it's much too dangerous. This is our last round, actually. You're lucky we found you."

"I know. I've cut it close all night."

He wanted to spill his knowledge of Andy Ryerson and the movie reels and the brand of magic the dead wielded, but he couldn't convince his lips to work. It was too outlandish and outright crazy, just like all of tonight's events.

"Government conspiracy," Stan said randomly. "Someone's putting the fear to us. That's how they work. They want to slaughter the city of Chicago. To make the country think terrorists pulled it off, or some bullshit to let America roll onto is belly and wet themselves and let Congress pass any goddamn legislation they please. Phone taps, privacy fences, and next we'll go to war with Turkey instead of Iraq. This is over oil. Someone struck crude in the city. It's underneath the subway. Some hobo or transient accidentally discovered it."

Billy side-stepped the conspiracy theory talk, knowing the truth. "How many people are still alive?"

Stan stacked figures in his head. "Well, maybe a couple thousand, by my best calculations. And I know there's plenty more hiding. The last round, the whole Corporate Tower stretch was decimated. Every building was smashed to pieces. One of the alleys on Front Street, I spotted a heap of skeletons head high. They were intact as if someone just ripped them out of the body and tossed them aside. Other bodies were embalmed, and even stranger, they kept bleeding the fluid, as if they were producing it."

"My apartment building," Stan said, fighting tears, but at this point, his nerves and emotions were skinned raw. "Angie was strangled to death. Not with a rope, or hands, Billy. It was something else. Her neck had snapped in three places. And her eyes, fucking Christ, they'd popped out of the sockets. The pressure caused her skull to explode. That's the last image I have of my wife. *Goddamn them.*"

Billy hugged him. This time Stan's barrier collapsed, and he wept. "She's gone forever, Billy. Nothing's bringing her back."

Jessica stepped in, patting his back and consoling him. "But you've saved a lot of lives tonight, Stan. There's something good."

"The only thing good tonight," Stan sighed, wiping his tears and forcing a tough face. "And that's if whoever's killing everyone doesn't pay our emergency camp a visit. It's the last shelter in Chicago."

Billy stayed with Jessica for the duration of the ride. She cradled his hands. "What do you think happened to Nelson?"

"They're fine," Billy quickly answered with an awkward smirk. "Dr. Aorta's with him."

Jessica rolled her eyes. "Dr. Aorta isn't real."

"If you'd talked to those corpses on the fifth floor, you would believe it. We have no choice but to believe it."

"What about that address?"

"Shit. I forgot it. Dr. Aorta nabbed the slip of paper. I can't remember what road that apartment building was on for the life of me. I guess running from the flytrap heads and the five hundred-foot hooker jarred loose that information."

"Then what do we do?" Jessica's nerves were frazzled. "I'm playing devil's advocate here because my eyes trump common sense. A projector is playing reels of old horror movies in some dude's apartment, ghosts inhabited them, and the movies are coming to life. And we can't do a damn thing to stop them because you've forgotten the address," Jessica snapped. "We're losing air, I've almost been killed a handful of times, and now we're running again from certain death."

"It wasn't my fault I lost the address," Billy fired back at her. "Dr. Aorta took the slip of paper."

"I would've memorized it." Jessica shifted from his hold. "And saved our lives—a whole city's worth of lives."

Billy rubbed his aching head. It was difficult to shift with his broken rib. "Let's hope Nelson and Dr. Aorta arrive at the address. Something has to go our way tonight. It's our only hope."

Stan approached them as the subway came to a gradual halt.

"Okay kids, we're here. Let's go topside."

Stan rushed the subway stairs with a pistol raised. Billy and Jessica were instructed to hold back behind him. The other officers flanked each side of him with shotguns and rifles and flashlights. Navy Pier was unrecognizable; the tourist trap, the pride of Chicago second to their deep dish pizza, had fallen into decimation. The Ferris wheel was shut down and the shops were used as shelter for citizens, mainly mothers and their children. The street didn't end or begin, but instead, a wood blockade was set up two blocks from the Navy Pier entrance. The rest of the shops were shut down along the boardwalk. Carnival-sized tents displaying a red cross were spread out, a dozen by Billy's count. Ambulances and police vehicles reinforced the simple blockade. Officers stood in a line armed with steel batons and shields. Vans and other vehicles also created a barricade.

The officers were panting and covered in sweat. Billy had to help Jessica up the last few steps. She was gasping for breath, weak from the night of terror. The air was even thinner than before. Billy felt like he was breathing underneath a blanket. Grit covered his throat, and every so often, he coughed.

There were no words for what had transpired in the last forty-eight hours. A city had been slaughtered and picked off by B-movie monsters! He didn't bother leveling with Stan. Nobody would believe what he learned from Andy Ryerson. Stan and the police would be stuck on terrorists dressed up in evil costumes instead of the outlandish truth.

Through the blockades, a group of medical orderlies whisked Jessica toward the pier. The woman at the lead checked the skies and streets, while saying, "Come with us, ma'am. We'll take a look at you. Check you over and make sure you're not critically injured."

"What about Billy? He's more busted up than me."

"I'll be right behind you," Billy said. "I have a few questions to ask Stan first."

Stan jumped at his name. The body could put up a strong front, but not the eyes, Billy thought. The man was terrified, beyond sleep and downtrodden to the point of giving up.

Billy kissed Jessica before she was taken away. "I'll be right there, honey. This is important."

She understood and turned to follow the orderlies. They offered her a wheelchair, but she declined. Billy watched her until she vanished behind the blockades.

Stan smoked a thick cigar. "Billy, I'm just a cop. This takeover is beyond my qualifications. This is the goddamn apocalypse. I don't know what you want from me."

"Hey, I'm a meter-man, for fuck's sake. Whatever's out there, we're on our own. Terrorists or real-life monsters, setting this base up isn't going to stop them. Have any of them come here yet and attacked?"

"No." Stan flicked an ash and sneered. "We can't beat them, whoever they are. I'm just being honest. Think about it. They're monsters. Goons. Camel jockeys—whatever, we're headed straight for the grave at the rate we're going."

This wasn't the pep talk he'd anticipated, but Billy understood the man's resignation. He kept his head low, unsure of what else to say, when Stan said, "I told you about my wife, but I didn't tell you my daughter was also killed. No, not killed. *Destroyed.* A fist punched through our apartment building, and a giant hand—I shit you not—grabbed her and just squeezed the life out of the poor girl. I was lucky to escape the building in time before the entire place collapsed. Ninth Street, hell, the whole Corporate District is just about smashed." The words came out deadly serious. "And it was a giant who did it. A giant woman."

"I've seen her," Billy said. "This is real, Stan, not terrorists. That would be too easy an explanation. Shoot them dead and wash your hands of them. But it's not happening this time. These are, well, supernatural."

"What are you saying? Do you really believe in monsters?"

"I believe in the dead speaking to me." He had to tell Stan. He was the closest to someone he could trust. "Dead bodies talked to me. They said this is ghosts at work."

It finally struck Billy, and he grabbed Stan by the coat and demanded, "You have to take me to those medical tents. I must see the dead bodies. Anyone dead, I have to see them."

Stan's expression went from confused to offended. "Billy, it's been a long night for the both of us, but if you're saying—"

Billy skipped the arguing. He charged through the lines, shuffling between car bumpers, police officers rigidly standing in place, and shuffled down a flight of concrete steps onto the pier. Stan was shouting after him. Billy opened the first tent he came upon. Cots and stretchers held victims under blankets, many attached to I.V.s. Everyone inside was alive.

An orderly eyed him angrily. "Sir, if you're looking for a loved one, you're going to have to wait. This is an emergency situation, and I can only do so much at a given time...""

Billy moved on to another tent, but before he could poke his head inside, Stan restrained him and shook him angrily. Billy's ribs flared up, and he grunted at the surge of pain.

"Billy, you're a good kid, but you're talking about crazier things than what's happening out there. Talking to the dead, Billy, I...I don't know what to say."

Billy understood. "You think this is crazy, but it's not."

He wasn't sure what else to say. They stood in silence for a moment. Billy eyed the dark waters of Lake Michigan just beyond them. He didn't have a plan or the answers, but he had hope again when he caught sight of the tent four down and three over from them. He noticed two EMTs wheel in a body bag through the flaps.

A force inside Billy propelled him to the tent. He wormed out of Stan's hold. Stan shouted after him, "I'm shoving your ass in jail. You're making me do it, Billy!"

"Maybe I'll be safer in prison than this excuse of a base!"

Billy shot through the open flaps, shoving aside the EMTs who were halfway through advising him to stay out. This tent was larger than the others. He stamped through puddles of blood. The stench of the freshly dead, the way grocery store beef smelled after removing the cellophane packaging, struck him. The body bags were stacked like cordwood. Rows fifty long and six high filled the tent. His eyes kept scanning the room, unable to take it all in at once.

I have to do this.

Either I'm crazy, or I'm right.

Damn it, I saw what I saw.

Andy Ryerson talked to me.

"Andy, where the fuck are you?" Billy shouted at the bodies. "Talk to me. Shout, say something—HELP ME OUT! I FORGOT THE DAMN ADDRESS YOU GAVE ME!"

He spun around and around in search of a talking body. Any second now, Stan would burst through the front flaps, cart him out of the tent and lock him up. Jessica would be alone without him. Andy Ryerson shared something with him that could potentially save the city, and he fucked it up.

You have to keep trying.

Billy knelt. His knees absorbed the blood through his jeans. He unzipped the nearest body bag. A young woman, maybe sixteen or seventeen, stared back at him. Her eyes were open wide in death, her chalky white face untouched. It was her midsection that was damaged. From the sternum down to the navel, a slit gleamed with what he thought to be internal organs, but it was actually apple filling.

He pressed his shirt up to his nose. The ripe scent of the corpse and tart apples repulsed him. Stan seized him from behind and drove him into the floor. "My patience is worn thin! I'm sorry, Billy, but I'm detaining you. We've set up a temporary jail in the Abercrombie and Fitch store."

How appropriate.

The argument refused to die in Billy. He fought off Stan's hold. He shouted at the body bags, "Talk to me, please. Andy—any ghosts, you have to help us! We don't stand a chance against the monsters without you!"

Three other officers entered after hearing the commotion. "What the hell is this pervert trying to do in here?"

They aimed their service revolvers at him.

"Put your guns down," Stan insisted. "He's stressed. Out of his head, but harmless."

Billy ignored them. "We're going to die without your help. I can't let everybody die because I forgot a fucking address!"

The clink of cuffs. Billy couldn't avoid Stan any longer. He was lifted back up to his feet. His front was wet with blood. Billy met the scowling eyes of the cops. He was a criminal in their eyes. A drooling mad fool.

"My father was slaughtered by those things out there," Billy pleaded to Stan. "I'm not out of my head. I'm trying to help whoever's left alive to survive. This is more important than you could ever know!"

Stan didn't think so. "Well, this isn't the way to go about it."

"No shit," another cop muttered. "You're desecrating the dead."

"The dead are trying to save us. You and your police squad haven't been able to stop them, and that's not your fault. But do you think the monsters will just give up and go away if we stay here long enough?"

"We'll fight them with whatever we got," Stan insisted. "Now that we've made so many attempts to recover survivors, it's time we talked about our plans to fight back."

After a cough and belch of fluids, a death-stricken voice said, "*Your plan isn't worth shit.*"

The four cops, including Stan, turned to the female corpse that talked. She worked out of the body bag. Apple filling spilled out of her midsection and to her feet. "*Billy's right. There isn't much time. The monsters have cleared out the city. They wanted you in one spot. This is their climax to the evening. Once the last person alive in this city ceases to breathe, the bone dome over the city will lift and land over another city, and repeat the massacre."*

Billy could've picked everybody's jaws up from the ground, their shock was so apparent.

Stan cocked his head. "W-who are you?"

"Call me Andy," the woman creaked, black blood spilling from her lips. *"Midnight tonight, every creature will fall in on your base. That gives you barely an hour to form a defense. Collect all the weapons you've got..."*

The woman's corpse dissolved, every particle of flesh and bone melting into a black-green pile of sizzling fluid. Another corpse shifted in a nearby body bag. Billy was the one to free the body, this one a legless man who didn't bother to work his way from the bag. *"...form a chain of those willing to fight these bastards off. Their attack will free up the streets. My plan to save your asses involves Billy. You must protect him at all costs. He's one of the last remaining hopes for the city. One hour you've got to rally your troops, Stan. These monsters are real, and they will kill you."*

The glazed, off-yellow eyes pierced into Billy next. *"Be ready for a trip back into the city when they arrive, Billy..."*

The corpse stopped talking before it could melt. Everyone stared at the body, astonished. Nobody moved or breathed. Billy was forced to break the silence. "I told you the dead were talking to me. You should listen to what I say. Stan, let's do what Andy says. Gather everybody. The monsters are on their way. It'll be hell on the streets soon."

Stan blinked and returned to the moment. "Y-yeah. I understand." He uncuffed Billy and patted his shoulder. "I'm so sorry about all of that. I hope you understand why I didn't believe you."

"No harm done." Billy smiled at him. "Let's protect the survivors. Everybody who can fight, let's get them armed and ready to take on whatever's on the way."

"Go get your ribs taped up real quick," Stan insisted. "Then join

215

us. I'm assuming you're ready to fight too. Your dad would be proud of you. You managed to piss me off and make me agree with you all within ten minutes. Pretty impressive, boy. Keep it up."

Billy said, "Then let's get to it."

He left the tent and scavenged for the medical unit. Jessica was sitting on a cot alone, the abrasions on her arms taped up. She was spaced out until he sat down next to her. "What happened, where did you go? I heard a big commotion. Is everyone okay?"

Billy explained what had happened, and the battle they were about to prepare for.

Chapter Twenty-Nine

Ted searched the aisles of Piggly Wiggly for raw meat. He cut through the canned goods section, the baked goods wall, and caught sight of the glass display case of various meats. He shoved the push-cart into the employee's only side of the department. Ted piled beef, filet mignon, T-bone steaks, porterhouse steaks—and any meat that contained blood into his cart.

Now you're thinking.

Play by their rules.

It occurred to him that the movies were alive, so why couldn't they be stopped the way they had been in the movies as well? The climax of *Morgue Vampire Tramps Find Temptation at the Funeral Home* involved the caretaker of the cemetery, a Mr. Ruden Duvenick, filling a truck full of bloody meat mixed with weed killer to poison the vamps. The vampires were so attracted to the blood they didn't pay attention to the chemical additives. Then they melted into ruby red puddles and soaked back into the earth where they belonged. The sequel, if Dennis Brauman hadn't shut his movie company down financially, would've involved their blood seeping through the cemetery earth and covering a new set of nubile corpses and turning them into morgue vampire tramps.

It would've been a film worthy of Paul Naschy.

He scooted fast to the lawn and home care section and added six cases of liquid weed killer to the cart, the kind where the bottle attached to the end of a garden hose. Ted was near the back exit to load his truck when a titter froze him in his tracks.

"You've had your fingers in a lot of dirty pies, haven't you, Mr. Fuller? Pies you had no business sticking your fingers in, you nasty man."

Ted peered over the chip aisle and caught two tufts of singed hair bob from a blackened scalp. The smell of cooked flesh permeated thick as did the sickly sweet aroma of freshly baked pies. Smoke continued to issue from Mr. Baker's body. He didn't know how to respond, so Ted kept quiet.

"Where do you think you're going, huh, Mr. Fuller? Count it on your fingers, my friend. How many women had you cheated on before your wife left you?"

How does he know about that?

"I-I don't know what you're talking about."

The ragged and mean voice shot back, "*Yes you do!* You were quite the handsome movie director in your day. You filmed me, Mr. Fuller, and you fornicated with many of my victims on the set. Nina Hayworth. Rebecca Kelly. Jenny Kurtis. Oh, and Shannon Klenklen. She was quite the hot tomato. They were all in my pies. Yet somehow you felt so sorry for yourself when Katie divorced you. You stank of disgusting, dirty pie. Katie could smell it too. The rotten pie tells all!"

"Would you quit saying that?" Ted was growing guilty and scared of where the conversation might veer to next. "What do you know about me? You're from a movie."

"I'm as much a ghost hidden beneath this shell as I am a movie character." He played his free hand down his charred face, the other hand hidden behind a rack of corn chips. "The dead know everything about everybody, including you, Mr. Fuller. The ghosts of the dead wish nothing but harm to the living. The dead know magic, and they've possessed many of your films to bring terror to the ones we despise."

"Then what the hell do you want from me?"

Mr. Baker stepped into complete visibility. He clutched a long-bladed steak knife, at least seven inches in length and two in width. "I want the dirtiest piece of meat from your body for my pie. It's a

218

delicacy—your tender meat. The juiciest meat, Mr. Fuller. May I ask you to unbutton your trousers? One cut, and I'll be done. You'll never hear from me again...*unless it can grow back!*"

Ted was backpedaling. He knocked over a display of 2-liter soda bottles. He turned and bolted when Mr. Baker bounded for him.

"MY PIE MUST BE COMPLETED! If you keep running, I won't let you sample it when it's finished."

Ted's shoulder blade was sliced by a knife. He yipped in agony and landed on his back, the pain blinding him for two seconds. Then the reality was upon him. Mr. Baker crouched above him. He was working the button of his pants. "Come on out from in there!"

Ted pushed off from the floor, crawled backward and gained a four foot separation from Mr. Baker. He scrambled and searched for a way out. Blood trailed down his shoulder, warm and quickly turning cold. The charred baker came at him again. "You're playing hard to get, Mr. Fuller? I thought people loved pie."

He struggled to return to his feet, using the shelf behind him for support. He touched a row of store-baked bread wrapped in cellophane. Cookies in plastic containers came next. And then his life-saving weapon: baked pie. Ted held up the cherry pie, the surface speckled in sugar crystals.

"What is that?" Mr. Baker said, backing away. The pie was to the baker what a crucifix would be to a vampire. He shielded his body from the pie. "Inferior goods! Keep them away from me! Don't touch it. Drop it, Mr. Fuller. That pie's an abomination. It's no good for anybody. I consider it poison—POISON!"

Ted tore the top of the box and poked his finger into the cherry filling. He ate a quarter of a piece. "It's so good. You shouldn't knock it before you try it."

"I'm not eating that trash, and I'm not cooking you with that shit in you!" Mr. Baker pointed the knife at him. "I'll come back for you, Mr. Fuller, when you've had a chance to excrete that awful dessert from your body."

Mr. Baker rushed from the grocery store, fear and disappointment playing on his face. Ted released a sigh of relief. He dropped the pie and licked his lips. "Thanks for saving my life, pie."

Mr. Baker feared other baked goods and their subpar quality. He considered store-bought pies the ultimate sin. Any dessert without human flesh, or organs, or blood was toxic.

I should've thrown it at him. Why didn't I think of that? He could be dead instead of still out there.

He remembered the end of his film. A group of local bakers banded together to murder the villain, but in their shop, one uses a shotgun, and Mr. Baker lands on a shelf of cooling pies. The pies sizzle and burn his skin. The man's outer exterior is destroyed and his true self is revealed; the baker is a zombie who exists on human flesh. He was cursed by another baker upon his death for running many of the mom and pop bakeries out of business when he stole their recipes and opened a mainstream bakery in the community. A gypsy reversed the curse and allowed Mr. Baker to finally die from the shotgun wound he received. Ted admitted the plot was ridiculous, but that was the genre and what put cars in the drive-in.

He said he was as much a ghost as he was a character from my movie. Why would ghosts want to be characters from B-horror movies?

The answer was in the devastation around him. They couldn't reap so much terror and destruction by becoming Abbott and Costello or Groucho Marx.

Ted returned to his shopping cart. He wheeled it back outside to the Ford truck. Outside, he expected the relief of fresh air, but it was warmer now. Ten degrees warmer, he thought, and it would only get worse. The oxygen was depleting by the minute.

He began tearing through the cellophane wrapping and hurling wads of raw meat into the cab. Fat grains of greasy meat wet his hands. "I need more than this. This isn't enough."

Barely half the cab was filled.

Vampires like blood.

He checked his watch. It was eleven-twenty.

It was time to visit the local blood bank.

The Chicago Blood and Tissue Donation Center was sandwiched between the all-night Five And Dime Laundry—empty now—and The Salvation Army. The city was deathly quiet. He hadn't encountered another person in blocks, including corpses. He saw what looked to be a body dragged somewhere, the streaks of blood ending in Otto's Garage. Mr. Baker was hard at work on his next batch of pies, he assumed.

Ted entered the waiting room of the blood bank. A receptionist sat in a chair, her body limp, her head dangling backward, her neck chewed in one big bite. He carefully walked into the back hall. The donation rooms. The storage rooms were in the back. A padlock had been broken.

Don't tell me someone's already stolen the blood.

It would make sense. Talon marks clawed up the door and the padlock. Refrigerators with glass doors were raided, many of the blood samples stolen. Ted knew the vampires were the culprits, but they were so erratic in their seizure, they left many samples behind. He collected the remaining blood packs, many covered in sticky blood.

Apparently somebody couldn't wait to indulge.

He rushed in and out, in and out, with arms heaped in blood packs. Ted split them open with his keys and poured them into the raw meat stew. After the red gravy covered every inch of meat, he dumped in the liquid weed killer. Ted returned to the blood bank to double check if he'd left any blood behind. He was stopped in the waiting room by the dead receptionist. She was barely audible, every word a cough of blood out her open esophagus.

"Wait... until... midnight... I know... *uuu-whup*... what you are... trying... *graaack—graaag-graaag-gruuughaaaack*—to do."

"Why wait until midnight?"

He couldn't believe he was asking the corpse a question. Tonight had been one guilt trip after the next, and a confusing and unbelievable trip at that. He wasn't prepared to let a corpse tell him what to do unless he understood why.

"Answer me! Why wait until midnight?"

Doris, according to her name tag, didn't move to reply. Her face was motionless. Dead.

"I'm sorry, Doris. You deserve respect. Nobody deserves to die like this."

"Thank you," the corpse finally replied, making him recoil in fright, and she laughed. "Sorry, I had to do that. The monsters, you see, the ones from many of your films, are striking soon at Navy Pier. Many survivors are holed up there. The monsters are waiting until midnight to stage a mass assault. That's your chance to destroy the projector. Andy Ryerson wanted me to tell you this."

"Andy Ryerson—my God!"

Doris's face melted in wax globules to reveal the white skeleton beneath. The rest of her oozed from her sleeves and skirt until the bones crumbled down, the skull striking the carpet and rolling underneath the desk.

Ted stared at the human mess on the floor until he snapped out of the moment. The monsters would attack Navy Pier. *What if I can't destroy the projector?*

He parted the front blinds of the window and kept his eye on his apartment two blocks south of him. His room light was on. The profile of four vampires and the flicker of the projector reels assured him reaching his apartment wouldn't be an easy task.

"Looks like I have no choice but to listen to you, Doris."

Ted checked his watch.

Fifteen minutes to midnight.

Chapter Thirty

Sheriff Roger Elliot approached old man Red's farm. The cows that used to be in his pasture were absent, as were the goats and the chickens that used to be in their coop. This was now a farm only by appearance, not function. The sheriff was called to the farm to address the screams heard around the property. Six people had disappeared in his town, and a town like Cold Creek being so close-knit, six disappearances had the residents locking their doors at five o'clock and keeping their kids off the streets.

The squeak of a wheel barrow alerted him. "Who's out there?"

Nobody replied. He continued toward the noise. Sheriff Elliot hopped the wooden fence to the other side. He avoided cow patties, but this time, it wasn't a cow patty he almost stepped in.

It was a human liver.

"Holy Mother of Tits and Ass," Sheriff Elliot gasped, accidentally spitting out his entire wad of chaw instead of the juice. He bent down and clutched the liver in his hands. "This isn't cow shit. No, it's not cow shit at all."

The wheel barrow squeaked again. He drew his revolver. "Come out, Red. I need to speak with you. Show yourself."

The command failed to bring Red out of his hiding place. Sheriff Elliot kept moving through the pasture. Pieces of flesh on the ground, blood-stained straw and grass, and a stomach and length of intestine increased his pace. It was at that moment he finally called for back-up.

"Betsy, I need Darrel and Piper here quick. I have an emergency situation at Red's farm."

He jumped the other end of the fence and slopped through the pig pen, which was empty of pigs. Mud and feces were kicked up in his face, but the fear of what was happening on Red's property kept him moving.

He called out again. Desperation cracked his voice. "Damn it, Red, let's talk. Why are you hiding from me?"

He came upon a man standing beside the red and white barn. The blue and white checkered flannel shirt, the straw hat, the black boots... He was certain it was Red standing there.

"Red, you old bastard, you got wax in your ears or something?"

The man didn't turn around.

"Red, talk to me. This is police business. Take this visit seriously, would ya?"

He was feet from the man. Without warning, the man whipped around. It was Red, but his eyes were large black orbs, like those of a mosquito. Everything else was human, except those horrible eyes. When Red opened his mouth, four rows of shark-like teeth filled his maw.

"Gorrack!" The voice projected like a tinny-sounding record with crackles and pops.

Sheriff Elliot lost hold of his gun when three tines from a pitchfork pierced his chest.

"Gorrack!"

The weapon was dislodged, and he landed onto the ground. Red's wife, Gertrude, helped Red carry him to the shed. Sheriff Elliot gasped and burped and choked on blood, in the preliminary stages of death. "No...no...help me please!"

It had been six people missing earlier, but now it would be many more, the sheriff realized. Instead of hay bales, bales of human corpses were rolled up together, cooking in the July sun. He was added to a half-formed bale and tied up with chicken wire.

When a shovel struck his skull, the last thing he heard from Red's alien mouth was: "Gorrack!"

Georgia was convinced *Flesh Farmers Harvest the Living* (aka *Gorrack!*) had played long enough. It was fifteen minutes until midnight. They wouldn't have much time before the attack on Navy Pier began. So many warm necks awaited them. Blood flowing in veins, hearts churning out the red delicacy. She salivated at the thought.

Anne, her auburn hair slathered with so much blood it dyed the strands a bright crimson, hugged her from behind. "What's next? Which movie? We've already played *Beta* and *Skinpreys*."

Georgia curled Anne's hair with her finger. "I have one final film before midnight. I need numbers. The flesh farmers will help, but this will put us to where we need to be. Everyone in the city must die. I'm not stepping out of here until we've accomplished that."

Anne glanced out the curtain to the city. "Ted's out there, you know that?"

"I'll take care of him," Georgia said flatly. "He's weak. He can't win. Me against him, I will slaughter him. We'll drink blood straight from his heart after you're through with Navy Pier."

"It sounds delicious." Anne was intoxicated by the mention of sharing blood from Georgia's lips. "You and me naked under Ted's running blood, it would be *beautiful*."

Georgia kissed her with a wet, sucking sound. "Finish Chicago, my dear, and we can continue this orgy. Start flying out, my darlings. I'll protect the projectors. I will play the final film for tonight."

Anne kissed her one last time. "You heard her. Bleed the rest of the city."

The three leapt out of the window and changed from human to reptile in seconds. Their wings sprouted and flapped on to their destination. Georgia was alone, and she did the only thing she could with the final ten minutes before those on Navy Pier would be executed and Ted would arrive to attempt to kill her.

She changed out reels and played *Preggers*.

Mid-Point Medical Center's OB floor was silent at midnight, including the creeping Hymengorat. The strange thing was five feet tall. It was comprised of black amphibious flesh, a concave face, hydrocephalic head shaped like two cantaloupes, lobster eyes and two separate slits for mouths. Every feature was coated in a clear jelly. Its limbs were slender and fifteen feet long, the knee bones and elbows shaped at the edges like triangular daggers sharpened to kill. The Hymengorat crept its way past the empty waiting room and the nurse's station. With its grasshopper-like arm—one of eight—it reached for the door to room 321 and opened it. Through the darkness, the monster shot up onto the bed. The end of one leg was sharpened into a needle. The tip of it injected a tranquilizer into Mrs. Adam's neck. She was instantly paralyzed and unconscious. Another leg reached up through the sheets and between her legs and injected its seed, a grenade-shaped egg shiny with primordial ooze.

The pregnant woman's eyes opened. They blazed red, like twin light bulbs. Her head lit up. Then the belly also lit up as if a bright red bulb glowed from within. Inside the belly, the shape of an insect taking control of what was now the human mother took form. The actual baby within the womb was expelled onto the sheets. The Hymengorat wrapped the child in a blanket and discarded it in the trash.

The monster tick-tick-ticked a strange language: "Merap-merop-merap-merop."

The mother-to-be rose to her feet in mechanical and forced motion. The demon child controlled the woman from inside her belly, and with each shift, every thought, and every action, the little beast slowly plotted the deaths of many.

The naked woman followed behind the Hymengorat to infect and enslave the rest of the expecting mothers on the OB floor.

The Hymengorat issued one final hiss before exiting Mrs. Adam's room, "Preggers."

Chapter Thirty-One

Nelson was relieved they were well on their way to their destination. Four more blocks and they'd arrive at Ted Fuller's apartment building. Whatever was causing the horror films to come to life, they would snuff it dead, Dr. Aorta promised. He continued to collect himself from the close call with the five hundred-foot hooker in mid-air. Riding in the Boxer with a movie character was also an amazing experience. He wanted to ask for an autograph, but it was a character, not a human being, he kept reminding himself. Plus he didn't have a piece of paper and a pen.

The CB radio beside the control panel went off with a sharp crackle. *"This is Fred Holland, Chicago Chief of Police. If anybody is left alive out there, please report to Navy Pier. You'll have food, clothing, shelter, and most of all, safety."*

Another person stole the microphone and said fast, *"This isn't about safety, this is about fighting! Get your asses down here now. We're about to be attacked. They're on the horizon. Those monsters will kill us all unless you help us make a stand. Those of you who want to protect your families and loved ones, put your efforts into the battle and get your asses down here."*

"It sounds like most of the city is already down there," Nelson said. "The monsters finally found them."

"Yes, the monsters did find them."

"What do you mean?"

Dr. Aorta shot him a sideways grin. "I can't help you, Nelson."

"But we're blocks away from stopping them. What do you mean

you can't help me? We destroy the projector like you said. This'll end. Nobody else will get hurt. Why turn back now?"

"That wasn't a part of the battle plan. We tricked Andy, and we tricked you. I don't care to save anybody! Chicago be damned!"

Nelson attempted to wrench the doctor from the wheel and reclaim the Boxer. Dr. Aorta drilled him in the jaw and another fist hammered the top of his head.

He was knocked unconscious.

"Andy Ryerson thought he could stop us," Dr. Aorta laughed. "But he was wrong." He kicked Nelson in the ribs. "I'm joining my fellow spirits on the killing floor, and there isn't a damn thing you can do about it, boy."

The Boxer fishtailed and then drove in the direction of Navy Pier.

Chapter Thirty-Two

The remaining survivors of Chicago wasted no time arming themselves. The police were left with a few rifles, shotguns, and service revolvers. Three blocks south of Navy Pier, Kolar's Hardware harbored the majority of their arsenal. Billy chose a sledgehammer as his weapon. Many others chose hammers, electric drills, saw blades and nails driven into wooden planks, and from a section of Chicago under construction, one carried a concrete saw, and another, a construction worker, was at the helm of a wrecking crane. Others began stuffing rags down wrecked cars' gas tanks and stood vigil with a lighter to use the vehicles as bombs. A group had ransacked Rick's Sporting Goods in the nearby strip mall, many carrying wooden and aluminum baseball bats. A luckier few were armed with bows and arrows, hunting rifles, and other small arms. Five minutes were left, and many continued to scramble for protection, or a place to hide, or weapons.

"You should hide in the mall," Billy pleaded with Jessica. "It's not safe out here."

"If you're going to fight, so am I."

"Damn it, I don't want anything happening to you."

Jessica seized a hold of him. "I fought off the Intestinator by myself. And besides, if you guys die out here, I'm no safer in Mitchell's Donut Shop than I am out here with you."

Billy clung onto her, giving in to the fact this was a helpless situation. In moments, the monsters would be upon them, and his masculinity and his love for Jessica would mean absolutely shit in the face of unstoppable evil. His only trump card was Andy Ryerson.

He said the dead would protect them.

Three minutes and thirty-two seconds to midnight. It's about time you do something, Andy.

Jessica kissed him, and then she slipped a ring on his finger. "I stole these from Helman Jewelers in the mall. Will you marry me?"

"That's my girl," he laughed, taken aback by the fact she'd stolen two rings. "I can't believe you did this."

He wore the white gold band. Simple. The way he said he wanted it. When she handed him her ring, he nearly barreled over. Eighteen-karat diamond ring, gold band. The price tag on it proudly boasted eight grand. He slipped the ring on her finger. "I love you, yes, of course I'll marry you."

"Then let's kill some fucking monsters," Jessica declared, kissing him one last time. She removed a Colt Python from her jeans pocket. "I found this in the jewelry store too."

"Mother of God."

Billy eyed the streets beyond the barricade. Shadows played in the distance, though they couldn't be seen clearly. They had two minutes and counting to midnight.

"This might be our last moment together," Jessica admitted. "If we don't die now, our air supply will dwindle to nothing eventually."

"It's a shit situation," Billy agreed. "But if we don't kill them now, they'll kill others. And they won't have any idea what's hitting them like we do."

"They're almost here!" a citizen screamed. Many started lighting the rags jutting out from the junked cars along the blockade. "The monsters are everywhere!"

Billy's gut twisted.

Jessica let go of his hand in horror.

"I love you, honey," he said, knowing she wouldn't respond again. "Stay near me, okay? I'm not letting anything happen to you."

Jessica didn't reply. Kurt Vonnegut could've prewritten a speech for him to instill comfort in Jessica, and it would still fail in this situation, he thought.

Bail me out, Andy.

Save our asses.

Billy had no idea it would be a long wait before Andy could help him.

The flytrap heads were the first creatures to be seen, and there was row after row of them, hundreds of them coming. The living were vastly outnumbered, and there were so many monsters left to show themselves.

"Here we go," he whispered. "He comes hell."

Billy braced himself for battle.

Dennis Brauman boarded up the windows of his house after the police stopped answering their phones and the random screams of riots and terror became rampant. He kept Helen, his wife, locked up in the basement. She was content with her bottle of raspberry-flavored vodka, wave radio that hadn't worked for the past six hours, King James Bible, and a hundred-bottle supply of water and enough canned goods to survive three months. The radio air waves played noise, but it was the sound of a patient flat-lining: *eeeeeeeeeeeeeeeeee*. He couldn't shake the notion of how familiar that was to him. He'd heard it or seen it before, but from where? from what?

Outside the window between the notches of broken table—Helen's cherished oak coffee table six generations old, good solid wood—he caught shapes moving in the sky bearing the harsh red glow of eyes and jagged outstretched wings. The House of the Holy Resurrection Church across the street had been burned to the ground hours ago. He put five hundred thousand dollars investment into that church. Everything he worked for was for the bettering of humanity. He'd dedicated his life to upholding the decency of public morals.

Today, everybody had a new reason to fear God. And that's why he didn't want to sit in the basement with Helen. He'd done bad things in

231

his lifetime, and any second, whatever demons, or redeemers, or angels serving God's word would come tearing through that door and reveal him for who he really was, and he didn't want Helen present for that.

It might not happen. You don't know what's out there. Whatever it is, you're still a good man, Dennis. You've worked for the Private Film Coalition of Public Morals. You were a good father. You saved Becky from that pornographer/so-called horror film maker. You're a good citizen to your community.

Dennis moved back to the kitchen to find a shot of courage from a bottle of whiskey and ended up discovering that the piano bench covering the kitchen window had been removed. Whoever had breached the barrier had been quiet about it. He caught trails of blood on the windowsill and the shape of footprints.

How did I not hear them?

Fear ignited within him. "Helen—*Helen, are you okay?*"

He raced through the living room to the basement door, which hung wide open. *Oh God—oh no! I'm a phony. I'm a fake. I'm sorry. Take me, not her—me, not her!*

Dennis sidestepped his fear and entered the basement. The light switch didn't work, but there were flickering movements of white, blue and red below. He ended up frozen on the last step and craned his head at the disturbing scene before him.

Suddenly the door to the basement was thrown closed and locked.

He gripped the stair rail. Icy sensations encompassed him, and he kept shivering and quaking. He stood in place, horrified and disgusted. Then a venomous female voice, eking out her throat in a slither, spoke to him. "You made a career out of telling people what they couldn't watch. You censored movies, outright stole property that didn't belong to you—you and your National Legion of Decency. There's nothing decent about you, Dennis Brauman. You're a closet pervert, and there's nothing worse than a freak in the closet. It means they do bad things in secret."

Film strips and canisters were spread out on the basement floor.

Hundreds of them. The tins glowed a dull silver in the dark. He turned to Helen, to the image playing on the wall, to the profile of a woman hiding in the shadows, and back up to the top of the stairs to the line of light and the shape of feet standing behind the door.

"W-w-what did you do to Helen?" He fell to his knees, and then onto all fours. "*What did you do to her?*"

The woman in the dark replied, "I offered her the chance to watch your life's work."

Dennis crawled through the films, parting them like snow, as he attempted to reach Helen.

"You're a hypocrite, Mr. Brauman. Now Ted Fuller will have his films back and so much more. We're packing these up and saving them for later. That's what life here will be like from now on, a long movie playing out. Movies were always better than life."

The woman stepped into a patch of light.

He recognized the reptilian woman from one of Ted Fuller's films.

"You stole those films out of my storage locker, didn't you?"

The woman's eyes spat red fiery sparks. "*Yeeeeees!*"

She lunged at him and seized his neck and jerked it back toward Helen. She was propped in a sitting position on a chair. Her mouth was open wide in fright. The expression was so gnarled and fixed, her death must have happened in a second.

"Oh, but look at the screen—this isn't a horror movie! Over half the films we found hidden behind that cinder block in the wall beneath the stairs were STAG FILMS! You've polished your chubby to the classics."

Dennis was ashamed, disturbed by what used to be arousing now turned morbid and associated with death.

She seethed through clenched fangs, "You were so fixated on public morals you forgot your own!"

The screen displayed six women on a bed giving each other oral sex, but there they were on the screen, and then there they were in his basement surrounding him. Buxom and young, they strutted to him, petting his hair, lifting off his shirt, playfully unzipping his pants and tugging them down to his knees, while random moans and fake orgasms kept repeating in the background. Helen seemed to watch him, the bright artificial light spilling out the lens animating her pale blue face with life.

Lips kissed down his neck and belly. Dennis was lowered to the mattress on the floor covered from head to toe by nubile, horny women. The vampire woman watched them at work, fascinated, and offered soft words to cheer them on. And finally, the vampire woman said loudly, *"You always said there was no difference between porn and horror movies..."*

Two of the women clenched Dennis's neck and broke the spinal cord in one bone-jarring snap.

"...I guess you were right."

Chapter Thirty-Three

Ted had witnessed many things in the last fifteen minutes. He used the alley of the blood bank to take cover. He saw three vampires rocket out of his apartment window and fly into the night. One stayed behind, her profile visible in the window.

Why didn't all of them leave?

The slasher girls outside the apartment were armed with various bludgeons and sharp weapons. He counted over sixty of them. They were heading north, but where, he thought. Men and women filed from apartment buildings, businesses, and even the gutters with split-faces, the brains beneath gleaming under the streetlights. He ducked behind a garbage compactor at the burning sight of the Pickler. As he continued to walk, every drop he left behind was a puddle of flaming embalming fluid. Mr. Baker had stolen a Mazda pick-up truck and had loaded it with canned preserves, pounds of sugar, baking sheets, bread rollers and an axe. A steamroller chugged down the street, the man at the helm a skeletal corpse in a hardhat and a reflective orange vest. He also carried a shotgun. Ted had seen the movie before. The man blew the kneecaps off of his victims and flattened them with the steamroller. Then a hulking man with a bulging belly followed him; the hole at his navel widened and shrank as if breathing. The pink viscera would poke out every few seconds issuing drops of blood.

More villains were on their way.

No—not them! Good God, what else is coming?

Men in checkered flannel shirts marched the streets. Thirty of them, by his rough count. The majority were armed with pitchforks, scythes and machetes, but also chicken wire—or more accurately, bale wire. "*Flesh Farmers Harvest the Living*," he mouthed. They followed the crowd, each in straw hats, chewing a piece of straw or a wad of tobacco, and eying the landscape for another body to ball up into their human bale.

Death Reject was among them undetected. The sunken corpse couldn't remove his smile; whatever was transpiring through his head, it defined pleasure in death, pleasure in delivering agony to the living. Ghosts, just as the blonde vampire said at Denton Hall, were inside them, playing out their revenge against the living. A sick feeling washed over him. Overwhelmed with guilt and helplessness, he battled not to vomit.

The cinematic parade wasn't over yet. Naked bodies were the tail end of their advance. Pregnant women, he realized. Four or five dozen.

"*Preggers*," he whispered. "That's a Howard James movie. If Howard was still alive to see this, he'd shit a brick."

Their eyes were bright red bulbs, and within the belly, the red bulb light gave shape to an alien life form at the helm. The creature plucked organs, bones and muscle tissue like a puppeteer controlling its puppet. Ted waited until they were four blocks away before starting the truck and pulling up right outside his apartment. Ted ran full-out to hide behind a set of parked cars and waited for the vampire to come out.

It's just you and me, bitch.

After five long minutes of doubting his plan, Ted saw the window open, and the vampire poked her head out to leer down at his trap.

Chapter Thirty-Four

Stan met Billy and Jessica at the edge of the barricade. "They're just on the horizon. Take my service revolver. Get ready."

"Give it to Jessica," Billy insisted. He clutched his sledgehammer. "I can't wait to wallop one of them over the head. Besides, I can't aim a gun for shit."

"Stand back," Stan warned them. "The police are taking the front lines. Maybe we can hold them back."

Stan issued a series of orders to the cops standing in a line armed with shields, batons, high-powered rifles and handguns. "Don't let them walk onto the pier. If they do, it's hell on earth for these people. They can't fight. NOW GET UP THERE AND DO YOUR JOBS!"

The dozens of men stomped behind the blockade of cars to form a line. The monsters were seconds from arriving. The line stopped, and a streamroller plowed through a line of vehicles. Two cars exploded, the lit rags finally igniting the gas tanks. Then another and another boomed and went up until ten cars were engulfed in flames and spitting thick black smoke into the air. The shrapnel did little to slow the monsters down. The plan backfired; instead of harming the monsters, it kept them behind a screen.

"Billy, fall back!" Jessica seized him with every ounce of strength and forced him back toward the shops. "If you love me, you won't let yourself die."

He was snapped from the moment. She was right, he realized. Their plan wouldn't work. They had no real way of fighting them. They fled from the scene and retreated into a Nordstrom. Inside, contemporary music played over the loudspeaker, a strange medley of Tori Amos and Kenny G. Billy watched the spectacle through a slit of boards in the main display window.

Ba-bam! Ba-bam! Ba-bam!

A series of booming gunshots, a row of police went down, rose blooms spitting out from their knees. They were sent flailing onto the street. The steamroller crunched their bones, fiercely snapping, and crunching, and flattening them.

"Don't look, Jessica."

Fifteen others were hidden in the store. They were against the farthest wall near the men's cardigans. Billy finally noticed they were also close to the back exit. He caught a whiff of the gasoline smell. The clothing in many displays was sodden with it; the place was set to burn if they broke through.

Maybe we're not helpless after all...

Billy's chest tightened and he suffered shortness of breath—and not because of the inadequate air. Purple sunken flesh around the eyes, the rest of the skin off-yellow, the color of the stain on the filter of a smoked cigarette, naked from the waist up, bones proudly etched through the soft tissue, Death Reject walked through the smoke of the dock. The grim features suddenly turned to joy—the promise of death smile.

Two seconds, WHUPWHAM! He detonated from the core. Rib bones, sternum shards, cracked humerus pieces, femurs, metatarsals and organs all turned into violent debris. Many were unharmed by the mess by using their shields, but Billy caught one officer who suffered a rib bone through the throat.

The next wave of attack, young girls in plaid mini-skirts sprinted toward the police bearing swords, axes and bludgeons. A double-edged axe literally sliced a cop's head in half through his helmet, spurts of blood shooting feet above his head. Another was sliced through the waist by a sword. Bullets shredded the girls, but many wouldn't stop attacking until they were pulped through and through.

The steamroller continued to shove aside the burning row of cars one-by-one. The flytraps were skulking through pockets of smoke to attack new victims. Billy caught the Intestinator suspended from an overhead light on the dock, slowly coming down like a spider from its web as his guts unrolled to lower him. Billy couldn't watch anymore. He shook his head, listening to the screams and desperate gunfire.

"There's not many of them left," Billy sighed in horror. "This isn't going to work. I have to reach that tent and those corpses."

"What are you talking about?" Jessica met his eyes. "We're not stepping out there."

"We won't have any choice soon enough. They'll rip through this barricade in no time flat. So what if we torch the store? We run outside, and there they are, and there we are."

Jessica clutched onto him. "We're not surviving this, are we?"

"If we die, I'm not taking it lightly. Andy Ryerson has contacted me twice through dead bodies. I need to be around corpses, damn it. He said to wait. He said he'd help me when it really counted."

"I'd say now is the time it counts."

As Billy glanced out the window again, seeing the battle continue, he wouldn't have to wait a moment longer for Andy Ryerson's help.

Stan blasted his shotgun at the woman whose face split in half to unveil a living brain beneath. Its chest erupted, and she faltered dead. Their skin was so soft, so easily destroyed, he thought. They weren't human—obviously—but almost a half-way replication of human.

His shotgun was empty, and his belt had run out of shells. He crouched to his feet and picked double-edged axe from a severed arm. He plucked each finger from the handle one by one.

Jesus, Mary and Joseph...

He ducked when the pavement kicked up shards, damaged by gunfire. The steamroller was headed in his direction. The gunner had murdered half his men and flattened them into the pavement. He checked the remaining stores. The people inside were safe for now.

"Die, you greasy pig!"

A cute girl in pigtails of blonde hair and a checkered black and white flannel skirt—the total package the equivalent of a Catholic schoolgirl—drove a knife in his direction. She missed. He kicked her in the stomach, but she rolled to the side and returned a kick to his balls. He landed on all fours shrieking in pain.

"Your manhood must be removed!"

He wheezed, "What are you talking about?"

She let out a girlish shriek of attack, but she slipped in blood, spilling backward. He forced himself to keep fighting, and he was about to land the axe into her back when an automatic weapon delivered thirty bullets into her body.

The machine gun fire continued, this time pushing Stan up against a hatchback and pumping his chest full of bullets.

Officer Paul Richards picked off the monsters from the rooftop. He was a marksman in the military. The Browning 240 with a Pathfinder infra red scope shot out the skull of another split-faced demon. He caught the silver glint of the eyes embedded in the brain all turn to red and yellow pus once the hollow point round was delivered into its cortex.

"Take that, you bastards!"

He blasted six more rounds, this time preventing the schoolgirl with a mace from landing it on Officer Luke Greenwood's head. Luke came alive with relief and shot the schoolgirl point blank in the face. Everybody on the force had seen enough to forgo procedure or mercy in order to save their asses.

He adjusted his sights to the person driving the steamroller. The face was literally a skull with a layer of blackened flesh, crusted with putrefaction. The man was dressed as a construction worker, hardhat included.

Your hardhat won't save you from my bullet.

He tightened his aim. Teased the trigger. Waited two seconds for the best moment.

And then he couldn't focus. All he could hear was vicious slurping and sucking sounds. His field of vision tilted, spun, and then his sight blanked out altogether.

The morgue vampire tramp sucked from the torn neck stump in her clutches as she flew back into the crowd for another victim to attack.

Adam Briggs wasn't a cop, but he stayed on the frontlines with two six-shooter replicas crafted after Jesse James's pistols. He kept them clean and workable for years for show, but now he finally got to use them. He was currently trapped against the wall of the Maine Dock Eatery, a seafood joint. The walls were closed up within, and he couldn't hide inside. He pounded against the boarded-up door, but nobody came to his rescue. What surrounded him were flannel-wearing, chaw-chewing farmers. Their eyes horrified him. Fourteen of them aimed their pitchforks at him, ready to impale him.

He was good at counting the bullets he'd fired—if he was good at anything at all—and knew only one remained in each gun. Adam had no time to reload. Seconds, they'd be upon him.

"SOMEBODY PLEASE LET ME IN!"

Maybe nobody's in there.

No, they're just not going to open the fucking door!

Adam fired at the closest one, a farmer with sun-baked skin and a five o'clock shadow of grizzled gray and black. The forehead split open in a V-shape from the bullet entry and spat out neon green ooze. The farmer fell forwards, somehow landing on his own pitchfork.

"Take that you dumb bastard! YEAH! FUCK YOU!"

More of the farmers in the background were hoarding dead bodies. They were stacking them—forming them into bales of human corpses.

Baling wire held the mess together. Mangled and terror-stricken faces glared back at him—living or dead, he couldn't look them in the eye.

He dropped one gun, now empty. The last gun he clutched with two hands. He stared from the gun, to the farmers, the gun, to the bobbing pitchforks, the gun, to the beads of blood dripping from the jagged points, the gun, the bits of flesh caught between the jagged points, to the gun, then the second wave of farmers, and Adam finally swallowed the barrel and pulled the trigger.

Wesley Hooper had manned the wrecking ball for his entire career, demolishing a variety of condemned buildings to create new space for industrialization, but this job was the most exhilarating. He swung Becky—the biggest ball breaker he'd known in his life—into a flying demon. The ball broke half the bones in her body, and the demon flapped with the use of only one wing and crashed into the harbor.

"This is a no fly zone, bitch!"

The ball had enough momentum to swing back down onto the dock and punch through a legion of schoolgirls—three of them completely exploding into bits of gory matter. "School's in session, bitches!"

The ball lost its momentum. Wesley prepared another attack when he was thrown from the crane. A body latched onto him, its legs wrapping around his hips, its arms around his arms. "You crazy fucker, let me go!"

The corpse counted under its breath, "Five, four, three..."

The body clutching him was ice cold. Purple-gray-blue flesh covered him. A corpse.

"...two—ONE!"

Exploding bones and shrapnel pierced Wesley's body.

Detective Kelly Odentag's waist was wrapped by what appeared to be a rope, but it was not rope. An inch thick, purplish-pink, swollen, pulsing and breathing, the coils were very much alive. She was being dragged on the street, pulled forward. The lasso had wrapped around her as she was lighting another car on fire via the gas tank. She crashed into dead bodies as she was propelled forward, her back bruised and bleeding. She was coated in the blood of her fallen co-workers and fellow citizens.

Kelly was lifted up and over a mashed vehicle and landed back down on the street. She was semi-conscious now and wished she was dead when she saw what dragged her. The viscera squeezed around her belly so tight her innards spat out both ends of her body.

Ernie Rivers led the team that had been hiding in Salty Big Pretzels. He wouldn't listen to another person die—cop or second-class citizen. The pretzel shop had a surprising number of useful weapons, and he clutched a dough cutter in each hand. Adrenaline guided the five of them from the shop.

The monsters were now approaching the docks.

Salty Big Pretzels was surrounded by an unspeakable army. Naked women crawled from their perches. They were pregnant, he realized, their bellies extended, covered in a slimy sweat. Then their eyes lit up a blazing red. Within the confines of their belly, a red glow revealed an outline of a strange creature with a hydrocephalic head and eight arms, insect in appearance. The creature within pressed and yanked on innards to force the woman to perform their bidding. The cold and clammy hands of one pressed against his throat. Ernie froze up, the dough cutters useless. He dropped them, shaking and gasping to breathe.

The woman wouldn't release him. The grip continued to strangle him. The red pulsing eyes were road flares, phosphorous and melting. He was pressed up against the woman's body, and he could feel the creature within her shift and it made a *tick-tick-tick-tick* noise of a crawling beetle.

He clenched his fist and drove a punch into the belly with a squeak and expelling of gas. Between the woman's feet, the alien was coughed out of the womb. The baby looked like a giant wet ant, three sections for the body, but its legs were those of a crawfish. He stamped the shriveled form to death, brown juice spilling from it as he kept smashing and grinding it with his heel.

Ernie couldn't save the other two couples from the pregnant women. They surrounded them, pounding them with their fists, choking them, slamming their faces onto the dock, doing anything they could to snuff the life from them. It was too late for Ernie too. He was kicked from behind the knees. He collapsed forward onto the pavement.

A charred face stared back at him, the wax globules of flesh and blackened skull forming an interested expression.

"It's all about early prep...once you reach the oven the pie could already be doomed."

The baker had picked up one of Ernie's dough cutters and sliced down his abdomen through his clothing. The other cutter in the baker's hand was dragged across his throat, hot crimson spilling down his chest. A bucket was on each side of him. The man worked expediently, dredging up his organs and slopping them against the dock. Before Ernie died, he was stuffed with blueberry filling.

Chapter Thirty-Five

Nelson woke with blood crusted on the inside of his nostrils. Dr. Aorta was at the control panel. Screens displayed scenes outside of bullets tearing up the fronts of stores along Navy Pier, destroying and loosening barricades. The clatter of shells and the burst of fire were deafening. He cupped his ears, the *whah, whah, whah, whah* tunnel effect a throb in his ear drums. The screens also showed the carnage of ruined police cars and corpses on the ground. They were losing the battle, and Dr. Aorta was no longer a hero.

He wasn't much for hand-to-hand combat, but the element of surprise was on his side. Nelson acted. He seized Dr. Aorta's throat and wrenched him to the floor. He shoved his fist into Dr. Aorta's mouth and drove it into the back of his throat. Dr. Aorta coughed and thrashed, but no air was passing through the man's lungs. He wasn't sure if he could murder a ghost in a movie-character's body, but he was shocked when Dr. Aorta's face turned blue, and his resistance weakened. After minutes of thrashing, the man went altogether still. Nelson dislodged his fist, covered in a mucous-thick saliva.

"And I wanted your autograph..."

Nelson stepped over the body and manned the machine guns on the Boxer.

"Don't shoot them!" Billy demanded. "They're on our side."

"The hell with you, they'll kill us all," a man in his fifties in a black business suit shouted, stepping out of the crowd. "They're zombies."

"Yes, but they're trying to help us. They're on our side, damn it."

Jessica joined in on the effort. "He's telling the truth. Just watch."

Another woman joined the argument, a younger girl in a sheath dress splattered in brains. "Listen to yourselves. Zombies aren't good in any situation. I watched my boyfriend get beheaded by guts, for God's sake! None of them out there are on our side. They're all dangerous."

"I say tear down the barricade and let them in," Billy yelled. "You have to trust me."

"I'm not trusting anyone who wants to throw us in harm's way," the business suit shouted. "If they try to break through, we have to hold them back."

Jessica hugged Billy before he could say another word. "How do we know they're on our side for sure?"

"They're coming out of that tent," Billy insisted, pointing between the boards of the front window. "They're not from a movie. They didn't appear out of nowhere. They're real walking corpses. People you once knew."

He pointed at the head of the crowd. "You see, that's Stan. God rest his soul, he's not from a movie. He's real. He's fighting for us from beyond the grave."

Nobody cared for his point, and Billy accepted the defeat. He turned to Jessica. "They'll tear through this barricade like it or not. I guess we'll hold back until they do so. Andy better have a plan, or else we're all dead."

The recently dead eyed them through the barricade holes. Fingers and arms reached through, pounding the wall and shaking the foundation. Boards were loosened from their posts. Glass was shattered and window frames taken apart. Their moans carried, though they didn't form words. Billy couldn't figure out why they didn't demand they release him.

"We have to use the back way," Billy insisted. He tugged Jessica by the arm, not meaning to hurt her but doing so anyway. "There isn't any more time to talk about it. Let's go!"

They swung through the maternity clothing section and hooked a left around the bath accessory aisle to an employee's only room. The double doors shot open, and they were met by a group of zombies. Were they the good ones or the bad ones? They'd decimated the blockade of trash barrels and wooden planks. In their panic, those already hunkering down in the store had forgotten to double check the back exit.

Closer, the walking dead approached them. One seized his arm. He brought his teeth down upon his arm and tried to bite down.

Jessica screamed, "These aren't our friends!"

The corpse lifted up his hands in defense. "Hey just kidding, just kidding! Don't shoot me in the head, please."

"Andy?" Billy gasped. "Is it you?"

Andy guided them through the open doors. "I have ten minutes in this body before it collapses. I've summoned enough spirits to maintain these bodies, so time is short."

Billy had to ask, "How come the bad ghosts don't melt away like you?"

The eyelids were half-obscured by sagging flesh when they turned to meet Billy's. "There are many more evil spirits than there are good spirits...our soul energy is much weaker than theirs."

Jessica's mouth hung open. "Oh, so I see. That explains everything."

Andy pointed with a gnarled finger; every second, the body continued to rot: cavities crusted, darkened, and tightened and collapsed with feasting bacteria. The flesh seemed to give birth to maggots and earthworms. "We run through this back stretch behind the shops and leap from the edge of the pier and swim back toward the city. There you'll find cars. I'll follow you, Billy, and help you start any car of your choosing, and I will personally drive you to the destination. I have a vendetta, you see, against those flying bitches—and you wouldn't understand, so don't ask. Just do as I say."

The plan wouldn't be as easy as it was laid out. Billy declined to count the number of corpses that gathered around him—a literal army spilled from the shops. Jessica drew closer to him, closing her eyes and wincing softly. "This can't be real. This can't be real. We're going to die. We're going to die."

Andy touched Jessica's shoulder and said, "You have the best soldiers to protect you, lady. We're dead—and don't have a thing to lose!"

Billy and Jessica were shoved forward from behind. He wasn't functioning except on instinct: move legs, move arms, breathe and watch out. Jessica's breathing grew erratic; she couldn't control herself. He tried to comfort her, but they were parted by the flooding of corpses from the Salty Big Pretzels shop's back door. EMTs, police— doing more to defend them dead than alive—and local citizens surrounded them.

"There's so few left alive in the city," a random corpse spouted, "if you guys die, surely the bone dome will be relocated, and everyone else in the country will be on the chopping block."

"If that happens, there won't be enough zombies to stop them."

"Never mind, destroy the reels."

"So stay alive!"

"No problem!" Billy shouted over the grumble and din of the dead. "Please, protect Jessica—she's all I got left!"

Fire cascaded from the top of American Eagle Outfitters. The flames, spouting out like liquid to reach them, turned the dead into kindling, their flailing doing nothing to fan out the flames.

"I won't let you go, Billy," Andy said, dodging the flames. "The Pickler won't harm you, I swear."

The dead covered him when the flames came his way. He felt the heat and experienced the chemical smell, a caustic incendiary burning. Overhead, from each side, the dead covered him like a tarp. He couldn't see through the bodies and appendages. Billy had lost Jessica; even her screams had subsided.

"Where's Jessica?" Billy kept demanding. "I can't let her die, you understand me—do you understand me?"

Andy said, "She's being protected like you are. Now keep moving."

Red demon eyes glowed at his feet. A naked woman had squirmed through the pile and latched onto his legs. The grip was vise tight and attempted to crush the bones of his ankles. A boot swung down and stamped her bulging belly, spitting out an ant-like creature that deflated and leaked brown juices.

"What in hell was that?"

"It's from a movie about aliens implanting themselves in expecting mothers and using the mothers' bodies as a vessel as a weapon to terminate humanity," Andy explained. "They call them *Preggers!* Equipped with man-stopping strength, testicle-stomping fury—"

"Okay, enough! I get it!"

Billy treaded through strewn bodies. The zombies were somehow holding their own. They reached the edge of the dock. The covering of undead flesh released him.

"It's time to swim, Billy—"

A scythe swiped Andy's head from the neck. The head flopped over the edge of the dock and into the water. Farmers surrounded them, mixed with more of the schoolgirls—one with a mace swinging over her shoulder, another with a samurai sword, another with a chicken wire garrote, and five with a machete in each grip. They called out: "I bet you still want to fuck me!" "His dying wish will be a quickie!" "I'll give him head—his own!" "I'll throw a pair of my panties in his coffin as a souvenir!"

He believed the zombies were fighting bravely, but so few of the walking dead were left, maybe three dozen, and that meant Jessica was no safer than he was.

This plan is going to shit.

Overhead, the five hundred-foot hooker kicked and bludgeoned through buildings. Her abdominal cavity was hollowed out, the flaps of skin hanging out like an open coat, her body dripping bloody rain. She was closing in, beginning to step into the harbor, her eyes intent on him.

The flytrap heads weren't in clear sight, but their fierce bone-clacking was audible. It sounded like they were walking in droves of fifty. The Pickler was a burning pyre turning the stores into fiery pillars. A man in a baker's outfit was stoking the flames to cook bodies, the bodies themselves speared through the anus and mouth by modified stop signs. He saw the Intestinator wrap his intestines around five zombie heads and snap them with derision and pleasure. A steamroller finished off the fallen corpses, squishing and squashing them into paste.

From the harbor, the very edge of the dock, roaring waves foamed and crashed against the wood pillars. The dock was moments from being decimated. From the black depths of the harbor, a gaping mouth surfaced, the length of a freight car.

Billy shouted in horror, "It can't be!"

The monster was a replica of a purple and blue betta fish, except enlarged to the size of a school bus. Scaled tendons reached out from the gills to try and knock Billy's feet out from underneath him, but he jumped and rolled to avoid the deadly grip. Muscles rippled from each side of the fish, the fins branching with veins as thick as elevator cables. Its eyes were demonic red, clear globes sloshing with blood.

"BILLY, I'M OVER HERE!"

He caught sight of Jessica at the opposite end of the dock. He couldn't reach her without combating the schoolgirls, farmers, the Intestinator, and perhaps the five hundred-foot hooker. Billy attempted to reach her despite the enemies, but the beta's tendrils wrapped around Jessica's midsection, and she was sucked down into the brilliant-colored gaping jaws of the betta beast.

"JESSICA!"

He replayed the scene in his head. Was she chewed up, he asked himself. He couldn't tell if she was swallowed whole or devoured. *Does it make a difference, the fucking fish ate her!*

Billy backed up to avoid a mace smashing into his skull. The woman was bitter, spittle oozing down her lips. "You pigs always have a way of backing out of your commitments, huh? You'd knock me up and insist I have an abortion, wouldn't you?"

Before he could respond, the force of the waves snapped a leg of the dock, and he was thrown into the black harbor with hundreds of monsters at his back.

Chapter Thirty-Six

Ted's knees ached and his feet were filling with pinpricks waiting behind the row of vehicles for the vampire to check out his trap. She was interested. Human eyes disintegrated into blazing red globes. The smile somehow glowed in the dark, a mere stencil of a human prototype, but the lips were bent and jagged and much too long to be real. She was perched in the window, blonde hair caught in the wind flapping silky clean, though pieces of gristle and fat were clotted in the strands. The city's outcries of terror were muffled from a distance, and Ted blocked it out.

This is all that matters.

Destroy the projector, destroy the monsters!

The blonde—Georgia, he recalled her name—flew down, her skin changing from flesh to black plated with a *plick-plick-plick* sound. The attraction—though sullied by the evidence of violence painted on her body—was erased. Breasts turned to flat muscle. Nails curled into eagle's talons. She resembled a flying Draco lizard.

She landed onto the truck bed with a squish. Georgia was pleased with the spread: fresh blood from the blood bank and raw meat. She hunkered down on all fours grunting, gobbling, masticating, swallowing, slurping and mewling in ecstasy. He'd designed their pleasure moans to be exaggerated and pornographic when he shot the film. Sex was big in the late seventies, he recalled. Porn was serious cinema. Anything boasting naked female flesh, sex and a smattering of gore could sell in domestic and overseas markets. And that was another reason he quit films; the horror market had lost its heart and soul and guts and spine. He was bored with today's films, though he had often wished—and finally got his wish, unfortunately—that the old days would return.

"Isn't this what you wanted?" Georgia asked through a mouthful of pink beef that spewed blood with each bite. She could read his thoughts. "The good ol' days of Stan Merle Sheckler? You've marketed so many films in your years, Mr. Sheckler, that nobody saw. Nobody would give you more than twenty-five grand to make a picture. That's shit. Chump change. You fear obscurity, but look at you, you are obscure. A rarity."

"That's Dennis Brauman's fault," Ted challenged her, furious. "I did what I was supposed to do to entertain my demographic. I worked hard. Busted my ass. And Brauman's rich religious ass canned my career."

Why am I arguing with this bitch?

She pouted; the action was strange with her face greasy with raw meat. "Deep down, you wanted to bring us back to show him up, didn't you? I showed Dennis something. I sure did. *Mmmhmmm.* I showed him something you'd loved to see."

Georgia descended over him, picking him up under the armpits like an eagle would a field mouse. He flailed, moaning and groaning in fear she'd drop him from four stories high. She forced him through his apartment window and into his living room. He landed in their lair. Corpses were strewn on the carpet with their throats eaten, women splayed with their guts emptied and their flesh intentionally painted red—vampire art, he thought, what had also appeared in the film. She pointed with an extended pointer finger. "Look. Ahead of you."

Dennis Brauman was barely recognizable. He was splayed standing up, naked from the waist down, his beige leisure suit top still on, and his chest torn through, his heart missing. "I told him how you felt, Mr. Sheckler."

"Quit calling me that!"

"I told Dennis he had no heart," she cackled, throwing her head back. She moved to the wall playing with Dennis's hanging open mouth. She used his mandible to frame words. "He said 'God would have nothing to do with such a parade of ugly humanity...sex, boobs, bush shots, dismembered body parts, foul language and movies designed by the dark recesses of the mind', but I showed Dennis who he really was, Mr. Sheckler. I did it for you. You deserve redemption. This is your redemption. You thought people weren't afraid of horror movies anymore. Now they're real. Now they'll piss and shit themselves because of you. You have accomplished so much by bringing us back."

"No, no, no! I brought you back because I was confused. I had a contingency plan if something so crazy could work. I was going to blow you bitches back to hell with a shotgun. I seriously didn't think playing the reels would've caused you to come to life. I didn't believe it. I, I didn't."

"Why did you have to go and say that?" Georgia released Dennis's mouth, which dropped back open in a natural expression of shock. "You miss filmmaking, don't you? You have plenty of new ideas. And so do me and the girls. Ideas that could last forever. Movies fade in time, and in this market, it's one fix after the next, today's new release becomes yesterday's news. Your movies won't be like that, Mr. Sheckler. Not while we're around."

Every time she said "Mr. Sheckler," it drew gooseflesh. He'd been spared this long to hear this bargain. Their new plan.

I have to play along.

He eyed the projector in the corner. The lights were on in the room, and the screen was whitewashed. Two more projectors rattled from the living room.

Unplug them. Stomp them into pieces. Do something.

Ted couldn't move. He couldn't destroy all three without facing Georgia, and that was a confrontation he'd lose.

Then it occurred to him: *Why isn't she dead? She ate the poisoned meat.*

Georgia's tone was a creak, "Ahhhhhh, yes, now you're thinking.

Why am I alive? You're forgetting one important detail about the poison. It isn't the right brand. The brand that killed me in the movie was Sherman's, not TruLawn. Can't you remember your own movies?"

"That was over thirty years ago!"

"Our working relationship would never work, you see," Georgia said. "I can't trust you, and well," she dabbed the splotch of blood from each corner of her mouth and tasted it, "you probably can't trust me."

The flying Draco façade vanished in two seconds. She was nubile again, breasts bared to touch, skin unblemished by blood, bush perfectly trimmed and primped, her lips ruby red and natural, and blue eye shadow. Everything about her was seductive: his very definition of sexy. Thirty years ago he could've laughed at the self-gratifying concepts he injected in his films, but now, there wasn't a shred of humor to contrive.

He leapt at the projector nearest him and unplugged it. He punched and broke the lens, but it wouldn't be enough. Two more projectors worked in the opposite room. And Georgia sneered, the vampire in her returning. She shredded his chest with her talons and picked him up. "THEN I'LL SEE YOU IN HELL WHEN I FINALLY RETURN THERE!"

He was flung through the window and suffered the four-floor plummet down.

Chapter Thirty-Seven

The harbor was wave after wave of crashing fury, each torrent a new attempt at sucking Billy down into the suffocating depths. Hands clutched at his ankles to force him down. Fists pumped to smash his face in, each source a different monster hell bent on seeing him drown and die in agony.

Great idea, Andy, send me to a place where they can simply drown me.

The Beta jumped up and then crashed back down into the water, diving headfirst. He had seconds to swim out ahead of the crowd and reach land. Water obscured his vision, each attempt at seeing clearly a new sting to his eyes. The steamroller followed alongside land taking random shotgun shots at Billy—and each new round closer to accuracy. Coils of intestines sprang up from the water and tangled with his arm, but he bit at the mess and pierced the rubbery outer covering and caused a visceral retreat. Schoolgirls slashed the water with blades, their grating words mottled yet disheartening in large numbers. The pregnant women with red globes for eyes bobbed closer to him, their hands outstretched to grapple him.

Andy, this was a fucked-up plan! Where are the dead now, huh? Who can save me?

His back ankle was sliced with a butterfly knife, the girls cheering in high-pitched glee—a high school pep squad on a sugar high—as blood colored the water's surface. He unleashed a water-choked howl. He batted harder, faster, his skin tingling and aching and turning numb from the effort. He was six yards out from land. Out of breath, out of arm strength, losing blood, losing vision, his body kicked itself into overdrive to survive.

A flytrap head swam out beside him. The brain between the teeth cackled, the noise alien as it was a challenge. Billy acted on impulse and jabbed his finger between the spokes of teeth and stubbed out the eyes in the brain. He yanked his hand back in time for the flytrap to snap closed and for the body to falter and sink into the harbor. Pounding his arms faster, he once again dodged pink viscera that attempted to tie itself around his neck. He dove under, using his legs to surge ahead. Below, fiery eyes met his descent. Vampires, demons and pregnant women, they bit for his arms and legs, but he lunged back up to avoid them. Three yards from reaching land, he could pull himself up and run—and that's if he had any juice left to survive a block's distance of running.

Ba-Bam! The next shotgun blast took out two of the three schoolgirls about to plunge a sword into his back. *Thanks, idiot!* His shoulder blade was lacerated by the other girl, a straight razor her weapon of choice. He was punched on top of the head, a pregnant woman sending him under again. He was dazed, every angle spinning out of control: distorted demon eyes, foaming water, the undercurrent packed with new power to force him below. Billy couldn't struggle any longer.

And then a familiar voice shouted after him, "Grab this, man! You're so close."

Billy's memory failed to pinpoint the owner of the voice. He was too busy trying to twist free from the mixture of enemies to fully think.

"Catch this, Billy! I'll pull you in."

A lifesaver struck the surface. Something to reach for, Billy thought. He grabbed a hold of it, though three hands seized his neck and shoulders to anchor him down into blacker depths. Fingers attempted to gouge out his eyes. A hand shoved itself into his mouth, and though he clamped down to bite it, the owner wouldn't release it. Talons clung into his legs like fishhooks. The screams came in unison.

"*Shaleeeeeeeeeh!*"

He kept hold of the lifesaver.

If you're going to save my ass, whoever you are, you better do it now.

Billy was suddenly ripped from underwater by a powerful force. He was flung several feet into the air, those holding onto him along for the ride. Water sprayed in each direction of him. He was hurled from the water and onto a dock with a crash that recreated the same impact as when he broke his ribs the first time. Now, he was stunned, overtaken by the vision-stealing agony. He closed his eyes and released caterwaul after caterwaul.

"I've got you covered, Billy!"

He opened his eyes in time to catch Nelson race toward him carrying what looked to be a grenade launcher, but it was a single cartoonishly big cannon with a cartridge holder that belonged on a Tommy-gun.

PHOOOP!

The edge of the dock near them imploded, the planks chomped in half, the explosion turning schoolgirl faces, blazing pregnant eyes, clacking flytrap heads, and the guts closing in on them into a mass of blood. The blood and bodies flew so high, Nelson had to carry him towards the Boxer to take cover.

"We need an umbrella," Nelson joked. "Here, get in here quick—they're everywhere!"

Billy crawled into the Boxer first, landing awkwardly inside. Nelson shut the entrance top once he was inside. Billy was alarmed at the corpse on the ground; it was Dr. Aorta. The doctor eyed Billy like he was alive. The corpse was boiling at the skin, his words gurgling, "I told your friend the address, now destroy the reels and the projector. There's nobody else left. You're the only ones alive!"

"Will do, Andy," Billy said, gasping and wheezing, grateful but guilty at being alive since Jessica was dead and inside a horrible creature's belly. "Will you rest in peace when this is over?"

Dr. Aorta's body slowly turned into liquid, the current a pudding consistency running out of his sleeves and pants. "You worry about destroying those reels and the projector, and I'll worry about eternal slumber."

The body collapsed; the vile liquid kicked up a wretched stink. Billy covered his nose. "Christ, this has been one shock after another tonight."

Nelson didn't waste time. He drove the Boxer from the dock, crunching over corpses and failed blockades on the way until he was back onto the main road. Chicago was unrecognizable. Rubble and fallen buildings left devastation in place of the familiar.

Ba-boom!

The steamroller was right behind them, the corpse driver determined to halt them.

"My machine guns are dry," Nelson said. "The only thing I can do is out-drive him."

Nelson clutched the steering wheel. It wouldn't be enough, Billy thought. There were many monsters in the city ready to tangle with them.

STOMP! STOMP! STOMP!

Billy watched the console. The five hundred-foot hooker was dashing toward them. Half her skull was pulp and her torso was hollowed of insides.

"That bitch is determined to kill us!"

"I know," Nelson growled. "She won't stay dead!"

Billy shook his head. They couldn't catch a break. Yes, he was still alive, but for how long? Nelson voiced the same sentiment. "I can't out-drive these things. I can barely drive this hulking vehicle. We're screwed. I'm sorry, Billy. I tried to save the city."

"We all did," Billy sighed. "Jessica's dead, man. That creature in the harbor ate her. Just like that."

"I'm sorry," Nelson said, though his attempt at consoling was a bumbling one. They both suffered tragedies tonight. "I thought I could beat them."

STOMP! STOMP! STOMP!

Ba-bam! Ba-bam!

"I DON'T WANT TO DIE LIKE THIS!" Billy was about to crawl up topside to fight to the death when he caught Dr. Aorta's phalange point at the wall. He turned his head in confusion. The wall was blank of buttons, but there was a dip in the aluminum. He touched it with his hands. *Beep.* A hermetic pop. A wall came down and a shelf of weapons were revealed.

Billy cheered. "You've found the mother load. Good fucking job!"

"You keep driving," Billy challenged. "I'll deal with them outside."

He chose a sniper rifle with a scope. There was an odd device on the side of it, a black box that ticked as if the machine gun had a pulse.

"Careful, Dr. Aorta's weapons are full of surprises."

"No problem—I hope."

Billy went topside. Nelson slowed the vehicle. The giant woman was a block's distance. He aimed the scope. When he fired, it didn't blast like he thought it would. Instead, it fizzled and sparked, emitting a red lightning bolt. The lightning bolt turned into a full-out net and wrapped around the hooker. Her skin melted immediately, and seconds later, without a chance to react, she dissolved into blood. The flood was upon them. Jets of blood cascaded down, floods of blood. Shutting the top hatch of the Boxer, Billy hunkered in with Nelson. Moments later, they were lifted up by the wave of blood. The front was smashed by the force of the tide, the vehicle rendered into half its normal size. They were lifted up high, and then dropped back down when the blood wave had passed.

Nelson and Billy forced open the hatch. Nelson came out with hands stocked with goodies, including the gun Billy left behind. "We can't go to the prom without condoms."

"What?"

Nelson was taking the role of Dr. Aorta, Billy thought. *Let him use contrived tag lines as long as he's covering my ass.*

Billy laughed when Nelson gave him his old weapon. "Then let's go to the prom with extra-lubed Trojans."

"I didn't know you were into men."

"Fuck you. Let's get on with this."

Billy's gun had physically changed. The black box was the same, but now it was an M-16. He didn't question it, and like everything else tonight, he had to trust his eyes over common sense. Nelson clutched a six-shooter in each hand with blue steel trim, a banana clip sticking out of each side, the nozzles tipped with knives that looked to have been soldered on.

"Can we run a mile?" Nelson asked. "That's how far this place is. Martindale Street. Look for an apartment building."

Billy laughed. "My fat ass has run all night."

"Mine hasn't," Nelson said. "I wish you luck. One of us has to destroy those reels. If I die, don't let it hold you up."

"That goes for you too."

Nelson offered one last idea. "It's been fun watching cheesy movies and eating junk food all these years."

"I'll never watch a horror movie again."

"Well," Nelson groaned, "I can't say that for myself."

"You're a damn fool!"

Ba-boom!

The steamroller smashed through a series of cars. The corpse was set on flattening them. Billy aimed the machine gun. A single burst of rapid fire exploded out of the barrels. Small spiked buckshot struck the steamroller with numerous *tings*.

A red dot flashed on each spike.

The concussion came first. Then static electricity. Then the jounce that sent them onto the ground, reeling from the force of the explosion. WHOOOOOOOSH!

The steamroller was enveloped in electrical currents. The hairs on their arms and head stood on end. Crackles of brilliant blue tore the vehicle in half, causing the engine to erupt. The corpse himself was torn into shreds by each pop of insane lightning until he was nothing more than dust floating on the air. The street was blackened, and singed, and kicking up white smoke.

Billy stared at his gun. It had changed again. This time it was a bazooka.

"You have to save me!" A man charged out of an apartment building, the top half of the building having been removed by a giant swipe of an arm. He didn't recognize the person shouting for them. Many more men and women flopped out of hiding places, crying in hysteria. "They're inside me. So many of them. I can feel it crawling inside of me. Taking over. We went swimming in old man Harper's lake. Sure, there was leeches, but these are different. They're mutated. Harper's been up to no good. He's crop dusted with the cheap stuff. I know because my father did the job. It's no better than agent orange."

From the man's eyes, large black leeches slithered and forced the eyes of his sockets. "They're skinpreys!"

"Skinpreys?" Billy gasped. "RUN LIKE HELL!"

Each of the victims shed the leech creatures from each orifice: one victim kept excreting them from the ears, another vomited a pile of them up, and most of them were boiling under the skin, the creatures eating their way out with their lance-filled mouths and beady blue marble eyes. Hundreds of victims revealed themselves. The sound of thousands of squirming, squishing, enclosing skinpreys sent Billy and Nelson up the street. Martindale Street eventually came into view, and when it did, so did the monsters at their backs.

Chapter Thirty-Eight

It's so simple.

Why didn't I think of it before?

Impossible. I'm a walking pile of broken bones.

One last thing to do.

So do it!

Ted had broken his right leg, shattered his arm when he'd landed on the street, and he was certain his hips and pelvis weren't in good shape either. He'd deflected off a garbage dumpster on the way down. Ted was lucky to be alive, in any shape. He had enough life left in him for one last try. He crawled because he couldn't walk, through the side door that led into the basement of the apartment building.

One last thing to do.

So simple...

A great wall of enemies charged in at them from all angles. They were surrounded and entrenched in B-movie warfare. Nelson was thrown across the street, tangled in the mean clutches of the schoolgirls. Pitchforks were shoved at Billy. He shot his bazooka in their direction. It made an odd sound, like spackle shot out of a giant tube at impossible speeds. SPLAT! A wad of white steaming goop like melted marshmallow cream landed on the farmers. They sizzled, melted and began crumbling into boiling piles. The substance was sticky, the corpses unable to move once they collapsed onto the street.

"My pies are always the best! ALWAYS FRESH!"

The back of his neck was sliced with a pizza cutter. "Ah Jesus!"

Billy's weapon changed into a long pole with a fan blade on the end. It buzzed as if it had a motor from within. The blade was spinning, slicing, a gas smell accompanying each chug of the motor.

"GIVE THEM HELL!" Nelson cried. "AHHHHHHHHH!"

Billy saw six axes bear down upon Nelson, each slicing him. The schoolgirls bathed in his blood, rubbing their faces in it, soaking their clothes in the red, and relishing another man's death.

"NELSON!" He used the spinning blade to his advantage, picturing Jessica and Nelson as they were before death, healthy and happy. "DAMN YOU ALL TO PIECES!"

Billy caught the baker across the face, his charred skeleton splitting in half leaving the lower mandible and a tongue extending like the feelers on a cricket's head. A flying vampire swooped down: "SHALEEEEEEEEEH!" He dodged the reaching talons and delved the blades into her left leg until it snapped from the body. She screamed, spinning in misdirection, and careened into the street. A wad of intestines wrapped around the blades, the pink coils turning into mist and spray. Then a burning skeletal hand clutched the weapon. Fluids trickled down the pole, and instantly, Billy's prized weapon was engulfed in flames.

The corpse said, "The dead don't need their organs after they die... I'll consider that the moment you perish, Billy."

Billy stumbled over his own feet. The fleet they had aimed to destroy stood above him, dominating his last moments of life. Skinpreys slithered over his arms and legs, coating them in an inch of slime. Schoolgirls regarded him as filth, sizing him up, swiping and swatting the air with their deadly blades covered in Nelson's fresh blood. Farmers rolled a bale of human bodies closer to him, Nelson's tangled in the mix, his eyes and mouth jammed with hay. The baker was half-headed, but managed to stuff peach filling into a corpse's torso beneath the traffic light. Three winged vampires, even the one-legged vampire, devoured and licked up Nelson's puddle of blood from the street, the group playfully splashing each other, dragging their blood-colored tongues against each other in ecstasy. More of the awful monsters paraded in the background, so many he couldn't take them in.

He clutched a trash can lid and shielded himself from the guarantee of a brutal death.

All Jessica could think was how humid it was inside the beast. The walls resembled the inside of her mouth and the walls of her cheeks: soft, pink, bumpy textured and fleshy. The ceiling was the same porous texture and a deep purple color. Somehow, light had filtered into what she would've expected to be a dark cave, though the light was unnatural—like a large spotlight's illumination. She landed into a forced somersault onto her back in a puddle. The puddle was above room temperature, and as it set into her skin, it began to burn. She yelped and backpedaled to a dry surface.

"That's only a taste of what's coming our way."

She wasn't alone. Twenty people at each side of her were hunched down pressed up against the wall. Their backs bobbed up and down as did their heads. A sucking and spitting noise repeated. She turned away in repulsion. "What's going on in here? What are you people doing?"

The man who spoke earlier wore a white lab coat and bore the resemblance of a young Christopher Lee. "Survival, my dear, is what's happening here. We have exactly fifty-five minutes to escape the beast."

"And what in hell is this beast we're inside of exactly?"

The person she assumed was a scientist, his breast pocket read Dr. Misery. *That can't be a real name.*

Then the obvious occurred to her: this was a character from a movie. The beast that swallowed her up was from a movie. *Am I the only one in here who's real?*

"The beast," Dr. Misery began, "is an experiment of mine. I wanted to grow beta fish into larger fish, perhaps so large it could feed many.

265

You see, I developed them to survive in salt water and humid regions so they could prosper in third world countries..."

But something went horribly wrong...

"But something went horribly wrong..."

"Enough of this crazy shit. How do we get out of here?"

Dr. Misery pointed at each of the victims on their haunches. "We have fifty minutes before that wall of tissue comes down and bathes us in acid for digestion. Then, we're nothing but digestible material." He smirked. "The beta fish can be defeated from within, and I'll tell you how."

The sucking sounds continued. The victims' breathing was muffled and labored. The echo of mastication was off-putting in this scenario.

"Then what do we do?"

Dr. Misery guided her by both arms and propped her in front of the fleshy wall. The spongy material dripped with a thick white mucous fluid. The doctor's voice bent when he said, "*We have to eat our way out of the creature...*"

Vrrrrrrrrrrrrrrrrrm!

Ted had worked himself into a standing position, the wall his crutch, as he walked down the apartment's back stairs to the bottom floor. He limped his way inside the building when the roar of a chainsaw resounded through another room. He kept edging toward the last room in the hall despite what he knew was coming for him.

It's always the last room.

Thack! Clap! Thack! Clap! Thack! Clap! Thack!

Three rooms from his destination, the blade of the chainsaw cut through a door. The door was battered down by several steel-sounding collisions. The door flew open. That's when a fleet of tools was sent his direction: hammers, wrenches, chainsaw, nail gun, table saw, power sander, all of it was hurled his way. They moved and were propelled as if ghosts were holding them in their hands, he thought. Any moment, they could be used on him. Ted had directed and watched enough horror movies to know his time was limited.

He lucked out, opening an unlocked door and shielding himself behind the barrier. Splinters and dust shot at his body, the whir and whine of power tools deafening.

The tools could tear him into pieces and send him directly into death. But he had reached his destination. He expected a hammer to clack against his head or a nail to pierce his chest. The tools simply faltered to the floor with a collective metallic crash.

"Stop, Ted!"

Georgia stood as a woman in the hallway. Naked. Unashamed. Her face begging. Eyes alight with shock that he'd survived this long, that he was this close to ending their reign of terror.

"Why should I stop? You've murdered and turned this city into a tomb. I want nothing to do with you anymore. After this, I hope my movies fall into obscurity forever. I can't be the source of any more death."

"You can have all the women you want," she said, teasing her tongue between her lips. "Look, Teddy Bear."

A warden entered the hall. She was dressed in a black uniform. Ted watched in awe as she undressed down to nothing. Blonde and buxom, curvy and sexual along every inch of her naked flesh, he simply shook his head at the show. Another battalion of walking sex pots, the slasher girls entered via the opposite rooms of the hallway dressed in skirts and stockings, flashing their tits and hiking their dresses up for an extra-special peek of their virginal beauty. Their murderous feminism ended and was replaced with promises of sexual freedom.

"We're yours," Georgia promised, tracing her hands along the bodies of the slasher girls. "I promise none of us will ever hurt you if you promise not to bring harm upon us. It's that easy, Teddy. Are you on our side, or theirs? The living will become the dead. They'll be just like us, and finally, we can live as equals, Teddy. We can never be completely human again. We can't lead fulfilling lives like the living and breathing masses can. They don't appreciate life. They don't know regret, loss and death itself. The dead can only live as vague profiles of their former selves—as you can see, we're creatures. But we're enjoying our new bodies, our new homes. In fact, it'll be a damn shame when every living person is dead. The fun will be over. We've had an enjoyable time killing everybody. Or maybe we could kill you in smaller doses. Let society recoup their losses. You people are always bringing new life into the world. Babies are born every day. So much flesh to create...and desecrate."

"If you're a bunch of ghosts, you've truly lost your sanity," Ted said. "You're simply a bunch of killing machines without any tangible goal. Even if you had one to begin with, you've lost it. The movie characters are taking you over. Their motives, their ambitions, their characteristics have become your own. Georgia, you didn't used to be a lesbian. In fact, you only wanted men—I remember one of your co-actresses tried to make out with you, and you rejected her. All of you are lost in the movie characters. It's turned you into psychotics. You can't return to being human beings the way you were before death ever again. And you can't keep killing everyone. It's not up to you when it's someone's time to go or not. I'm here to end this...I'm sending you back to where you came from forever."

Georgia shouted, "You haven't won! There's a plan B. You can't stop us forever!"

"Enjoy your plan B in hell."

The nail gun lifted from the floor. Seven shots spat out the nozzle. He was pierced through the chest, the seventh shot splitting his heart in half.

By then, he had already opened the breaker box and cut the power.

Chapter Thirty-Nine

Billy clutched the trashcan lid. He waited. And waited. He opened one eye. Then the other. He was alone on the street. Nelson's body was splayed on the pavement in six different pieces. He averted his eyes and scrambled from the scene in horror. He was halfway up the street when he recalled the purpose of coming here.

Destroy the projector and the reels.

He sprinted to the apartment building. Andy had told him that the projector was on the fourth floor. Rushing inside, he observed open rooms on the way up, blood on every wall, the residents murdered.

He kept moving.

Running up to the fourth floor, he located the room. Corpses were stacked at every corner, gore smeared on the walls. The stench was horrid. He scavenged the room for something to burn the entire building down with. He had to be creative and located a bottle of bourbon and a book of matches. Reels were littered on the floor, titles ranging from *Squid Man Versus The Living Dead*, *Dracula Lives in Saint Anne's Dormitory*, *Wolfman Defeats the United States Army*, *Hacksaw Cheerleaders Kill*, and many more. He smashed the three projectors into one pile, beating them into pieces before dousing them in bourbon and setting them afire.

"Burn," he kept chanting. "Burn! BURN!"

Fire spread along the carpet. Billy fed the orange current until the bottle was dry. By then, the walls were dancing with firelight. The place would be canvassed in flames in no time, he thought.

He walked down the stairs at a stagger pace. The beating he'd taken over the past hours had caught up with him. He was bleeding from his legs and shoulders in sizeable bite wounds. His ribs pained him the most, as did the loss of Jessica and Nelson. He imagined Jessica swallowed up by the betta creature. Nelson axed into pieces by Catholic schoolgirls from hell. The permanent outcome weighed him down once he crossed the threshold and stood in the street alone. There was nowhere to go, everywhere devastated, Chicago turned into the aftermath of a war zone.

The bone dome was missing, he noticed. Sunlight touched down upon him. He imagined God telling him to "hang in there", but at this moment, he couldn't accept signs from God. Too much horror had occurred to believe in anything holy.

The thumping of chopper blades resounded overhead. The National Guard had arrived. Ambulances and squad car sirens wailed in the near proximity.

"You're too late," he muttered. "Way too late."

Billy sat on the curb and watched the apartment building spew flames from the fourth floor. It wasn't long before an ambulance crew and police car stopped to provide medical care for him. The evening's losses didn't leave his mind well after he arrived at the nearest functioning hospital.

Chapter Forty

Billy was driven for treatment right outside of Chicago. He arrived at St. John's Mercy Hospital amid few survivors. Fifty people total had survived the horror; the rest of the city was one big catalog of casualities. He only knew this because a detective had woken him from a morphine-induced sleep—something the doctors provided for his bodily trauma—while talking to the nurse in the room. The drugs didn't prevent the truth from sinking in, for Billy. Jessica had died. Nelson had died. And they didn't perish peacefully.

Detective Bruce Johnston was the man standing above his bed, a tight-end-sized man with a connecting beard and an expression of "I needed coffee two hours ago" pasted on his tired face. "How are you feeling, Billy?"

"Like absolute shit. My best friend is dead. My girlfriend is dead. My father is dead. Everybody I know is dead." He took a moment before he asked, "Oh, and how about you?"

The detective replaced his pad of paper into his pocket. "Look, I'm sorry. You're not ready to talk to me. I understand."

The detective was visibly frustrated, but Billy didn't care. He was in the hospital for barely a day after he'd witnessed hell on earth, and he was already being questioned.

The detective almost exited the room, when he returned. "As an apology, you should see this."

The detective parted the curtain separating him from the other patient.

And there she was.

"Jessica!"

The detective turned to leave them alone when Billy called out to him, "Hey, give us a few minutes. I'll answer any questions you have, sir!"

Billy nearly ripped the I.V. from his arm launching over to her bed and hugging her with the vise grips of life. He kissed her face, took in her smell, and kept stealing glances at her and touching her arms and face to double-check she was real. "Y-you're alive. But I saw you...I saw you eaten."

Jessica's face went pale. "I was in the belly of that thing...and, I had to...I had to eat—"

"Let's not talk about it right now, okay? We're alive. Thank God, we're alive."

He sat on the edge of her bed. Jessica smiled at him, but tears were pouring from her eyes. "Did Nelson...?"

Billy lowered his head. "No. But he saved my life. He saved a lot of peoples' lives. If we would've died, those monsters would've moved on and killed even more people outside of Chicago."

Jessica clasped his hand in hers. "What do we tell the police?"

Billy shrugged. "I have no idea. If we tell them the truth, they'd think we're crazy, and if we lie, they won't believe us either. I say we tell them what we saw and be honest."

"That monsters did this?" Jessica shook her head. "I'm not so sure."

"Remember that website. They have pictures of the bone dome. Pictures of the monsters too."

"The government will cover it up," Jessica insisted. "Nobody wants to believe in monsters. I've heard there were only fifty survivors. Those are enough people to easily silence."

The door flew open. Detective Johnston re-entered. "There are enough people to easily silence, you're right. What you saw was real, okay? I'm not Big Brother, guys. I'm only doing my job. I'm here to let you know what happened is classified. You're under court order to keep silent what you witnessed. We don't have a clue what caused those awful creatures to come to life. Our jobs right now are to treat you and keep this situation from the general public. Let me say measures are being taken to figure out the truth behind the events."

"Have you been listening to our conversation?" Billy challenged him.

"It gets things done," Detective Johnston said dryly. "I've been doing this since the events in Anderson Mills. And I still haven't found the answers. Maybe never will."

He handed them two slips of paper. It was a Contract of Silence. Billy eyed the paper and the detective in disbelief. "I didn't know these kind of contracts existed. Fine, I'll sign if it'll get you out of the way faster."

"Very good. That's what I like to hear."

Jessica signed first, and then Billy.

"This is for your own good," the detective explained. "The media has no clue what went down. Nobody must know the truth about Chicago. We'll be watching you two from a distance. Just keep this to yourself. It's better that way. Enough harm has already been done, let's not make it worse...and you're right ma'am, people don't want to believe in monsters. It's been that way for a *very* long time. We're working on explaining what happened in Chicago. It's going to be a bitch, but we'll handle it like we did Anderson Mills. The people will believe the lies we tell them." One side of his lips curved up in a smile. "You'll be hearing from me every now and again. I wish you a good recovery."

The detective exited the room.

Jessica turned to Billy. "What do we do now?"

"Recuperate."

"And what else, smart guy?"

"We get married."

Jessica rolled her eyes. "Yes, of course, but seriously, we can't talk to anybody about this. This, this is a mammoth story that begs to be told."

"I destroyed the reels, honey," Billy said, shushing her. "This is better left unknown to anybody. Nobody would try and dig up the truth and repeat what happened. The monsters won't come back; this is for the best. Andy told me that was the ghosts' final way into the world. I've closed it off. It's that simple. So let's focus on realistic goals. Marriage. Eating ice cream. We need something pleasant besides this classified bullshit experience. I don't know how we're ever going to move on from this, but we will. Thank God you're alive."

Jessica gave him a big smile. "There is one thing I do know."

"And what is that?"

"We're not watching scary movies ever again!"

Epilogue

Plan B was real.

Three to five business days after the terror ended in Chicago, Jules Baxter, a sixty-year-old man who was seventy pounds overweight with skin the color of nicotine, finally realized the truth. Odyssey Cinema was a financial failure. The fresh tarred lot was empty on a Monday morning, the four-theatre cineplex like a ghost town, just as it was on Friday, Saturday and Sunday. Two months after opening, he couldn't make a single bank payment, never mind complete the payroll, though the three kids on his staff didn't care. They were in it for the same reasons he was. They loved the movies he loved. His leap of faith in the customers had resulted in a hard landing, Jules realized. Nobody cared for his taste in films. And he was near half a million in debt because of it.

Face it, nobody likes horror movies anymore.

"I should've opened closer to Halloween," Jules muttered, stepping out of his rusted cobalt-blue Impala toward the movie house. *I should've expanded...maybe played old classics as well as horror movies. Every day of the week could've had a theme. Bogart day. Abbott and Costello day. Hitchcock day. Newman day. Cruise day.*

Fuck that.

I only want horror movies.

Fuck the bank. Fuck the people that didn't come.

Fuck everything.

Odyssey Cinema was a simple, square, eraser-red brick building. Glass front. Inside, lime-green seventies tiles decorated the walls. The floors were painted black, though there were cracks and pocks in the flooring. The theatres themselves had an ugly orange carpeting on the walls and orange seats to match. It was the closet to 42nd Street anybody could come in this day and age, though this was in a suburb of New Jersey. Nobody greeted him inside; the lights were off. The place exuded the ambiance of foreclosure. He decided to flip on the front room lights for old time's sake. Monday's noon bill was a double feature: Lucio Fulci's *Zombi 2* and Herschell Gordon Lewis's *The Gore Gore Girls*.

I should've had scantily clad models dressed up as zombies. I would've called them...

"Nah," Jules sighed. He rubbed his balding head. "I'm sure someone would've protested that. Surely somebody would get something jammed up their asses about it."

He turned on the concession lights. The popcorn machine, the candy displays, all of it begged for customers.

I don't have the corporate power. Advertising for one, and I don't have the newest Disney movie to put butts into the seats.

Two weeks was what the banker had given him to decide on foreclosure or bankruptcy. He told his staff to stay home today. There'd be no business rush. Nobody actually. He counted the torn ticket stubs. Twelve people had come last Friday, and that was for George Romero's *Dawn of the Dead*.

Jules wandered to his office, a tiny closet at the end of the concession stand. When he entered, there was mail spread across his desk in a thick pile. Bank envelopes. Junk mailers. And a large, heavy box.

He checked for the return address, and there was none. His address was lettered in scraggly, blood-red writing. Jules picked the package up and lifted it. It had weight.

"*Hmmm*. This is interesting."

Without thinking, he tore the top strip off of the package. He worked through the bubble wrap, which was covered in a reddish-brown crusted substance. His fingers were sticky working out what hid at the bottom. He first retrieved a note, literally a scrap of paper roughly torn. More blood-red writing, what looked to be someone's finger nail putting the scrawl to paper:

This will put butts in the seats.

Play this at your next showing.

I promise delightful results.

Jules turned his head at the note. No signature. A complete stranger had sent him this package. They cared about his business, apparently.

"It's worth a look," he said without amusement. "It's worth a gander."

He retrieved a reel. It was small. Not very long by the thickness of the roll. He studied a strip in the light. Jules smiled.

It was a trailer reel.

"Wow. That's—wow. *Morgue Vampire Tramps Find Temptation at the Funeral Home.* And look, there's so many more trailers! God, this takes me back."

Jules doted on the trailer reel.

It was decided.

He'd be playing this first thing at his next showing.

About the Author

Alan Spencer spends an inordinate amount of time watching horror movies, writing film reviews for Cinesploitation, columns for Morpheus Tales magazine, and editing his upcoming novels. *B-Movie Attack* is his second novel from Samhain Publishing, the first being *B-Movie Reels*. Keep your eyes peeled for his next release in 2013 called *Psycho Therapy*. E-mail him at alanspencer26@hotmail.com or visit his blog at horroralan.blogspot.com.

Off of the screen and out for blood!

B-Movie Reels
© *2012 Alan Spencer*

Andy Ryerson, a film school graduate, has been hired to write commentary on two dozen cheap, b-horror movies. It seems harmless enough, and he might even enjoy it. But the people in the town around him won't enjoy it at all when one by one, the films he watches come to life. Andy chose the wrong projector to screen his movies. This one is out for blood. While Andy grumbles about low budgets and poor production values, a hungry butcher, a plague of rotting zombies, demonic vampires, a mallet-toting killer, flesh-eating locusts, and many other terrors descend on the unsuspecting innocent. By the time he realizes what he's done, the town is teeming with evil, and it's up to Andy and the few survivors left to stop the celluloid horror he's unleashed.

Available now in ebook and print from Samhain Publishing.

Enjoy the following excerpt from B-Movie Reels...

"Ladies and gentlemen, I am Gideon, your guide to grand illusion! Tonight, you will be shocked and awed. I won't patronize you with gags from kid's books. This is a real stage. What you see is what it is. No tricks of light, no aversion tactics, I won't pull rabbits out of hats, juggle fire, tear newspapers and reconstruct them, and I won't saw anyone in half because that's been done to death. But we do have a showgirl!"

Matthew Bard, a security guard at the Comedy Tavern, watched the show on amateur talent night with limited enthusiasm, as did the audience. He recognized Bunny Anderson on stage; she was the blonde adorned in a purple sequined outfit that revealed her long silky legs. She smiled and waved to the crowd of regulars, pretending to live up to a higher standard of showmanship. Gideon paid her thirty dollars to take the night off of her barmaid gig to be his helper. "Stand up there and look good," he'd overheard Gideon instruct Bunny at rehearsal. "When I call the audience up to the stage, usher them right to where I point. Easiest thirty bucks you'll ever earn, darling."

Gideon was dressed the part. The magician wore a loose purple silk shirt and black leather pants. A ridiculous Abraham Lincoln top hat rested on his head. His cheeks were poked with acne scars, and around the eyes, dark saucers lent the performer a strung out sheen. The gray hair on his chin was shaved into an upside down triangle. The overall attempt was ill-realized but good enough for amateur night.

Playing up the crowd, Gideon waved his nine-inch wand, gesturing as he spoke, "This is real magic, ladies and gentlemen. I am an oracle." He cupped his ear, acting like he hadn't heard his own question. "What is an oracle, you might be asking? It's what the Romans called those who could speak to the gods. But I am not an alchemist; I cannot cure diseases and save lives. I use the gods to entertain and delight. I have access between the living and dead worlds, you see, ladies and gentlemen. They've taught me magic beyond any illusionist's ability. I am a medium between the spirits and living world." Extending his arms as if to give the crowd a hug, he announced with startling vigor, "I am Gideon."

"So do something, Gideon!"

"Yeah, it's been five minutes—what the hell?"

"This is a magic show, right?"

Matthew smiled at the ribbing; the man was being heckled before he'd even started.

"I see you're ready to be amazed!" He shuffled to the left side of Bunny and then pointed his finger in the direction of the crowd. "I'm going to call out twenty people from the audience to sit in these chairs behind me. Any brave volunteers?"

Matthew watched the chairs, curious as to their function. He'd helped place them hours ago for ten bucks. He recalled the cool touch of Gideon's handshake through his silk gloves—like a piano man's— and the soft treble in his voice, the purr of a male lion. "Ten bucks says you can help me set up my stage. What do you say, my good man?"

Gideon selected twenty volunteers from the audience, and Bunny escorted them to their places. It was three minutes later the audience participants were seated and ready for the trick to unfold.

The performer dragged two metal poles on stage, one from which a purple curtain was unrolled, and he clipped that curtain to the other pole by two hooks. He reappeared behind the veil, the audience members hidden by a layer of fabric. "I will make these twenty people disappear. They are not paid or have ever seen me before. We are all strangers under this roof. I will invite you to walk on stage and double-check my claims." Hamming up his act, he boasted the promise, "I, Gideon, will make them vanish and then reappear!"

The crowd's interest heated up. They begged to be entertained. Hands clapped, while those at the bar walked in closer for a better view. There were about one-hundred and thirty people in "The Comedy

Tavern," including the ones on stage, each with faces ready to be dazzled.

"I will count to three, and with the wave of my wand, I will make them vanish."

The club's floors shook with the stomping of feet. Whistles pierced the air. Drinks were refilled and cigarettes lit. Gideon absorbed the skeptical comments before continuing the show.

"I'd like to see the asshole pull it off."

"This bar's too small for disappearing acts."

"Amateur hack is going to embarrass himself."

"Dork sure looks like he believes in magic."

The performer closed his eyes and extended his arms up to the ceiling, prepared to disprove their doubts. "I ask you to count to three, audience."

The audience responded with a boisterous shout: "ONE!"

"I call upon you," he whispered to himself, channeling a greater force. "I call upon the gods, make them disappear."

"TWO!"

The shuffle of many chairs at once, Gideon peeled back the curtain the split-second he knew the gods had acquiesced upon his wishes.

"THREE!"

The stage revealed, the chairs were emptied as many of the legs rattled the floor and then momentarily settled. The audience clapped, but then abruptly stopped their accolades when they noticed certain members in the crowd had disappeared as well. The bartender went missing in a blink; the shot glass and bottle of scotch in his hands shattered against the floor, dropped. The audience was less than half of what they were before the show began. A mix of worry and concern sent nervous chatter throughout the club. Matthew wasn't sure how to react himself, standing rigid and unconfident; his beefy size couldn't fight tonight's problem. He surveyed the people in their seats again, remembering those who'd been sitting one moment, and the next there was nothing, only the sharp scuffle of chairs.

Gideon addressed the audience, expecting the uproar. "Ah, the gods heed me. I will make them return. Let's hear it. Clap for me! You'll see my magic. It's real. I promise you, all is well. All is well!"

Bunny stood still on the stage unnerved, squinting throughout the audience to check if this was really happening. She drew back the purple curtain at his request, though hesitantly, afraid helping the man would make matters worse.

The audience didn't cheer this time, but Gideon understood why.

He too was concerned.

The magic had worked too well tonight.

Stumbling on his words, he spat out to the uneasy crowd, "I will count to three, and the gods shall place the audience members back into the living world. I am Gideon. Heed my magic."

He waved the wand back and forth (the action meaning nothing, and Gideon knew it too) and closed his eyes. "I call upon the gods. Return our visitors from the world of the ghosts and spirits to the living."

Gideon counted aloud since no one else joined in.

"One...two...THREE!"

The curtain was drawn back by Bunny. Instantly, the chair legs scuffed the stage's floor. Gasps rocked the club. Tables were knocked over and screams issued with alarming intensity. Patrons battled to escape the club, barreling into each other, shoving, and pushing, and fighting and cursing the horrible spectacles busying the bar and seating area.

Gideon buckled to his knees, taking in the horrors. "This wasn't supposed to happen. This wasn't supposed to happen this way!"

Matthew closed in on the stage, though he was hesitant to enter the morbid carnage.

His life was in danger too.

The audience members on stage did return, but they were altered.

Eyes had switched sockets, the orbs bleeding from the exchange. Legs and feet were mismatched. One body was only a torso with an arm replacing the head. Fish-net legs jutted from a man's big-bellied torso, the connection sealed by tangles of melded-together flesh and bone. A man's head was attached to a women's body, the pink dress sodden in crimson from the throat's strange flesh graft stitching. The twenty people were blended together, not a single one owning their original parts. They writhed in horrid agony, twitching, and bleeding, and screaming and pealing out in terror, their inflictions unimaginable.

Those that weren't dead upon returning were soon thereafter. The club was silent and near empty. Bunny retreated out the back exit, the final person to escape. The other security officer, Sam Wilks, was calling the police from the back room, his expression petrified and so pale.

Gideon wept on stage, curled in a fetal position and babbling. "This wasn't supposed to happen. They promised they wouldn't hurt anyone ever again. They promised. They promised me they'd be nice." Snarling as spittle flecked out his mouth, he shouted, "And look what they've done!"

Matthew avoided numerous puddles of blood, treading closer to the grief-stricken man. The stage was a macabre scene, and he did his best to avert his eyes from studying the victims. Raising his voice, he attempted to re-claim control over the chaos, "Come with me, Gideon. You're under arrest. It's over. Now come along quietly."

He wasn't a cop, but it was the best thing he could muster in the situation. Gideon didn't move or resist. Matthew removed his cuffs from his belt, afraid to touch the man. How safe was it to be near a person like Gideon? Would his limbs be switched out too?

The magician's mouth was an open maw. Sorrow affected his words. "It wasn't me. They promised to be good. I should've learned from the first time. They deceived me again. I should've known."

"Don't move," Matthew instructed adamantly. "I don't know what you're talking about, but I'm taking you to the police. You can explain it to them, okay?"

He forced Gideon's hands behind his back, sucking up his fears and putting the man in custody.

The man sobbed, "This wasn't my illusion...it was theirs."

Matthew fastened the cuffs, ignoring the man's cryptic confession. "Let's just let the police handle—"

Once he lifted the man to his feet, Gideon vanished.

Available now in ebook and print from Samhain Publishing.

THE BEST IN HORROR

Every month Samhain brings you the finest in horror fiction from the most respected names in the genre, as well as the most talented newcomers. From subtle chills to shocking terror, experience the ultimate in fear from such brilliant authors as:

Ramsey Campbell

W. D. Gagliani

Ronald Malfi

Greg F. Gifune

Brian Moreland

John Everson

And many more!

THE HOUSE OF HORROR

SAMHAIN

PUBLISHING

It's all about the story...

Romance

HORROR

Retro ROMANCE

www.samhainpublishing.com

CPSIA information can be obtained at www.ICGtesting.com
Printed in the USA
BVOW081221291112

306847BV00002B/99/P

9 781609 289256